Praise for David Constantine

Winner of the 2013 Frank O'Connor
International Short Story Award

Winner of the 2010 BBC National Short Story Award

"After reading David Constantine's story 'In Another Country'... I can't figure out why a US press hasn't caught on to his work. He's won ... the Frank O'Connor Award ... beating out Joyce Carol Oates, Deborah Levy, and Peter Stamm—and no wonder."—Nicole Rudick, *The Paris Review*

"The excellence of the collection is fractal: the whole book is excellent, and every story is excellent, and every paragraph is excellent, and every sentence is excellent. And unlike some literary fiction, it's effortless to read." —*The Independent on Sunday*

"Masterful... pregnant with fluctuating interpretations and concealed motives."—*The Guardian*

"This is a superb collection of stories: Constantine's writing is rare today, unafraid to be rich and allusive and unashamedly moving."—*The Independent*

"Sparkling."—*The Times Literary Supplement*

"Spellbinding."—*The Irish Times*

"Constantine is writing for his life. Every sentence and paragraph is shaped, tense with meaning and unobtrusively beautiful, his images of the natural world burning their way into the reader's mind."—Maggie Gee, *The Sunday Times*

"An exacting wordsmith, David Constantine is always in complete control of his material, every sentence exquisitely wrought to convey exactly the mood he intends."—*The Good Book Guide*

"Constantine's stories are not pre-prepared in any sense; he starts anew every time. Inspired by an image or specific instance, his work has a feeling of wholeness and growth."—*The Irish Post*

"Constantine is, quite clearly, a master draughtsman at work, and the short story is his ideal canvas."—*The Short Review*

"Flawless but unsettling." —Boyd Tonkin, *The Independent*

"This is a haunting collection filled with delicate clarity. Constantine has a sure grasp of the fear and fragility within his characters." —A.L. Kennedy

"So good I'll be surprised if there's a better collection this year."—*The Independent*

IN ANOTHER COUNTRY

In Another Country

Selected Stories

David Constantine

BIBLIOASIS
WINDSOR, ON

The stories in *In Another Country* first appeared in David Constantine's *Under the Dam, The Shieling, Tea at the Midland and Other Stories*, all published in Great Britain by Comma Press, and *Back at the Spike*, originally published in Great Britain by Ryburn Press (to be re-released by Comma Press next year).

FIRST EDITION

Library and Archives Canada Cataloguing in Publication

Constantine, David, 1944–
[Short stories. Selections]
    In another country : selected stories / David Constantine.

Issued in print and electronic formats.
ISBN 978-1-77196-017-5 (bound).--ISBN 978-1-77196-018-2 (epub)

    I. Title.

PR6053.O513A6 2015   823'.914   C2014-907953-2
                                              C2014-907954-0

Readied for the press by Daniel Wells
Copy-edited by Tara Tobler
Typeset by Chris Andrechek
Jacket designed by Kate Hargreaves

PRINTED AND BOUND IN THE USA

Contents

IN ANOTHER COUNTRY

When Mrs. Mercer came in she found her husband looking poorly. What's the matter now? she asked, putting down her bags. It startled him. Can't leave you for a minute, she said. They've found her, he said. Found who? That girl. What girl? That girl I told you about. What girl's that? Katya. Katya? said Mrs. Mercer beginning to side away the breakfast things. I don't remember any Katya. I don't remember you telling me about a Katya. I tell you everything, he said. I've always told you everything. Not Katya you haven't. She took his cup and saucer. Have you finished here? He had pushed them aside to make room for a dictionary. He was still in his dressing gown with a letter in his hand. *My* Katya, he said. I couldn't finish my tea when I read the letter. I see, said Mrs. Mercer. It worried her. Already it frightened her. Quickly she cleared the table. Excuse me, she said, while I shake the cloth. He raised the dictionary. A name like that, she said, coming back the two steps from the kitchen door, I'd have remembered it. She's foreign, by the sound. I told you, he said. His face had an injured look. One thing he could not bear was her not believing him when he said he'd told her things. You forget, he said. No I do not, she said. When then? That made him think. A good while back, I grant you. It was a good while back. What worried Mrs. Mercer suddenly took shape. Into the little room came a rush of ghosts. She sat down opposite him and both felt cold. That Katya, she said. Yes, he said. They've found her in the ice. I see, said Mrs. Mercer.

After a while she said: I see you found your book. Yes, he said. It was behind the pickles. You must have put it there. I suppose I must, she said. It was an old Cassell's. There were words in the letter, in the handwriting, he could not make out and words in the dictionary he could hardly find, in the old Gothic script; still, he had understood. Years since I read a word of German, he said. Funny how it starts coming back to you when you see it again. I daresay, said Mrs. Mercer. The folded cloth lay between them on the polished table. It's this global warming, he said, that we keep hearing about. What is? she asked. Why they've found her after all this time. Though he was the one with the information his face seemed to be asking her for help with it. The snow's gone off the ice, he said. You can see right in. And she's still in there just the way she was. I see, said Mrs. Mercer. She would be, wouldn't she, he added, when you come to think about it. Yes, said Mrs. Mercer, when you come to think about it I suppose she would. Again, with his face and with a slight lifting of his mottled hands he seemed to be asking her to help him comprehend. Well, she said after a pause during which she drew the cloth towards her and folded it again and then again. Can't sit here all day. I've got my club. Yes, he said. It's Tuesday. You've got your club. She rose and made to leave the room but halted in the door and said: What are you going to do about it? Do? he said. Oh nothing. What *can* I do?

All day in a trance. Katya in the ice, the chaste snow drawn off her. He cut himself shaving, stared at his face, tried to fetch out the twenty-year-old from under his present skin. Trickle of blood, pink froth where it entered the soap. He tried to see through his eyes into wherever the soul or spirit or whatever you call it lives that doesn't age with the casing it is in. The little house oppressed him. There were not enough rooms to go from room to room in, nowhere to pace. He looked into the flagstone garden but the neighbours either side were out and looking over. It drove him only in his indoor clothes out and along the road a little way to where the road went down suddenly steeply and the estate of all the same houses was redeemed by a view of the estuary, the mountains and the open sea. He stood there thinking of Katya in the ice. Stood there so long the lady whose house he was outside standing there came out and asked: Are you all right, Mr. Mercer? Fine, he said, and saw his own face mirrored in hers, ghastly. I'm too old, he thought. I don't want it all coming up in me again. We're both of us too old. We don't want it all welling up in us again. But it had begun.

No tea ready, said Mrs. Mercer, putting down her bag. He was sitting on the sofa queerly to one side as though somebody should be there next to him. No, he said. I didn't know what to get. The blood had dried black in a line down the middle of his chin. Besides, I'm not feeling too good. The one day in the week when you get the tea, said Mrs. Mercer. I know, he said. I'm sorry. She went to see to it. He came in after her and hung in the doorway of the small room where they cooked and ate. His unease was palpable. Whether to stand or sit, whether to speak or not. Two or three times he shrugged. In the end he managed to say: Where was the trip then? Prestatyn, she answered brightly. We went to Prestatyn. You always enjoy your trips, he said. Yes, she said, I wouldn't miss a Tuesday trip if I could help it. He had lapsed away again. His face was desolate and absent. His fingers, under their own compulsion, picked at one another. Yes, she said. We went to Prestatyn market and I got myself a blouse. I'll have to see it, he said.

11

I've been wondering, Mrs. Mercer said when they were face to face across the little table eating. Why did they write to you about that girl? So long ago it happened and didn't you tell me you were only passing through? I'm next of kin, he said. Mrs. Mercer put down her cup. I beg your pardon. I mean they think I am. She'd have no mother and father, would she, if you think about it. Besides, they were Jews. Dead anyway, of age. But very likely dead long before they died of age. And she was an only child, my Katya was. Yes but, Mrs. Mercer said. Yes but so what? I don't see that makes you the next of kin. Oh I told them we were married, Mr. Mercer said. I see, said Mrs. Mercer. I had to where we stayed. Not like nowadays. You had to say you were Mr. and Mrs. in those days. And wear a curtain ring. We never did, said Mrs. Mercer. We didn't have to, did we, Mr. Mercer said. We didn't have to because we really were. And you two weren't? No, no, said Mr. Mercer. I only said we were. You never told me you were another woman's next of kin. I did, he said. Besides, I'm not. And if I didn't it was so as not to upset you.

The meal went on and finished. They watched some television. They went to bed. In the dark it was immediately worse and worse. How old was she? Mrs. Mercer asked. Same age as you, he answered. Nearly to the day. I told you, you're both Virgo. Same age as me, she said. Still is if you think about it. They thought about it.

So quiet that house was in the night, so quiet all the other little homes around it were that held the elderly in them and the old alone or still in couples sleeping early, waking, lying awake and thinking about the past. So much past every night in the silence settling over those houses that all looked much the same on a hillside creeping up against the rock and gorse and tipping down to the river where it widened, widened and ended in the sea. We went from village to village, said Mr. Mercer in the dark. We had a map to start with but it soon gave out. We asked the way. Sometimes we had a guide from place to place. We had one when it happened funnily enough. To be honest, said Mr. Mercer, I was a wee bit jealous of him. You mean she flirted? Mrs. Mercer asked. I mean they had the language and I was only learning still and couldn't always follow. They laughed a lot, they made some jokes I couldn't understand. Also they went ahead a bit more than they needed to perhaps. Or perhaps I let them, perhaps I lagged behind on purpose and let them go ahead, I don't know why. We were on a path around a slithery purple rock and the glacier on the right of us below. They were laughing. I must have let them go ahead. Then the path went round the rock face left and they were out of sight. Last sound but one I heard from her was laughter when she was already out of sight. And the very last, her scream. When I got there she'd gone and the guide was looking down. His face was dirty yellow, I remember. Was she a blonde? Mrs. Mercer asked. No, said Mr. Mercer, her hair was black. I thought she'd be blonde, said Mrs. Mercer, being German. No, said Mr. Mercer, I told you when I told you the whole story, her hair was like yours, black. Like mine, said Mrs. Mercer.

Wednesday was library day. Same again? said Mr. Mercer. His hands were trembling, he had a scared look. Same sort of thing, said Mrs. Mercer. Mind how you go.

Whatever is in there behind the eyes or around the heart or wherever else it is, whatever it is that is not the husk of us will cease when the husk does but in the meantime never ages, does it? Explain him otherwise his agitation when he thinks of Katya in the ice: her bodily warmth and merriment night after night as Mrs. Mercer in the wooden houses among flowers in the snow comes up in him, an old man near the end, inhabits him as thoroughly as does his renewing blood. Sweet first girl, sweet unimaginable shock of the simple sight of her the first time without her clothes. What am I going to do about it? he asks himself aloud. Nothing. What can I do?

At dinnertime he said: This global warming... What about it? Mrs. Mercer said. I read some more about it in the library in a magazine. I've read that book you brought me by the way, Mrs. Mercer said. Sorry, he said. They're very worried in Switzerland especially. Where's all the water going? The glaciers are melting but the water's not come down yet. They think it's waiting, like a dam. I see, said Mrs. Mercer. They fear it will all come down at once one day. Very likely, said Mrs. Mercer. Then she said: When you tell me she's still there where she fell does that mean people can see her if they go and look? Yes, said Mr. Mercer. That's what the letter said. Still there apparently, just the way she was. Twenty, in the dress of that day and age. She'll come down when the waters break with mud and rocks and anything human in the way of it will be wiped out. But we shall be dead by then and turning in our own clay in the earth.

In the night, in the utter silence of the nights among those little houses where old people live, she felt him leave the bed and in the pitch-black reach his dressing gown and leave the room. She let him go. How it troubled her, all this. Not much to ask, peace of mind at nights and a bit of ordinary cheerfulness in the day, some conversation, something to laugh about and doing nobody any harm. And not all this. A slit of light came on under the bedroom door. She heard him fishing about above his head with the stick, tap tap, for the hook to fetch the trap door down and the ladder on it, to mount into the loft. He'll break his neck. But she heard the steps creak and the gasps of his exertion as he got up there. He'll freeze to death. How cold it was in the space under the roof above their little living space, bitter cold and draughty, where they stored the past, its bulk and minutiae, in boxes, parcels, bags, on sagging shelves, in hidey-holes diminishing with the rafters. She heard him on the ceiling above the bed, rooting around. The slithering of cartons. Heard the efforts. Then silence. She slept. Woke in a sudden terror over his absence still. Stood in her nightie at the foot of the ladder, cold even there, calling up to him till finally he showed himself, wrapped up and shivering, without his teeth, leaning over the hole, his face a blue grey with the cold and grief, he leaned down over the hole above her upturned face, its halo of thin silver hair, and tried to say nothing to worry about but couldn't and made a gibbering noise, the photos clutched two-handed against his heart.

He slept late and shuffled in without a shave. His hand was shaking. She poured his tea. That's enough now, she said. Yes, he said. But asked could she remember where she had put the big atlas. I just want to look, he said. Under the sofa, since it was more wide than fat. And my boots, he said. I beg your pardon? My boots. But those aren't the ones. No, no, but I always bought the same. She thought they might be in the shed under the old fish tank. That stick I brought back might be in there as well, he said. I daresay, said Mrs. Mercer. And will you make an appointment and get something to quieten you down?

He had found the photos and a book of hers he was carrying for her in his rucksack when she went ahead with the guide and out of sight fell down through the snow into a crack in the glacier. It was a book of poems in Gothic script with a Nazi eagle stamped on the inside cover. In the pages were some gentians, flat and nearly black. But blue if you looked long enough, an eternal blue. In the photographs she was just as she was: slim, in a long skirt, smiling, her black hair in a curve around her cheek. The white mountains were behind. The paths she stood on to be photographed often looked vertiginous but were safe enough in reality, until the last one. They were heading south, more or less, trying to find a way into Italy, as she said she had always wanted to. Her idea was there would be a last big climb, up very high where it would be hard to get your breath, and after that all the streams would run the other way and they would run down with them getting warmer and warmer through an unbelievable profusion of flowers and before long they would see the vines and that would be Italy. But some days they forgot where they were going and if a place was nice they stayed.

One thing I didn't tell you, Mr. Mercer said next morning after a quieter night though sleepless mostly, open-eyed and thinking. Oh? said Mrs. Mercer. You made an appointment at the doctor's, I hope. Yes, he said. This afternoon. I was thinking in the night one thing I never told you. Never told anyone come to that. Not a living soul. Nobody ever knew. I'm the only one in the world who knows it even now, only one alive, I mean. Well? Mrs. Mercer said. She was going to have a baby. My Katya was. More and more slowly Mrs. Mercer went on with her toast and homemade damson jam. He sat, turning over his empty hands. His face, she knew, had she confronted it, was looking at her with its puzzled and pleading look, the eyes behind the glasses rather washed out. I suppose I thought it might upset you at the time. I see, she said after a while when her mouth had given up trying to eat. I suppose you would think that. Then she took her own things to the draining board and left him sitting there with his.

They parted company; ate together, slept together, but were in separate circles. Almost at once, as though it were beyond his failing strength, he gave up pitying his wife and fell back down the decades into the couple of months of a summer in the Alps. Between thinking and muttering he went to and fro, up and down, never knew which he was in, and in her company, face to face over another meal or side by side on a walk to the post office, addressed her or himself. I wonder where you put that big medical dictionary. It wasn't with the Cassell's behind the jars. In the loft perhaps. The ladder to the loft was permanently down, encumbering the way into the little living room. A breath of cold hung over the opening. Or the warmth of their living space, being drawn up there, was converted into cold just above their heads. He was often up there, rooting around. In the mechanism of her love and duty she called him down when his meal was on the table. But also at nights he went up there and she heard him moving and muttering over the bedroom ceiling. Then she wept to herself, for the unfairness. Surely to God it wasn't much to ask, that you get through to the end and looking back you don't fill with horror and disappointment and hopeless wishful thinking? All she wanted was to be able to say it hasn't been nothing, it hasn't been a waste of time, the fifty years, that they amount to something, if not a child, a something made and grown between man and wife you could be proud of and nearly as substantial as a child. And now all this: him burrowing back though the layers, him rooting through all their accumulations, to get back where he wanted to be, in the time before she was. Once with a bitterness that twisted her mouth as if the question were vinegar she asked: How far gone was she? Six weeks, Mr. Mercer answered. We worked it out it would be about six weeks.

The foetus at six weeks is a tiny thing hung in the mother like a creature in hibernation. The medical dictionary was in the loft in a very cramped place where the eaves came down behind a sort of false wall made of hardboard. But Mr. Mercer found it finally and in it a picture of the foetus at six weeks and sat there under the bare bulb like an adolescent staring at it. What struck him most when he thought about him and Katya was their heedlessness. That was the word that came to him. We were heedless. Because really if it was bad where we were leaving, which was Bavaria, it was not much better where we were heading, which was Italy, and up there in the snow, the minute we set off what did we do but go and get a baby. Heedless. For obviously we should have to come down again sooner or later, out of the sharp air, the flowers and the snow, and face up to our responsibilities in a bad world getting worse. But then

again when he thought about it it didn't seem heedless at
all, because the thing he was most sure about, after all the
years, was how sure they were all those years ago that what
he wanted with her and she with him was to have a baby
and go on living and living together forevermore. And you
can't be called heedless when you know as well as that what
your purpose is in life and you act accordingly. And though
they weren't walking anywhere in particular, only to Italy
and where in Italy it didn't much matter, every day seemed
to have enough point to it getting from wherever they were
to wherever they ended up and finding somewhere nice to
stay as Mr. and Mrs. with her brassy wedding ring. And days
when they didn't go anywhere but stayed in bed and took a
little stroll in the vicinity when they felt like it seemed just
as purposeful as days when they set off at four in the morning deadly serious. What did we do for food, I wonder, he
asked himself up there in the roof space as though somebody
else was asking him. What did we have for money between
us to go on like that day after day, week after week? I can
only suppose, he said to himself aloud or in his head, that
God provided and kind people along the way. I have the
feeling, he said, that somehow people liked us and somehow
or other it gladdened them when we turned up. When Mr.
Mercer thought of himself and her he thought of certain
flowers and not the gentians that were beyond having any
ideas about but a bare and rather frail violet flower that came
up *actually in the ice*, as soon as there was the least gap of grass
or earth and the water unfreezing around it and running
fast, there you would see one or more of these frail flowers
sprung up. Then, and more so now, he wanted to call them,
these flowers, brave: but a flower was a flower and neither
brave nor cowardly nor anything else, yet the word brave
came to mind when he thought of that quick seizing of a
chance to spring up the minute the ice opened even only
a little. And that was how he thought of Katya and himself

after all that time with Hitler where they'd come from and Mussolini where they were going to, up there wandering around and making a baby the minute they turned their backs on civilization.

Tuesday again. Where's the trip today then? Mr. Mercer asked. It seemed to Mrs. Mercer he had aged ten years in a week if that were possible for a man his age already. The Horseshoe Pass, she said brightly, and the Swallow Falls, to see some scenery. You'll enjoy that, he said.

The minute the door closed after her he put his boots on that were not *the* boots but like them because he had always bought the same and packed a rucksack with the maps and some provisions for the journey. The maps were the very ones, in Gothic script with a pair of hikers on the cover in the costume of that time and place. He had found them in the loft with the photographs that he had against his heart now in a wallet with the letter to prove he had a right to see her in the ice if anyone in authority challenged him. When he was ready with a hat and stick and money from the place he hid his in under one of the joists, he wrote a message to leave on the table for Mrs. Mercer when she came home from her trip. Dear Kate, he wrote, I am sorry about the tea again but trust you will understand that I have to go and see her as the next of kin and am sure it will all be back to normal here with you and me after that. PS I've made another appointment for a week on Monday. I think I'll ask him for something a bit stronger to quieten me down.

Where the road drops away from among the same houses Mr. Mercer paused for a moment over the view, over the estuary, over the river widening and giving itself up into the endless sea. A sunny light was on that place where sweet and salt meet and the salt takes all the river in, all the streams of all the hills all along the way and feels not a bit of difference but continues vast and flat and through and through

undrinkable. Kitted up to leave with money and some bis-
cuits for the journey Mr. Mercer brought his mind to bear
on a six-week baby beginning in a girl of twenty in the ice
now after sixty years uncovered because the glacier had lost
its snow and discovered in there, fresh. The kindly woman
whose house he was standing outside must have watched
him for a good ten minutes from her front-room window
before she came out worried. And tried her best then, shaking him gently, speaking close up into his absent face, to get
through to what was still alive in him in there behind his
glasses and the glaze of tears.

THE CAVE

Lou's sister phoned. Was she still seeing her funny chap? Lately he was all Maya asked about. Indeed, she had begun to preach, which Lou rather resented. But since she had no one else to discuss him—or it, the whole business—with, often she weakened and confessed. Yes, she said, I'm seeing him next week as a matter of fact. And what will it be this time? Maya asked. A longboat to the Arctic Circle? Lying on deck under the Aurora Borealis? Lou said it wouldn't be anything so idle but what it would be she didn't know. She never knew. That was what annoyed Maya. She said it was demeaning, always waiting for surprises, like a little girl, always waiting for the next treat. But she wasn't a little girl, she was a grown woman, time running out etc., etc. Life's not all treats, you know. At which point Lou asked after the children. How was Chloë's piano? Did William like his new school? Was she, Maya, still doing all the fetching and carrying? How was Henry? Very busy? Was she seeing anyone else? As a matter of fact I am, said Maya. Time's running out, I do want a life of my own. And then she reverted, in what sounded like real concern, to her sister, *her* life, her infrequent meetings with the man she,

Maya, thought very dubious. All I mean is, does he mean it? Mean what? When he takes you off doing these extraordinary things, is he serious? He's *very* serious, said Lou. Or rather, *it's* serious. *It* is very serious. But I suppose you mean does he love me, will he marry me, will we buy a house, will he have children with me, that sort of thing? You love him, that's obvious, said Maya, and if he doesn't love you he shouldn't keep doing things with you that make you love him more. Obvious? Keep doing? More? Lou got tangled up and stopped listening. She wondered did men ever talk about women like that, hour after hour, about their women. She couldn't imagine that they did. She supposed some of them boasted. She couldn't imagine Owen talking to another man about her and boasting. For one thing, what did he have to boast about, in that sense? Maya, she said, coming back in, I sometimes think we're no better off than Jane Austen's women, and men aren't better off either, the way you talk. They mustn't do anything that might arouse in us expectations they cannot or will not fulfill. And if they do, they are bad men and we are fools. I only mean you should find out if he's serious, Maya said. Or what else is he after? Power? You worry me, Lou. You are on your own too much.

Lou was right to say that a longboat under the Aurora Borealis would not have been Owen's thing. Mostly when he wrote to suggest they might meet it was to do something he described as his job, or his job, 'sort of'. For example, during a bad fire on the moors he asked, the minute she arrived, would she like to climb up with him and see the damage? It was still burning when they got there and the usual roads had been closed by the police; but he knew a way round, from upwind, luckily enough, and they followed the fire as it cropped its way through the heather. Funny having residual flames about your ankles and kicking through hot ash. One discovery pleased him particularly. He had come across a poem about a hill fire in which the fire was described as advancing over all but 'leaving springs in hoofmarks'. In Lou's opinion, Owen did not give enough credence to poetry; but when they found several such damp survivals he had to concede that, for once, a poem told the truth.

Anyway, a week after Maya's phone call, there they were, Lou Johnson and Owen Shepperd, in the limestone country and it was not going well. Miserably she trailed along behind him like a child in disgrace not knowing why, sorrowful and furious at the rules she did not understand but hated and despised anyway, whether she understood or not. Why had he asked her? Why had she been fool enough to come? They were trailing along the busy street of a small town and she supposed it must be back to the railway station he was leading her and there, courteous and cold, he would see her on to a train and that would be that. Well so be it. Still she was miserable.

Then suddenly he halted, turned to her and said, Forget all that. Here's this. And he took her first by the arm then very firmly by the hand and stepped with her off the busy street into an alleyway between two ordinary shops. The way was not surfaced like a modern street but roughly cobbled and before long not even that, the limestone itself was underfoot and the alley had become a track, rising. So the street had a very thin border, only one row of shops, and you could step between them, if you knew the gap, into this! Owen said nothing, he seemed to be concentrating. He had on his face the expression of a man concentrating hard to get something right, to make something come true under his feet and before his eyes. But he held her hand tightly as though that should be proof enough and she shouldn't worry he might rather be there concentrating alone. They went on in silence, the way climbed, soon it was more a deserted stream bed than a path, they climbed under hazels and alders, in a mossy light, and the noise of the town quietened behind them and below. The town continued in her consciousness for a while, lingering as a murmur at the back of her mind, then she forgot it. The first words he said were, The water's just underneath.

Stepping off a public street into a quite different space and time was something Owen had done with Lou before. Once it was in the spa town, in late summer. He had written and suggested they meet, she agreed, they met, they were walking along, it was going well between them, in a friendly sort of way. He seemed glad of the occasion, sure of it, and quite suddenly guided her off the street through a broken door (it wouldn't open, they squeezed) into a long walled garden. The place astonished her. Only later, not having heard from him for weeks, did she again rather resent his ability to astonish her. Whenever Owen fell out of her favour she declared him, almost in her sister's voice, to be playing a very calculated game with her, the chief interest of which, from his point of view, was power. But the garden did astonish her. It belonged to a very big house whose many eyes and mouths were shut with steel against the vandals. Owen's interest lay at the far end, in the apple orchard. Scrumping, he said. Before the developers grub them up. And out of his rucksack he took several plastic bags and handed Lou a couple. The trees had been neglected, they wore mistletoe, moss and lichen on many dead branches as the marks of it; but nevertheless, keeping their side of the bargain, they had cropped. A few of each sort, if you wouldn't mind, Owen said. The old lady collected and some you can't find any more. Quietly they moved through the apple light plucking fruit that was shining pearl and shades of red and gold and underwater green. Owen could name some, but had a friend, he said, who would identify the rest and grow their progeny from pips. When he took out his notebook and became very serious, Lou drifted back to where the wreckage of a kitchen garden began and sat there, on the orchard frontier, under the last tree, eating an apple whose name perhaps only Owen's friend would know. The flesh and juice and sweetness without a name gave her a thoughtful pleasure that had an undertow of sadness, in full view of the stopped and blinded house.

And now, climbing the stream bed, Lou acknowledged that he must once again have schemed for an effect. Surely he knew very well where the particular gap was between the shops. But because of the bad mood and her trailing behind him dejectedly they might have forfeited the chance, their being in the stream bed after all was a mercy, and when he said that the water was 'just underneath' she felt a rush of affection for him and gratitude that he had wrenched himself out of his bad humour and rescued the good opportunity for them both.

The climb steepened. Owen went ahead. Then the course of the stream, the dampness, its covering of trees, its softening and adornment by moss and pennywort and fern, gave out and they had an open space before them and lapwings flapping up raggedly into a blue sky. Late afternoon. Some distance off was a grey-white scar. It's there, he said. What it was, Lou did not ask. I was sixteen when I came here last, he said, on my own. I doubted I would find the place again. I thought the gap would be filled in years ago. His happiness touched her. And the lapwing still! That's a blessing, they are so diminished nowadays. How I love limestone!

Owen lived on the gritstone, which has its own character and beauties. And—as he had told Lou more than once—he was content that the limestone should be some way off, within walking distance but still a sensible journey. It was a zone he could set off for and come into, a country of rock that changed from almost black through grey to white under the fleeting weather. He loved the shallows of water on the green grass in the sunshine after rain; the vanishings of water, its passage and collecting underground, its distant reappearances. All that and more, he said. Much more. And not that I don't love where I live.

Lou had gone there once, to Owen's house on the gritstone, uninvited, or at least without warning him. He had often said to her, Call in if you're ever that way, so one day she did, not having heard from him for weeks and without pretending that she had any other business in his neighbourhood. See how he pulls you, Maya said. But then she added, Your voice is funny. Is it bad again? Yes, said Lou it is very bad again. I thought the walk might get me out of it. So she bought the necessary map, drove for a couple of hours, left the car ten miles off, and walked. She did not expect him to be at home and was not even sure, the closer she got, that she really hoped he would be. Mile by mile the walk had inspirited her lungs, her voice came up, she tested it by singing. The walking itself—the movement, the attention—was so beautifully effective she began to believe she did not need him to be the object of it and, almost arrived, she had half a mind to turn and retrace her steps.

The village surprised her. It was intricately built up one side, the south-facing, of a narrow valley, the houses were fitted along terraces and access from level to level was by steep alleys and steps. Having no hope of finding his house, she asked at the shop, which was down below by the bridge. The woman directed her, and two or three gossipers looked on and smiled. It occurred to her that she had no real idea how Owen lived, not even whether he lived alone; but lodged now in the talk of the village she felt she had no option but to see her journey through. Besides, she was tired. The directions were inadequate, two levels up she had to ask again. A man who had been watching her pointed out the house, and soon she stood there in the garden of it, entering by the back gate not the front, and saw him in the window at a plain table, writing. For perhaps half a minute Lou had the advantage and considered him. She saw again—she had seen it often—how when he concentrated he seemed to need nobody and nothing but what he had in mind. He seemed in a circle of his own, and she stood outside, viewing him through the glass, banished. But then, not enjoying her advantage, she made a small movement of her hand so that he looked up, saw her, and she saw him not just surprised but at a loss, bewildered, fearful, as though appearing suddenly in his garden in the sunlight she was a phenomenon against which he was quite defenceless. It shook her to see him like that, and deeply confused her feelings.

By the time he opened the door, Owen had composed himself. But she had seen him strangely and differently, he knew it, she could see it in his eyes still, anxious, curious what she might mean by her arrival. But he welcomed her in and, watching him closely, Lou judged his warmth to be sincere. They stood in the kitchen, which was clean and bright, everything purposeful and in order, no clutter, nothing lying around. In style the larger room, where she had watched him writing, was much the same. There were many books, but neatly shelved; a few pictures, but with space around them; a plain brick hearth, nicely proportioned, with a fire laid in. Lou realized that she had always supposed he would inhabit such a house. It fitted her idea of him: that he was self-possessed, needed nobody, had things to do in a house conducive to doing them. But perhaps he lived like this by an effort of the will, by concentrating, by not allowing himself to be distracted? If so, then his discomposure, his look almost of panic when he saw her in the garden, must be counted a lapse, which he would duly make up for.

But how courteous he was, how glad she had sought him out! She must stay the night, in the morning he would walk back to the car with her, they would have at least half the day together. Such a treat! Lou watched him, he encouraged her credence. There was one spare bedroom. He apologized that it had no view—except upwards, to the crest of the hillside, sky, passing clouds. His—he showed her—looked out over the valley, received the sun. There was a guitar in one corner; a small table in the window; bare walls, one line drawing of a nude, a girl walking away; the bed. The room was like a bedsit, within the house, as though he could withdraw there, to a sparse place, and be content. So, she thought, he lives alone, the way a man will live who is purposeful and self-reliant. The word 'economy' occurred to her, not as meanness, not even as thrift, but sufficiency, the parts fitting and belonging, like the features of his face when he was attentive in a conversation or set on a purpose, like his clothes, his body, his quick decided walk. Why should he want her or anyone else? He gave her a clean towel and she went for a bath. After it, back in her room, she wondered whether to change or not, and did then, into the red dress that hardly crumpled in a rucksack.

Supper was cooking. Lou heard Owen on the telephone in the kitchen. He seemed to be making an arrangement. She stood by the hearth and looked at the two photographs that were the only things on the mantelpiece: two young women, one from many years ago, in a loose dress patterned with what might be jasmine; the other modern, in the same style of dress, doubtless from a charity shop. Owen came in. Have you had to rearrange your evening because of me? she asked. Yes, he said, and I'm glad. I was supposed to be keeping watch tonight, but I've swapped my shift, I'll do it tomorrow. Keeping watch? The lady's slipper, he said. There's a patch not far from here, I'll show you in the morning if you like. The last, or the first, it depends. We have to guard them all day and at nights. People know and would come and dig them up. So you lie out under the moon and stars and keep watch? It's my job, he said. Sort of. Once it was ospreys, now it's the lady's slipper. I see, said Lou.

Then Owen said, Can you see any family resemblance? He nodded at the photographs. Yes I can, said Lou. The smile, their eyes. The two women, side by side, looked out hesitantly and confidently, as though fearful of their own appeal, at whoever would look at them. They are both very beautiful, Lou said. She could remember Maya in that look, too beautiful, nervous at the power of it. Yes, said Owen. They are both eighteen. That one's my mother sixty years ago. The other's my daughter twelve years ago. Lou looked closely, from the photographs to him and back again. Yes, she said, I do see the likeness. And where are they now? My mother is in Manchester, I see her once a fortnight. Natalie, I don't know where she is. I never see her. Never? I did three times in the year of that photograph. I stood outside her college and watched her go in. But never since. I was afraid she would notice. Nor could I bear it. And I promised, you see. She's not allowed to know. I promised her mother. She thinks the man at home is her father. He thinks so too. I see, said Lou.

Owen gave her some wine. We don't know much, do we? About one another, I mean. We don't ask, said Lou. I would always tell you if you asked. But saying that she thought, I'm an entrance into nothingness so put your questions softly or the earth will open up. But you, she said. I always supposed you must be very deep and now you tell me there's a grown-up daughter in you, so I was right. Owen shrugged. Except she's not, he said. Her absence is. I like you in that dress.

That night Lou couldn't sleep. The house was friendly, all its small noises were kind, the village felt homely, she could hear a stream, finding down to the river below. All evening he had been gentle, they were easy with one another, their talk went to and fro quietly and clear. Everything was kind. But the sadness came back on her, sadness and terror. She saw the two young women, girls of eighteen, the mother, the daughter, hesitant but sure of themselves, fearful of their beauty but trusting it, looking out. And herself she saw whirling in panic through a hole in the years into loveless space. She lay in the neat white bed in the hospitable room and shook from head to toe, she writhed, she dug her nails into her palms. Then she said aloud, This is foolish, he is my friend, I am sure of that at least, he will not take it amiss. She got out of bed and viewed her ghost in the long mirror naked, white, thin, clutching its shoulders. And at that she slipped on the red dress and went in to him. He was asleep. She woke him. Owen, she said, let

me be with you, please. I can't sleep, I'm shaking to bits again.
Hush, he said. Hush now. What is it? Come in here, we'll sleep.

In the bare landscape, in the expectation of the particular
place ahead of her, Lou's feelings rose and widened. Between
the two simple planes of earth and sky she entered a happiness
she imagined most people had enjoyed, and many could still
go back to, in childhood. The ground delighted her, the rock
so evident through its pelt of grass, the blood-red cranesbill,
the tufts of thyme and many more such graces over the vast
deposits of sea-lily stone. And the sky, as a child might paint
it, white clouds pasturing on blue, larks dangling. There's
something else you don't know about me, she said. Owen
waited. I was in the Bach choir once. Prove it, he said. Stand
there on that pulpit stone and sing. Lou stood, folded her
hands like a penitent, looked up to heaven and sang:

When I was a bachelor, I lived all alone,
I worked at the weaver's trade
And the only, only thing that I ever did wrong
Was to love a fair young maid.
I loved her in the wintertime
And in the summer, too
And the only, only thing that I ever did wrong
Was to keep her from the foggy, foggy dew.

One night she came to my bedside
As I lay sound asleep.
She laid her head upon my breast
And she began to weep.
She sighed, she cried, she damn near died,
She cried, What shall I do?
So I took her into bed and I covered up her head
Just to keep her from the foggy foggy dew.

There she halted. Owen's look halted her. In the silence they heard the larks again, the irrepressible leaps and falls and leapings again of song. And something else, still faintly, ahead of them on the higher ground, they heard water.

They climbed. Soon the way levelled across a broad terrace where it was damper and there were orchids, tight magenta spires, and also the yellow bog myrtle; and this moistening, where the water sank, was the sign that they were getting closer to the place itself, the cave, where the water issued. Owen's few words ceased altogether. Lou paused to let him go ahead. He shrugged, made a little gesture of apology and helplessness. He was hauling back the years in broad daylight, even before they reached the cave the boy he had been was repossessing him. But Lou was not put out, she gathered her own happiness down from the sky and off the open country into this young course of water that they were climbing to the cave, its place of issue, that Owen had remembered and wanted her to know. She waved him ahead, content being in herself. The water babbled and sparkled, this was its phase of passage under the sun and moon, after the cave and before the yellow and verdant and magenta dampness, the sink. She followed Owen, who had more years in him, she watched his stepping up and up against the water hurrying down at him, higher and higher he stepped, to the cliff itself, over which the water leaped and offered itself as a rope, a silver ladder, for him and her to climb. She would always see it thus: the clear hank of living water let down over the scar for her to climb, to the phenomenon the man she loved remembered and had wanted her to see.

Owen stood up on the brink. From the last foothold, splashed by the toppling water, Lou got two good hand-holds, two good grips, each into wet clefts, her fingers feeling rock under the moss, and heaved herself up and through in one quick movement of pure ability and lightness. And there they stood, on a broad and stony and flowery ledge, the water sliding fast towards them, towards its fall, and nothing now ahead of them but the cave.

The cave stretched all across and came down at either end. Naturally, it resembled a mouth, but not one screaming, it was not open wide enough for that; but sighing, gasping, moaning, in pain or pleasure, yes, open that wide. The breaths coming out of it were cold. Even where she stood, on the brink with Owen, where the stream hurried over, Lou felt the cold breath of the cave. Doubtless it carried on the cold slide of water. She and Owen had that water between them, steadily fast, sliding between them to the edge, only a narrow divide they could have taken hands across. She turned from facing the cave to facing him, and saw that he was watching her very closely. They were high up, they might have relaxed side by side, looking back down the way they had come, all the way down to where the path went into the dark foliage and dived as a stream bed, dry or damp or flowing, steeply back into the river-level town. Instead, he stood staring at her, waiting, and Lou understood they had not yet arrived. The cave was astonishing in its spread, the water hurrying out of it was lucid and beautiful, the climb had been a joy; but still they were only on a threshold. Listen, he said. Then she listened to what she had been hearing, without knowing, for some minutes or perhaps for years: the sound of the cave, audible outside in the sunlight but coming from far, far in, from inside, in the immeasurable bulk of limestone behind and beyond the cave, from deep in there. That's what I heard when I came here on my own, he said. In a way I've been hearkening for it ever since. And I wanted you to hear it and myself to hear it again now with you. Then he reached across, handed her over the fast shallow stream, to his side, and led her in, under the quite abruptly downsloping roof of the cave, in till they stooped, in till they crouched, and where they could go no further, in the angle of roof and floor, there at the slit, the flat aperture, where the water emerged, they made themselves small and sat.

Though you could hear nothing else, the water behind the slit was not deafening, not at all; its force lay in the certainty that its origins were remote. When you see a star, you know that its light has travelled years to your eyes. Similarly this noise, to their ears: from remote space and time. So the commotion they could hear was the long-after sound, carrying in it the remembered horror of the making. The water, that, far back, had been in there at the making, slid out in absolute silence, shallow, clear, very fast, and bubbles rode on it, clear domes travelled out of a zone of utter darkness into the cave-light on a sliding fast surface and very soon, silently, popped, and the air in them joined the air that Owen and Lou, bowed over them, watching intently, breathed.

In the way that human beings are bound to, Lou was thinking, What is this like? And ideas came to mind, rough gestures towards the thing itself: like a heart and a pulse, though not of any beast she knew; like an engine, the thrumming of a steady—but varied—working; like an oven, a furnace, if you could think of its cold as heat. But it was easier to compare this thing whose utterance was close and that was really of the earth, to phenomena she would never be anywhere near and was at liberty merely to imagine. The background noise of space, for example, the aural context of all the galactic debris still dispersing. So Lou spun ideas, as any human would, to try to say what the sound of the cave was like; but in the midst of her ideas, despite their interference, she knew with a thrill of horror, that what she was listening to, though nameless, was familiar. So reading a poem, often what dawns on you is a thing you knew already but had forgotten or didn't know well enough and now the lines with a vengeance will remind you and make you know it this time close and true.

Owen looked mesmerized, entranced, as though his first and remembered deep impression was deepening further now and more than he could bear. Lou touched his arm, and he started. She pointed towards the daylight at the mouth of the cave and after a little moment, which seemed not a reluctance but a coming to, he nodded and followed her. They went out to the brink and sat there looking over the open land, still sunny, down to where the little town must be.

What did you do when you came here last time, Lou asked, all those years ago? I ran away, said Owen. I wanted to sleep in the cave, I had ideas of that sort. But as soon as I lay down there was only that noise behind that slit. I couldn't bear it, so I decamped. Lou said nothing. After a while Owen said, I was going to ask what you would like to do. If we left now we could be back in town before dark and perhaps find a train or a bus. Is that what you want? Lou asked. If you were here on your own again, what would you do? I don't think I'd be here on my own, said Owen. But if I were, I think I should try to stay. Then we'll stay, said Lou.

Where they sat, the water toppling over made quite a loud and cheerful noise; but behind them, as they watched the shadow extending slowly over the open land towards their heights, the noise inside the cave became, if not louder, certainly more insistent. Why did you want to listen to it again? Lou asked. Because, Owen answered, I've often—and in some periods constantly—wanted to live as though I could always hear that cave. I don't want to live forgetting there's a noise like that. I mean, in some ways it isn't so very mysterious. Somewhere inside there must be a waterfall, quite a big one. Very beautiful no doubt, if things are beautiful that nobody can see. And what we can hear is the chute, the impact, the milling, the overflowing of water through tunnels till it finds that slit. All magnified, echoing, distorted. After heavy rain it would sound different. After no rain different again. But essentially the same, for all its variations, and always strange. Like the flight of the stuff of the universe: you might grasp the principle, but the act of it, the working out, is infinitely strange. But I can talk like this because we are sitting here together facing away and the sunlight will last a while longer.

Up close, in the dark, when I was a boy I understood nothing at all, I heard the noise, only that. And it would be the same today, I guess, up close in there on my own. I thought we'd sleep in the mouth, said Lou, nearer the open air. I thought the same, said Owen. Still it will be cold and loud.

The shadow was climbing. They moved along to the far corner of the cave where, as you might say, upper lip and lower met. Owen dug out from his rucksack first a bag of food, then an old army blanket. This latter resource Lou smiled at. I've got something similar, she said. From Marks & Spencer's. Not so serious, but very handy. She produced it. We can lie on that and have yours over us. She went back to the stream, filled her water bottle, and returning saw, first, that he had also fished out a bottle of wine, and, secondly, that, above his head, under the coping of stone and fern and moss, a wren had gone in to nest. The smallness of the bird— she could almost feel its heartbeat—and the constant booming and droning from in the cave, the two together, brought a rush of tears to her eyes, and she knelt down by Owen in a state he could perhaps only guess at, to take the cup of wine.

They were still in the sun, but not for much longer. She watched him eyeing the shadow. She wanted him not to worry. I see it will be cold, she said. But it isn't now. So they ate and drank on the ledge, without haste. But then he was brisk, stood up, said they must get ready, and walked away, round that edge of the cave out of sight, she supposed to pee. She went round the other corner, taking her wash-bag, and met him back at the stream where it toppled over, and face to face across the water they cleaned their teeth. Very domestic, he said. Then back in their alcove he said she must put on everything she had with her, which she did, or almost. And when they were on her rug and under his blanket, lying on ferns and their heads on the rucksacks, and the wren chirred loudly against the steady engine of the cave, she said, Funny how I put on clothes to go to bed with you.

Then she added, I'll tell you something, though my big sister told me I shouldn't. Why did she tell you you shouldn't? Owen asked. She said I'd be more in your power if you knew. I see, said Owen. Don't tell me then, if you believe what she says. But you're not in my power, I don't want that power. Whether or not, said Lou. It's nothing much, only silly. Before I come and see you, because I never know what we'll do, I always go and buy myself something pretty, just in case. Like your red dress? No, for underneath. I see, said Owen. But you don't, said Lou. The thing is you don't. No, I never do, he said. Now, for example, said Lou, I'd freeze to death if you did. All the same, said Owen. What else does your sister say? She says I should ask you if you are serious. But you know that I'm serious. That's what I tell her, said Lou. I tell her you are *very* serious.

Night moved in quietly and very gradually. The evening let go its colours, their great variety, into the state of pallor into which the dark could seep. Stars flowered delicately on a fainter and fainter wash of blue and pink and green; then hardened, began to glint and pulse, on the risen tide of their own element, blackness. Under a house roof or under the street lamps you never see them coming into their energy. You have to be out, lying under them, aware of the thinness of the habitable skin of the earth, and the stars in a dome come crowding over you and the spaces between them fill with black infinity.

Sheltered from half the sky under their eave of rock, Owen and Lou had the cave behind them. They lay in the mouth of it as though in the bowl and under the lid of a half-open shell, and the din of the engines of water, as everything else was hushed, entered their consciousness through tunnels in the rock and tunnels in their ears, totally. Lou doubted whether thoughts and the unspeaking voice you employ within your head would be at all effective, as a self-assertion, against that constant pulse. She understood why the boy Owen had fled and wondered where out of earshot he had gone and shivered.

Her face was cold but in his arms under the blanket in all her clothes the rest was warm. After a while she said, My sister says we never do anything ordinary. She says it's not grown-up to only do extraordinary things together. Your sister…, Owen began. Then he asked had she, Lou, ever been underground, really underground, in a deep cave, and put the lights out? Because if she hadn't, they could do that together one day, if she liked. He knew somebody who would take them down. I mean so you can see a true darkness. Really underground with the lights out you can't see the hand in front of your face, put it as close and stare at it as hard and for as long as you will. Lou said no thank you, where they were now, together with the noise of it, was dark enough. Owen agreed. I thought I had to, he added, for my work. I was with someone who knew about the creatures that can live in dark like that. They are white and don't have any eyes. I thought I ought to see them so he took me down and showed me how they live. You and your work, said Lou. Yes, said Owen, and the reason I wanted to hear this cave again is so that I won't forget how much there is on earth we'll never see.

Lou wanted him to say that her being there with him was some consolation, at least, for what he couldn't see; but he stayed silent, the silence filled up with the noise and soon she said, You see a lot, you understand the way life hangs together. I hadn't thought much about the web of life till I met you. It's torn, he said, it's tearing worse and worse before my eyes, day and night, we mend what bits we can but it's all a rearguard fighting, little halts we make now and then that feel like victories, but the way is hurrying to ruin as everyone in the business, whichever side they're on, knows very well. His voice was level; a level sadness. And in the end what does it matter? That in there, that machine, will go on in some shape or form whatever we do. When the accident of our being here is cancelled out, what's left will start up again without us, by the old laws. Which is another reason for always being able to hear that noise. They are the mechanics that will survive us when by our doing—melting the ice, raising the seas, opening the deluges of the firmament—we have helped them wipe us out. And there we are.

Owen was a long time silent. They both were. The pulse of inhuman life in total darkness continued unperturbed. Lou began to be very fearful. Something more cavernous than he seemed to have any inkling of was opening up in her, as she had feared it would. But then in the same level voice against the cold breathing of the cave he said, And of course it's loveless. That's why I came to listen to it again. Beautiful it may be, intricate and powerful beyond our imagining—but loveless. It is sentient life that loves, in varying degrees, we humans most. Every creature fears and in various ways, many finer than ours, they know. But we love most and know most, the most connectedly. We know the damage, for example. So we can't watch ourselves, the accident, hurrying to ruin without grief. Going back by the old mechanics into the old chaos of fire and flood, is sad to watch. No other thing on earth feels sad like that because nothing else on earth can know and love the way we do.

Frightened by a gap in speech, because it filled up with the churning of the waters behind the cave, Lou asked Owen what he knew of his daughter. Nothing, he said. Her mother stopped writing to me twelve years ago. Really I don't even know whether she's alive or dead. Did you love Natalie's mother? Yes I did. And did she love you? She said she did. But she wouldn't leave and come away with you? She had one child already and she loved her husband. So you love your daughter and you never see her? Yes. And can you do anything for her? Her mother wouldn't let me. She said Natalie must never know. Not even when her mother and father and the man she thinks is her father are dead must she ever know. But those photographs on your mantelpiece? They're not there usually. I only put them out every now and then. And when you appeared so suddenly that day I left them there for you to see. No one else sees them.

Lou dwelled on Natalie, on her mother and on the man she called her father. She felt anxious for them, as though they had been entrusted into her thinking, and were vulnerable. They floated on a lie, the truth, falling from heaven, would sink them. Lou imagined them floating on the surface of the underground roaring in a bubble. And bubbles in hundreds meanwhile rode out through the slit on the cold rapid slide of water, lasting in the lighter darkness until they popped. And warm against the man, Lou must have slept and breathed with him a little of the air shipped out from inside in those hemispheres.

Some while later, sleeping very near the surface and the waters under the earth seeming louder and louder, Lou became aware that Owen was speaking, but to whom, if anybody, and whether in his sleep or waking she could not have said. The voice was close and rapid and even if she were indeed the one addressed, still it felt like eavesdropping. She could not unhear it, any more than she could unsee the sight of him through the garden window the day she suddenly appeared; the words and the sight accrued to her like a power she had not sought but could not disavow. Perhaps he had been speaking for some time and only now, surfacing through their broken sleep, could she hear and understand. I was very young, he said, and perhaps when she said she would keep the baby a secret, though I did love her, in some part of me I thought this lets me off, I can start again and live my life on my own and no harm done. I suppose a woman always knows how much she will love her baby but perhaps a man does not, even if it's a love child, perhaps he can't imagine how he will love his child and be loved by her or him and be fastened in lifelong. Or perhaps he can, said Lou. Perhaps he sees as well as the woman he slept with sees. And so you didn't insist very much when she said the best for all concerned would be you keep her secret and go away. We kept in touch, she wrote me letters once a year at least.

And then soon after Natalie's eighteenth birthday came that photograph and a note she was starting art school in Newcastle on a certain day. I stood five mornings there, it was only on the third I saw her and on the fourth and fifth again. That last day was very bad. I saw her and it went through me. I thought will I ever see the girl again? I left the place, I was almost running down the street, away, and then I stopped and turned and walked very slowly back and there she was, coming out again through the big glass doors, with a look on her face as though she had forgotten or remembered something. And stood on the top step looking down at me, into my eyes, in a puzzled sort of shock. And when I think of it now there was nobody else around, only her and me, and the noise of the street or in my heart and head was like the noise in there, in the dark, behind that slit. After that her mother never wrote to me again and I kept my side of the bargain and never tried to learn about her further life. Funny to think of her, said Lou, going her ways in the world and you going yours and never crossing. If there was a god with nothing better to do he might have amused himself with your lines of life. Yes, said Owen, I read of a man who met his daughter abroad somewhere and fell in love with her and neither knew. They slept together on an island for a week or so and he begged her to marry him and it was only when she agreed and they went home that piece by piece the evidence of who they were came in. Is that what you're frightened of? Lou asked. You've seen her, you've got her photograph, it could never happen. Not like that, it couldn't, not like the man on the island, said Owen. Not in ignorance.

Lou pondered this; the cave too, so it seemed, mulled the business over, but indifferently, only as an engine, on and on. Like bubbles riding out on the fast cold water, the image of the girl looking down and the man looking up, both seeing deep into one another's eyes, became very clear to Lou and she said, perhaps aloud, perhaps already asleep and to a man asleep, Like falling in love, I suppose, there and then, the way it happens to some people, the lightning, so go your separate ways and trail the earth apart and you will never forget her nor she you. She slept in Owen's arms, the furnace of cold in the innermost heart of rock continuing to roar and to breathe little bubbles into the human world. Meanwhile outside, above, the stars pulsed on their black infinity.

Sleeping, Lou acknowledged more thoroughly than she would have cared to do in daylight that she and the noise in the dark behind the cave were old familiars. Owen had said he needed to hear it again, to be reminded that such undergound noise was there; but Lou, brought to the site by him, lay sleep-ing-listening to a thing she had known for years, and what appalled her now was how much deeper into it a soul might go. Suppose, she thought, or thoughts took hold of her and swirled her round and sent her out under the squeeze of rock as bubbles into the world where humans live, suppose it's all like that, only a mechanism and whether we live or not it will go on and on and whether he loves me or not is neither here nor there and I might as well be the water falling from a terri-ble height that he says must be beautiful, if something nobody sees can be called beautiful. Dread filled her up, the trembling took hold of her, deeply asleep she felt even closer to the noise, deeper down in it, staring to see and seeing nothing, eyes wide open and seeing not a thing but knowing that creatures were in there with her, white as death, white as the underbelly of a flatfish, big, flat, fast and blind, their eyes over millions of years of useless effort having evolved away. Lou tried her best to answer back, she babbled all she knew by heart and many good new things occurring to her while she slept, she pitched them all in her small human voice against the never-to-be-exhausted fund of noise within the cave. Then failing, so she felt, defeated, she gave up making sentences and screamed, widened her eyes and screamed and screamed.

Hush, Owen said, hush now, nothing's amiss. It's only the noise. We're safe out here under our blanket, you and me. Feel my heart, she said. Whirring like a wren. Was it like that night in my house when you couldn't sleep? he asked. Worse, said Lou. Your lovely house, I could hear a little stream falling down to the river by the bridge where I asked the gossipy women how to find you. But in me nevertheless in your friendly house, to my shame, oh it was very bad. She was quiet, she listened to the noise, the churning, milling, steady mechanical cold breathing. Was I talking? she asked. Yes. Could you understand? The words, I could. What words? What did I say? I'll tell you one night when we are quiet, if you want to know. Sleep now.

Sleep rose and fell in her, in levels and layers with the noise of the underground waters. Sometimes her sleep felt threadbare, and she shivered with cold; but in other passages, Owen wrapping her more tightly perhaps, she went deeper under, and found it not only warm but strangely tranquil too. Later, when she thought of this sleeping with him, these depths of warmth and tranquility seemed to her quite peculiarly blessed. Hopeful too, that she could sleep with him like that. And another thing: every time she surfaced and said a few fragments more on subjects troubling her, he answered at once, just where she would have wished him to, so that her feeling, later, was that he had been attentive all night long, not awake necessarily, but so tuned to her sleeping, its rise and fall, its shallows, depths, fretfulness and calm, that whenever she needed him listening and answering, there he was. She remembered very little of what in the latter part of the night they had exchanged in the way of words, but the sense of it all, of their embracing and sleeping and speaking while the vast heart of the back and beyond of the cave pulsed, throbbed, thudded and dispatched its flotillas of bubbles into their breathing space, the sense of all that, she would never forget.

The light crept up as delicately as it had faded. Lou became aware of it as a faint alteration on the lids of her eyes; she opened them, dozed again, opened them next on a hazy visibility. The wren chirred loudly and flitted. Lou found that her right hand was gripping quite hard into the clothing over Owen's heart. And in a rush of happiness back came a memory of the strength of the grip of her fingers in the clefts of moss and rock when she hauled herself by the last body-length of the let-down hank of pure water in one light movement through and safely up.

She felt for Owen's cold face, the rasp of beard, and further, for his eyes—first one then the other they fluttered at the centre of the palm of her right hand. He eased himself free, wrapped her more tightly, put on his boots and a hat, and left. The blanket alone was by no means enough. So much warmth in a man. Still she lay, watching and listening. Outside was lighter, but misty. Under the coping, the ferns were beaded. The breathing through the slit of the cave issued over her cold. And she exulted—to have kept warm, like a bird, like a small animal, to have slept on a ledge with the din of the underworld droning all night in her ears, her and the man, with his arms around her, warm enough together, surviving.

When Owen came back he appeared strange to her. He was bare-headed and his hair, shining with droplets of mist, had a grizzled look. But he was grinning like a boy. See here, he said, see what I've found. She sat up and peered into his proffered hat. Berries, like big blackberries, the drupels with a grey-purple bloom over them, like plums. Dewberries, he said. I hoped there might be some. He laid them by her, she took one very gently between three fingers and a thumb, examined it, its collected succulence. Dewberry, she said, and popped it into the warm room of her mouth. Meanwhile Owen dug out a small gaz from his bag and brewed a mug of black coffee. Boy scout, she said. Hunter-gatherer in the fog. She loved him when he couldn't help showing he was pleased with himself. After the small ceremony of breakfast, she asked him did he have a towel in that bag of his. He did, he produced it. Now go for a little walk while I see to myself.

First Lou went to the back of the cave where the clear water slid out with the bubbles. She made herself small, to get as close as possible, and listened. Listened hard. It was a pulse, a great heart beating and pulsing, it would live forever. So the rock-earth respired, air riding on water came forth. Then she went out, taking her bag, to the brink where the water fell. She could see nothing ahead or below, only mist. But the mist, not so very high above her, was colouring faintly blue; and above that, very distinctly, were larks. Quickly she undressed, ran off to the far corner, squatted like a beast, ran back to the water, stood in it, stooped and with copious freezing handfuls sluiced and washed herself. Stood towelling then on the brink, facing out. Nobody sees me, she thought. Like the chute in the dark in the cave. And here I am, fit to be looked at, and shivering for no other reason than that I am cold. Then she put on the underwear she had bought for their meeting, then her jeans, socks and boots. Next the red dress, and over that her sweater and fleece.

Owen came back. They packed. Owen, she said, can we walk all day now? Do we have to go back into the town? I don't really want to climb down the waterfall. Not that I couldn't, you understand, but it was so lovely climbing up. I was going to say, said Owen, that we can walk across to the gritstone from here, if you like, all the way back to my house, if you would like. I looked at the map while you were seeing to yourself. That is exactly what I would like, she said. And will it be warm? I'd say so, he said. In an hour or so. Good, said Lou, I want some sun. I know I look funny at the moment, bundled up. But things will improve as we go along, you'll see.

44

THE LOSS

Nobody noticed. Apparently they never do. Or if they do, they misunderstand. It might be one of those sudden pauses—a silence, a gap— and somebody will say: An angel is passing. But it is no such thing. It is the soul leaving, flitting ahead to its place in the ninth circle.

Mr. Silverman looked up, looked round. All the men were still there, the men and the one or two successful women, all still there. He resumed his speech. Perhaps he had never faltered in it. He continued, he reached the end. He invited questions, some needed answers almost as long as a speech. Then it was over, he saw that he had been successful. They were smiling, they wanted what he wanted. One after the other they came and shook him by the hand, called him by his first name, congratulated him, wished him a safe journey. Seeing them dwindle—soon fewer than half remained—Mr. Silverman became fearful and, in some degree, also curious. Truly, had nobody noticed? He feared they had, and all the world henceforth would be gilded with pretence. Or he feared they had not, and he must go on now in the fact, enclosed in the fact, and nobody noticing. He took a big man by the sleeve and turned with him to the window in an old gesture of confidence. The big man—whose name was Raingold, who liked to be addressed as Ed—inclined to him, listening, frequently nodding, bespeaking friendliness with every fibre of his suit and with every pore of his naked skin where it showed in his hands and in his large and dappled face. But Mr. Silverman, speaking quietly, aware that at his back there were others waiting to wish him on his way—Mr. Silverman felt that it was too warm in the room and too cold outside in sunny Manhattan and that the plate glass between the warm and the terrible cold was surely quite impermeable. Mysterious then, the loss, the quitting. Would an adept be able to see his loss, like the dusty shape of a bird against the glass? It must be that the molecules of glass give way for the passage of a soul intent on reaching hell.

They were very high up, somewhere in the early hundreds. The surrounding towers of steel and glass seemed to be swaying slightly or rippling like a backcloth, but it was only an effect of light and shadows and clouds and reflections in the freezing wind. The towers were quite as stable as before. Yes, said Mr. Silverman, tugging at the good cloth of Ed Raingold's sleeve, went very well, I should say. What would *you* say? Went *very* well, Ed Raingold said. And he added, beaming down, You can do it, Bob. In Mr. Silverman's wonderment, in his honest puzzlement, there was a fine admixture of contempt. Had nobody noticed? Did it really not matter whether he had a soul or not?

At death, as is well known, the body lightens by a certain amount: twenty-one grams, in all cases. Aha, we say, that must be the weight of the human soul. The cadaver varies greatly. I saw a teenager the other day who must have weighed twenty stone. It was in the new mall at the old Pier 17. The food in there is on an upper floor and she stood at the foot of the escalator, wondering did she dare ascend or not. She wore a decoration in her hair, like antennae, such as elves and fairies are seen wearing in Victorian prints. On the other hand, one of those infants in, say, Ethiopia, can't weigh more than a pound or two. But the loss at death, apparently, will be the same.

But waking next morning Mr. Silverman did not feel lighter. On the contrary, he felt heavier. Imagine a blob of lead implanted in you overnight; or that some organ, roughly kidney-sized, has been converted to lead during your sleep. So it was. Hard to say where exactly: at the back of the head, in the region of the heart, in the pit of the belly? It seemed to shift. Wherever he pressed his hand, there it was not. Perhaps it could dissolve and occupy him thoroughly, like a heavy flu. He dozed and dreamed.

Shaken awake again by his early-morning call—he had an aeroplane to catch to Singapore—Mr. Silverman sat on the bed and tried to weep. He shook, he strained, he sobbed, but the tears that came were not much more than the wetness of a few snowflakes on his cheeks. No relief. He took a shower, he wandered naked around the overheated room. Again and again, touching, he received little shocks, from doorhandles, switches, a metal frame—quite sharp little shocks. They startled him, in little jolts they frightened him through his fingers to his heart. He collected them, each time giving forth a small yelp, until the room was dead. Then he looked out of the window. He was high, in the nineties, the sun was visiting the upper reaches of the towers. Down below—Mr. Silverman looked down—all the silent hurry was deep in shade. Which was worse? The measurement of remoteness in no company but his own? Or proof of it when he clutched at Ed Raingold? Mr. Silverman foresaw an icy interest in the ways and means and relative degrees of horror.

Car. Airport. Aeroplane. Singapore. Passing—so muffled, steady, multitudinous the tread—towards Baggage Reclaim, Mr. Silverman saw an extraordinary thing. There was carpet, glass, more and more glass, and falling from everywhere like vaporized warm piss, there was the usual music: but the extraordinary thing was a bird, a common sparrow by the look of it, high up against a ceiling, perhaps only an inner ceiling, of sunny glass, beating and fluttering. Natural that the creature should seek the light and whatever sustaining air was still available outside, but incredible that it should ever have got where it was now. Nothing living ever came in there, blind-dogs or bomb-dogs perhaps in the service of humans, but nothing else that lived, except the humans in transit. Perhaps not even microbes got in there, only the humans, marching in their gross forms, but never a bird, certainly never a common sparrow, but there it was, fluttering, beating its life out against the sunny glass. That was the last pure astonishment in Mr. Silverman's remaining years. A sparrow against the glass ceiling on the way to Baggage Reclaim! It was also, he acknowledged later, the last occasion on which he might have wept. Yes, he said, had I stepped aside and gone down on my knees on that thick carpet and bowed my head into my hands, knowing the bird against the ceiling high above me, then, God be my witness, I could have wept, the tears would have burst through my fingers, I might have cupped my hands and raised them up like a bowl, brimful with an offering of my final tears. Mysterious, the afterlife, lingering a while between New York and Singapore, between landing and Baggage Reclaim, an afterlife in which he might have wept.

But Mr. Silverman was met at Arrivals by a smiling driver holding up a card which read: Mr. Bob Silverman, Fidelity Investments; and soon, among smiling people, he was proceeding through his routine. Two days of meetings and presentations, all successful. He steered the company into wanting what he wanted. He had a clear mind, he set out the facts and figures clearly, he made shapely arguments, his conclusions were ungainsayable. No wonder he was so successful! He was a born persuader, persuading came as naturally to him as playing golf or the violin did to other mortals. And all the while it was like ventriloquy. He stood aside, listening to his own voice; he could even see it, his own embodied voice, and himself standing aside, observant.

In Singapore the rooms were, if anything, rather cool and the air outside (the little of it he had felt in passing to and from the car), if anything, rather warm. But the rooms were very high, in the hundreds, and the towers all around, very densely rising, looked—to Mr. Silverman—liable to crumple at any moment. The men coming up to congratulate him and to wish him a safe onward journey were less tall than he was, they were slighter, but they were dressed like him and from behind their glasses they beamed on him with an almost ferocious admiration. When their numbers dwindled, again he clutched at a sleeve, stood at a window, speaking the words and the body language of an old condescension. But he felt the leaden implant somewhere in his body, and suffered little starts of indignation that it mattered nothing to these successful gentlemen whether he stood and moved and had his being among them with a soul or without. Alone then, he had the distressing thought that perhaps it had never mattered; and a shadow fell like lead over all his past, all the life before his loss withered and died when he entertained the certainty that it had never mattered, he would have done just as well, he would have got just as high, even without a living soul in him. It had never been required of him that he have one.

He was met at Heathrow by his wife, Mrs. Silverman. He looked her in the eyes, to see would she notice. She seemed not to. He kissed her with some force on the lips. Was it palpable there on the lips, as a shock of cold perhaps? Apparently not. She had brought the two children with her. It was easier than finding someone to look after them. She asked him had he had a successful trip. Yes, he said, very; watching, would she notice? Then he asked after her life in the interim. Busy, she said, and detailed the difficulties. Then husband and wife were silent, driving in dense traffic, and the children on the back seat were silent too. He sensed his wife returning to her own preoccupations and he saw beyond any doubt that what had happened to him would never happen to her. She was fretted to the limits of her strength, she had days, weeks, being almost overwhelmed; but below or beyond all that there was something continuing in her for which it was indeed required that she have a soul. Bleak, the few insights in Mr. Silverman's remaining years. Before a man struggles to retain his living soul he must first be persuaded that he needs one.

Mr. Silverman began to notice other men and women to whom the loss had happened. Angels wandering the world in human disguise are said always to recognize one another. Likewise the clan to which Mr. Silverman now belonged. In one gathering or another, to his mild surprise, he knew and was known by his desolate kind. They were from all walks of life. At least, he met them in the few walks of life that he and Mrs. Silverman had any knowledge of. Successful people. For example, at a Christmas party somewhere just outside the M25 he was introduced to a successful academic. They saw, each in the other, the fact of it. What to say? Nothing really. There was no warmth between them. They stood side by side, their backs to the company, looking down a garden at the fairy lights in a dead tree. The academic, a Dr. Blench, said: Most of what we know about the ninth circle comes from Dante, of course. And he had an axe to grind. But the ice must be true, wouldn't you say? Mr. Silverman hadn't read Dante, didn't know about the ice, but at once acknowledged, after a few more words from Dr. Blench, that what Dante reported on the ice must indeed be true. The thing I haven't quite worked out, Dr. Blench continued, is why he says it is traitors that it happens to. I mean, are you a traitor? I don't think I am. So perhaps he got that wrong, even if the ice is right.

Driving home round the M25 Mr. Silverman thought about treachery. Was he a traitor? Was he even a liar? Whom had he betrayed? Whom had he ever lied to? He glanced at his wife. She was concentrating on her driving among all the lights in a good deal of rain and spray. But he thought again: it will never happen to her. When she can relax a little she will revert to her own concerns, and for those a soul is necessary. Still he did not think that his worst enemy or the Recording Angel could assert with any truth that he had betrayed his wife. Two or three times on his business trips he had been with a prostitute. In Tokyo they sent one up to his room on the 141st floor, without his asking, as a courtesy. But always he told Mrs. Silverman when he came home, said how sorry he was, how joyless it had been. He could not honestly say that she had forgiven him. He would have to say she had made him feel there was nothing to forgive. She appraised him, shrugged. She lingered over it briefly, as though it were a strange but characteristic thing. She seemed to be gauging whether it touched her or not, and to be deciding, with a shrug, that it did not. For a while he had even sustained a sort of affair, with a woman in Frankfurt, a secretary at several of his presentations. She told him he was a very persuasive man. They had sex together for a while whenever he flew in. But he confessed that also to Mrs. Silverman, said it was nothing very much, and she contemplated him and the fact of it briefly and seemed to concur: it was nothing much. So he was not a traitor, he was not a liar, not to her at least, his wife, his closest companion on the upper earth. To whom else then?

Nothing much more to say about the remaining years—many years, interminable, as it sometimes seemed—of Mr. Silverman's living death. Heeding the sort of information that must inevitably come, by accident or by grace and favour, to a man in his position, Mr. Silverman shifted some money very advantageously, for the benefit of Mrs. Silverman and her growing children. He told her so, with some wan satisfaction, quite without personal pride, and she appraised him as she had done when he told her about the prostitutes and about the secretary he had for a while had sex with in Frankfurt: thanked him, nodded, as though it were both very strange and very characteristic. And he watched her vanishing behind her eyes, to where she really belonged.

Mr. Silverman thought a good deal about the ice. He connected it with his inability to weep—and rightly so. One evening in the lift, ascending very rapidly to the 151st floor in Manhattan or Tokyo or Frankfurt or Singapore, he found himself the sole companion of another of his kind, a bigger man than himself, in a suit of excellent cloth, wearing a confident loud tie and a very big signet ring on his left little finger. The man—Sam's my name, he said—told him at once about a particularly bad ending (if it was an ending) that had just come to his knowledge. The doors opened, Sam and Mr. Silverman stood together on the hushed corridor. Sam continued. The man in question—he must surely be one of us— had taken an ice axe to his own face, raised it in desperation against himself, in the firm belief, so the story went, that his face, indeed his entire head, was enclosed in a bulky helmet of ice, in the desperate illusion raising the ice pick against himself, to make a way through to his eyes, to give exit to the tears that were, so he believed, welling up in there, hot melting tears welling up and not allowed to flow.

AN ISLAND

20 October

There weren't many on the boat—mostly birders coming over to observe the departures and for sightings of any rare vagrants. I eavesdropped a bit, on deck and in the bar they talked about nothing else. Before we left, one of them got texted that a red-eyed vireo had just been seen on Halangy dump and when he told the others they were taken up in a sort of rapture, big grown men with their beards, bad-weather wear and all the equipment. They made sounds that were scarcely words any more, little shouts and squeals, a hilarity, in the enchantment of their passion. I loitered on the fringes.

After a while, when we were clear of the harbour and coasting quietly along and had passed the first lighthouse, I went downstairs, right down to the lower saloon, below the waterline, and lay on a bunk under a blanket. There was nobody else down there. I felt okay on my own in the big throbbing of the engines, I felt them to be in my chest, like a heart, but I was okay, I kept seeing the faces of the birders when they received the news about the red-eyed vireo, I heard their voices, the transformation wrought in them by their enthusiasm, and it seemed to me that I knew what it was like to be in a company of friends in a common passion that would do no harm. Then I must have slept, but not deeply, near the surface, in the rapids of sleep, not restful, and in the whitewater hurry of the images the clearest, flitting not abiding but as clear as the blade of the moon when it cuts through the clouds, was you. And I believed you wouldn't mind if I wrote to you now and then. Everyone needs a fellow-mortal to address. You won't mind?

When I went up on deck the islands were coming into view. I watched them materialize in their own domain of light. It seemed to me a quite peculiar blessing that a place so manifestly different, far away, out on the borders, could be approached by me.

At Halangy I went down the gangway among the birders in single file and soon found the boat to Enys.

So here I am, camped snugly in the angle of two walls for shelter against the expected weather, the site to myself, the season ending and the small birds resting up here in the tamarisk hedges before they launch themselves across the ocean.

Sunday 25 October

The island is barely half a mile wide at its widest. There's a channel of the sea on the east and open sea on the west and my home (for now) is midway between, just under the winds that mostly come from the west. My first evening there was a pause, a complete silence. My second, and all through the night, the weather came over me like nothing I have ever been out in or lain under before, so thorough in its strength, loud in its howling, the wind, the rain, the waves after hundreds of leagues without impediment making their landfall here. Weather knows itself at last when it finds some terra firma to hit against, and best, most thoroughly, knows itself when there are some habitations too and creatures in them who can feel what it is like. Soon after daybreak the rain ceased and I went out in the wind, crouching and gasping for my own small breath in it. The scraps of abandoned fields were strewn with stones, wreck, seaweed, dead things that had lived in salt water. The waves slid up the sheer face of the northern headland and spilled back milk-white off the crown. Nowhere are we higher than a hundred feet above the sea. I crawled along the chine in a blizzard of spindrift through the tumuli home to this tiny lair with every stitch of dress and pore of exposed flesh sticky and proofed with salt. My little stove was a wonder to me, its hoarse flame, the can of drinkable water, the inhalation of the steam of coffee.

Since then, though the wind has dropped, I can always hear the sea, like a vast engine working just over the hill. It's as though I've been taught something, had my ears and my heart opened to a fact of sound I was ignorant of and now I shall always be able to hear it, even in the city where you live, there on the pavement in the din of traffic if I paused and bowed my head I would hear this sea.

Tomorrow night I'll be closer still, but more secure. The woman who runs the campsite has offered me accommodation in a shed. I can fit it out as I like, she says, there's a table and chair and a camp bed in it already and she'll lend me a bigger stove. In return, I'll paint the wash house here, do a few repairs, clear up, make myself useful. If she thinks me odd, she didn't say so. Generally someone blows in, she said, about this time and quite often over the years they've been about your age. You'll pick up more work if you want it, she said. If you're handy, if you want to stay. And it suddenly seemed to me that I *am* quite handy, that I do want to stay, that I'll be glad to be an odd-job man for a while and possess my own soul in patience in a shed within a stone's throw of the sea.

It's dark an hour earlier from today. I know you don't like that day of the year.

If you did want to write, c/o the campsite would find me. In fact, c/o Enys would, enough people have seen me by now on my walks or at the post office.

26 October

I went in the church today. It's down by the quay. Every now and then I remember—I mean, feel again—why I was ever with the monks. Four solid walls containing stillness, the light through the windows. Really it's only that, the possibility of being quiet and of receiving some illumination. I don't think that's too much to ask once in a while. Afterwards I mooched among the graves. There aren't many different names, half a dozen families seem to own the place. Newcomers get cremated and are remembered on tablets by the gate. The sea is so close, who wouldn't want to be buried or at least remembered here?

I like my shed. It smells of the sea. It's roomier than I expected and with electricity too because there's a workshop on the same plot, not used now but still connected. Mary lent me a heater as well as a stove, I trundled them down in a wheelbarrow with the rest of my gear and now I'm nicely at home. I cleaned the place out, mended the roof where the felt had blown off, shaved the window so it closes tight... Things like that. A few other jobs want doing and there are all manner of tools lying idle in the workshop. Help yourself, Mary said. Tomorrow I'll start on the wash house. That's the deal.

I've put my notebook, my writing paper and my couple of books on planks from the sea laid over two packing cases.

That's what Mary meant by a table. It's to write on, read at, eat off—under the window that faces out towards the sea. The chair's a real one, decently made. It came in off a wreck many years ago. The bed I shall call a truckle bed because I like that word. I took your photo out and did think of standing it on the planks to glance at while I write to you—but I shan't. I keep my eyes on the page, the nib, the black ink, the making of the letters and the words. If I stare out of the window towards the dune that hides the sea, if I let the vagueness come over, if I don't keep my eyes by force on the here and now, I see you at once, it's my gift and my affliction.

31 October

The last boat of the season arrives and leaves today. That's not as final as it sounds, there's a helicopter from Halangy once a week and I daresay I could scrape together enough for the fare if I panicked and had to get out. But the way things are now I don't think I shall panic. I'm as well off here as anywhere. Wherever I was, there'd still be the want of you.

Yesterday, if you'd been watching, I think you would have laughed out loud. (Your laughter is like nobody else's, it always made me feel there were deeper, freer, more abundant sources of mirth than I would ever have access to.) The birders arrived. I looked up from writing and there they were, about thirty of them, all men, in army camouflage, with their heavy tripods, cameras and telescopes, they must have come over the hill to this west side and they lined up barely twenty yards away, with their backs to me, in silence, in the mild early-morning light. After a while I went out and stood behind them. None paid me any attention. And when I asked I got two words in reply: rosy starling. I could see where they were looking—through the opening of the hedges, slantwise about three hundred yards down the length of the dune—but I couldn't see any bird. Then they all gasped and made the sounds of communal glee I had heard on the boat, then a great shout and they gathered up their equipment and began to run heavily away. The one I was standing next to, a fat man even more laden than his comrades, set off last. The others were almost out of sight and hadn't waited for him and nobody turned round to see was he following or not. His cumbersomeness troubled me for the rest of the day.

Sunday 1 November

I couldn't sleep for some hours last night. I thought very *brokenly* of you. Or, to be more exact, very *breakingly*—you were breaking, or my power to remember or imagine you was impaired, like sight or hearing, and back came the worry that everything I ever held true will crumble, perish and turn to dust from within, from within me, the power to uphold any faith and hope and love will erode, perhaps very quickly the way a cliff might collapse that was riddled through and through and nobody had known. I got up, to be less at the mercy of all this, and went out to the dune, the tide was high, close, but the washing, sliding, unfurling and withdrawal of it was very muted under cloud and in a light fog. That bay is a horseshoe, its headlands and an island behind and some reefs in part barricade it, so that in a storm the ocean breaks through very violently, being fretted, slewed and rifled by these hindrances, but last night it made a lingering and gentle entrance, at leisure, dispensing itself, its immensity, easefully and as though mercifully. Having seen this and after my fashion understood it in a light without moon or stars, a light embodied in drifts of vapour, silvery, I went back into my shed in the embrace of the tamarisks and behind closed eyes I insisted on that gentle incoming and could still hear the sounds of it, the breathing of water over shingle, and this morning I felt something had been added to my stock of resources against disintegration: an ocean entering quietly and giving bearably.

There was a bonfire last night, on the beach that twins with mine, over the hill. They built it well below high water on the fine shingle and the weed. I haven't stared into the heart of such a fire for years. It was mostly old pallets and wood-wormed timbers, but loppings from the pittosporum hedges too and their leaves flared and vanished with an almost liquid sizzle. I noticed that flames can live for a second or two quite detached from the substance they were burning—in the air, just above, they dance and vanish. There was hardly any wind so that the fire extending in sparks reached very high.

I met a few people. Several came up and said hello and I got a couple of offers of labour, cash-in-hand, which I need since what I do on the campsite I'm paid for with my shed. The hotel manager offered me some painting and decorating. He has closed for the winter. He kept open last year but this year trade is worse. Amiable chap, a bit nervous. Then a young man who farms at the south end asked had I ever cut hedges and I said yes, I had, years ago. He said there'd be plenty to do for him, if I liked. When I was with the monks I simplified the whole business into the two words: work and pray. The work was all with my hands, and by prayer I meant concentrating on whatever good I could imagine or remember, so as not to go to bits.

The women had made soup and hot dogs and there was a trestle table with beer and wine on and things for the kids. You helped yourself. I put my last ten-pound note in the kitty. I felt very blithe. And when after that I got my offers of work I wondered at my ever losing faith.

Much later, I came back. I wanted to watch the sea overwhelm the fire, and I did so, very closely. The hissing and the conversion of flame to steam were remarkable but best I liked the ability of fire to survive quite a while on blackened beams that floated. The sea swamped the *ground* of the fire but strewed its upper elements for a briefly continuing life on the surface left and right. True, the waves were soft. Breakers would finish it quickly.

20 November

The island is used to people passing through—or people trying to settle and failing. There are the few families who rule the graveyard, that stock won't leave and it will be many years before they die out or get diluted and lose their identity among the incomers who take root. A family from Wolverhampton, another from Bristol, another from Halifax are powerful and one of them may dominate in the end. But if they want to be buried they'll have to go elsewhere, here they'll have to make do with a tablet on the wall by the way in. So some do settle, they blow in and root tenaciously. But the chief impression you get is of instability. Whether it's sex or panic, I can't tell, but every year there's some breakup, rearrangement and departure.

I think they quite like the people who are passing through. The island economy, such as it is, depends on them. Of course, they're a risk as well, any one of them might become the solvent of a marriage and perhaps of a small business too. There was a baker here till a few years ago, then a girl came to help in the café and he left with her for London when the season ended. I guess some wives and husbands watch very anxiously who will land when the season starts again; others will watch hopefully. And it is certain that several in houses on their own have watched year after year, have gone down to the quay when the launch came in and have idled there and were never looked at by a stranger who might have stayed. They watch long after the likely time has passed. One such, a very lonely man, against all the odds and beyond all rational hope was chosen, as you might say, by a visitor not half his age. She stayed three years, then left him and the islands without warning.

I've got more than enough work now. In fact the manager offered me a room in the hotel but I like my shed too much. I'd pay Mary some rent but she won't have it, so I've begun tidying her workshop. Well, more than tidying it. I'll clear all the junk out, repair outside and in, see to the tools. She says that's a job long wanted doing and who would do it but somebody blown in? She's a Jackson, one of the old families, widowed, her two sons fish for crabs and lobsters, she has a couple of holiday-lets. The workshop was her father's, that's his boat there in the nettles. He was in his workshop or out in his boat most of the time. There was something wrong when he came back from the war. He more or less gave up talking, she said.

The hotel manager, Brian, is on his own. His wife left him at the start of the summer holidays, went to the mainland. It's not even that she fell in love. Suddenly she'd just had enough and she left him, taking the children. He dresses well and is altogether particular about his appearance and his environment. He's a rather fussy employer, which I don't mind. I see through his eyes, at heart he is terrified. He talks a lot to me and I don't mind that either. I guess he's ten years my junior. This is the first year he's had to close and it worries him. Not that he owns the place. A very rich man does. You don't have to stay here, I tell him. If it fails. No, of course not, he says. With my qualifications I can go where I like.

He's taken three other people on, all young. A boy from Melbourne on his way round the world, called Chris. A girl from Manchester, Elaine, who used to come here as a child and should be at university but couldn't face it and is having another year off. And Sarah, from Nottingham, who has finished university and is wondering what to do. I could have had a warm room on a back corridor with this attractive trio. I don't think they would have objected to me.

The hotel is shut till the end of March but Brian opens the bar a couple of nights a week and the regulars arrive.

I make an appearance when I feel up to it. If asked, I tell the makings of a tale about myself. Nobody probes. Either it's tact or they're not very curious. My kind come and go, every year there's at least one of us. Mostly they talk and I listen. I'm a good listener. From the hotel back to my shed is no great distance. I go past the Pool, quite an extent of water with only a bar of sand between it and the sea. The Pool is very softly spoken, even when there's a wind, at most you hear a steady lapping. The sea on my left, unless it's very low tide, makes an insistent noise. At high tide walking between the two waters it feels peculiar being a drylander who needs air to breathe. Some nights the dark is intense, the pale sand, the pale dead grass and rushes either side, are all the light there is. There's a lighthouse far out to the southwest, the wink of its beam comes round, and another, closer, to the north, but all you'll see of that one is the ghost of the passage of light on the underside of the cloud. I use my torch as little as possible. I like to feel my way, in at the opening of the tamarisks to my wooden home.

27 November

The work in the hotel is easy enough. We paint and decorate and we clear things out. Some days I drive the quad and trailer and take old fridges and televisions to the tip. Yesterday I fed fifteen hundred of last year's brochures into the incinerator, a rusty iron contraption with a tall chimney, we call it Puffing Billy. Children are mesmerized by it, Brian says.

Brian misses his family. They are living in the house they kept in Guildford just in case the venture here failed, which it has. He is not from Guildford nor is his wife. They moved there from the north, following the opportunities of his work. Brian detests Guildford and so does his wife. It distresses him that she would rather be there than here. And that she has nobody else, that she didn't fall in love and move to a new place with a new man so as to start again, that also distresses him. He has not even lost out to somebody more desirable. It is simply that she doesn't want to be with him. So she leaves, and takes her children with her, as of right. He hasn't the heart to contest it. Really, he agrees with her. In this beautiful place, a paradise some would say, she can't be happy with him, she can't even make do with him. Instead she takes herself and the children off to a place she detests, just so as not to be with him, and in his heart of hearts he can't blame her. It is not even passionate, she does not passionately hate him, wish to kill him, avenge herself on him for her wasted years. She just wants to be away from him. He tells me this in the bar when everyone else has gone. But he is quite sober, he is not a drunkard, nor is he a gambler, nor in a million years would he raise his hand against her, he scarcely ever raises his voice, he has never hit the children nor even frightened them by throwing things and swearing. It is not rational that she should leave him. It is not in her material interest. Still, she has. He hopes at least the children will come and visit him next Easter when the season has begun again and there are boat trips to the other islands. He will take a day off and perhaps they would like to go fishing. He tells me all this in the empty bar, quite late, still cleanly dressed in his suit and tie, and his watery eyes over his trim moustache appeal to me not for pity but for an explanation. And yet he knows it needs no explanation. I am in my work clothes, which are not much different from any other clothes I've got, my nails are broken and there's paint on my fingers. I know that he confides in me because he assumes I am passing through. Also that I leave his warm hotel and go back in the dark to a place of my own barely half a mile away but out on the rim, as far as he is concerned, eccentric, and when he looks me in the eyes and shakes me by the hand next morning, altogether affable, he knows or thinks he knows that he has nothing to

fear from me. I think he assumes I am at least as unhappy as
he is. And he is certain that before very long I will go away
and he will never see me again.

Does Brian interest you? I am trying to interest you in him.

30 November

I learned this from a lone birder, itself a rare creature, who
wandered, fully accoutred, into my precinct early yesterday: that in the winter, and especially about now, first thing
they do on their computers every morning is check out the
weather over the western Atlantic. They pray for winds,
colossal storm winds, blowing our way, because on winds
like that the nearctic vagrants get blown in. The worse the
storms, the longer-lasting, the better for us, he said. Birds
making laborious headway from, it might be, Alaska to, say,
Nicaragua, for all their struggling get blown off course—
three thousand miles off course—and land up here. Mostly
singletons, my birder said, rare things, first-time sightings,
and mostly, so far as anyone can tell, they don't, except in a
thousand photographs, survive. The star last year was a great
blue heron, a juvenile. The winds blew steadily for a week
or more and the birders waited—not for a great blue heron
in particular: a varied thrush or a laughing gull or a Wilson's
snipe would have made them happy enough. The GBH, as
he kept calling it, was beyond their wildest dreams. The
creature landed exhausted on Halangy, in the reeds of Lower
Moors, around midday on 7 December and was observed
and photographed by scores of enthusiasts, summoned from
here, there and everywhere, all afternoon, feeding, until the
weather worsened, torrential rain came horizontally in, the
light declined and the juvenile vanished, 'never to be seen
again.' My birder liked that phrase and repeated it, in tones
of wonderment: 'never to be seen again.'

6 December

You mustn't think I live too monkishly. I'm never very cold and I eat pretty well. I found an old army greatcoat in the workshop and I put that round my shoulders when I sit and read or write. I can get most things it occurs to me to want at the post office near the quay and, besides, there's a shopping boat to Halangy once a week, though if the weather's very rough the supply ship from the mainland can't sail. I went to Halangy last week and spent a good bit on books. The one bookseller is giving up and he wanted rid of his stock. I bought a couple of things I know you'd like and now they and the rest sit on a shelf I made of a plank of driftwood.

Altogether my shed is quite well appointed. When I take junk from the hotel or from Mary's workshop to the tip I always look through what other people have thrown out. I got the brackets for my shelf from there, and an Italian coffee maker, a Bialetti, one like yours, that works okay, and two nice cups. Two wine glasses and a beer mug also. There was a mirror I might have had but I didn't want it in the shed. I've the wash house to myself just up the hill. Mary gave me a dinner plate. I'm okay. I don't think you would like the long hours of darkness but I don't mind so much. There's work in the evenings at the hotel if I want, and there's the bar some nights. But often I prefer it here. I do a bit more at the workshop. It's coming on nicely. And Mary gave me a little radio so I lie on my truckle bed and listen to that sometimes. You might think the news would be easier to bear being so remote but in fact it's worse. I suppose I'm not distracted. The little box in the dark is very close, the voices say the bad things direct into your ear. When I've had enough or if I don't feel up to listening to the radio I lie there and listen to the sea instead. And I think—though it's not exactly thinking, more like being a shade already in the underworld among the whispering of other shades in chance encounters out of time. You are among them some nights, though always as a visitor, you always make it clear you don't belong there. I've wondered lately when it was I stopped expecting or even hoping to be happy. I push the date back further and further, into my youth, into my childhood, vengefully, as though to wipe out my life, I cast my shadow back, longer and longer, to chill all the life I ever had in darkness though I know it is a terrible untruth I am perpetrating.

Here's okay. I do like the people and they interest me. And I like the work, especially in the fields southward. I cut the hedges. Nathan has given me a field to start with that hasn't been cut since he took over, the tops have shot up six or eight feet higher than they should be. He said the trimmer, fixed on the tractor, would hardly work and could I manage with loppers, a bowsaw and the ladder? It would be slow work, he knew. I answered that suited me perfectly. I'll tash it with the pitchfork and come round after with a buckrake on the tractor. Fine, he said. So when the weather's kind I skip the painting and decorating and cut fence all day, on my own, content. I find the old slant cuts from years ago, where the height should be, and work along level with them. It's mostly pittosporum, a silver grey, they remind me of the olive branches, perhaps it was on Ithaca. They make a whoosh when they fall over my shoulder through the air. You cut an opening in no time and there's the sea, running some mornings a hard blue, then suddenly black, jade green, turquoise and you see stilts of sun far out probing over pools of light, and shafts of rainbow almost perpendicular, just beginning their curve, then they break off. If I stay I'll have cut the hedges of all of Nathan's fields. That will be something done. And why shouldn't I stay?

Nathan and his wife are making a go of it. She's local, he arrived. There's no future in bulbs and flowers any more so they're growing potatoes, broccoli, carrots, spinach, staw-berries, all manner of things in abundance. The hotel buys from them and so do the self-catering visitors. His wife works as hard as he does. They'll make out all right, you can see it in their faces, the way they look at you, candid and appraising. They're settled, they'll make their way, their children will grow up here and have a good inheritance.

9 December

I had a shock this morning. I was at my table writing, concentrating hard, trying to be exact, vaguely conscious of the daylight strengthening, the sparrows and starlings in the hedges, the sea risen up under the dune, and I raised my eyes, for the right word, to get nearer the truth, and saw through the glass a face so close I had for an instant, long enough for a lifetime, the conviction that I looked into a mirror and the face I saw was mine: a big lopsided grinning face, baldheaded but for some white remnants, the eyebrows albino-pale, the teeth all angles, the blurting tongue very red, the eyes of a blue so weak it looked dissolved almost to nothing in an overwhelming blankness... Twelve hours later, writing this letter—I call it a letter—to you, I don't conjure up the face by force of memory to let you see it too, I can see it on the window pane, this side not outside, on the black glass which when there is no light in the tamarisk grove does indeed more or less distinctly reflect my own. The worst is its mix of senility and childishness— that raised the hairs on my neck, not for nearly a year have I felt such convincing proof that the heart of life is horror. He raised a hand and tapped on the window, his big head wobbled and wagged from side to side, then his hand went to his mouth, to cover his chortling, as though he remembered it is rude to laugh however ridiculous the stranger you are looking at may be. When he did that—made the gesture of consideration for my feelings—I knew there was no harm in him and tears came to my eyes, my face was wet with tears, I wiped them away, I smeared the salt of them across my lips, and seeing this he uncovered his mouth, showed me the palms of both his empty hands, made little grunts and mutters of pity for me, his features worked, sorrow possessed them, and I stood up, opened the door, to welcome him in. That was too much, too suddenly, he backed away, but as though he didn't wish to, as though he'd stay if he could be sure there was no harm in me. I put out my hand, as you might to a bird or an animal that—you supposed—had come to your door because it needed food or care, and he paused at that, near the useless boat, about fifteen yards between us. Then he shook his head, as though tired of it, as though dispirited, as though not wanting my company after all, and slouched away, out at the horseshoe opening towards the dune and the sea.

A minute later, while I still stood there in my borrowed army greatcoat, I heard a woman's voice calling from behind my shed, from in among the old bulb fields, calling his name, Eddie! Eddie! in a tone which sounded familiar with the tribulation but still not able to bear it. I turned, she appeared, she was bare-headed, wearing a big coat, which she huddled around her unbuttoned, over a long floral dress, and her feet in wellington boots. Her hair was as white as the sea when it slides back off the headland down the sheer cliff into the making of the next assault. Everything in the child-man who had lumbered off towards the shore was written in the lines and in the aura, in the whole spirit and bearing of her face. My son, she said. He's gone towards the shore, I said. She made a little cry, called out again, Eddie! Oh Eddie, don't go hurting yourself! and hurried away. I followed and saw her find him, scold him, wrap him in her arms, lead him by the hand down the sand path between the Pool and the sea.

17 December

I witnessed a thing last week you might have liked. There's a spit of pebbles at the south end covered at high water but running out to a lichened castle of rocks that stinks of birds, grows a rank verdure and is never covered. I came over the hill, one of the pocked-and-blistered-with-burials small hills, and saw a man out there on that low-water rope of stone and he was busy building. I got off the skyline quick, to watch. I was in the dead bracken, blotted out of view, like a hunter, watching him. About midway, where it would be covered a fathom deep, he was building an arch. I watched two hours, wrapped in Mary's father's army greatcoat, while the man exposed and utterly intent worked at his arch. I saw that to get the thing to stand he must build inside it also as it grew, supporting it all the way and especially, of course, where the curves, the desire of either side to meet in a keystone on thin air, began. He, by his cleverness, aided those pillars in their wish to curve, become the makings of an arch and meet. How he worked!—with tact, with care, with nous and cognizance of what any stone of a certain size and weight and shape could do and couldn't do. And when it was made and the arch was fitted around and relying on the merely *serving* wall of stones, I prayed a prayer such as I hardly ever prayed in all my time with the monks, that his keystone would hold and the two half-arches, so needing one another, so incapable of any life without, would by their meeting and their obedience to gravity (their suicidal wish to fall) over the void would hold when one by one he took his servant necessary stones away. It held: stone rainbow on its own two heavy feet, because the halves of its bodily curve had met and all desire to fall became the will to last miraculously forever. The man, the builder-man, stood back and contemplated it and nodded. Walked all round it, pausing, viewing it from every angle, nodded again, glanced at his watch (acknowledging he would die) then set off fast from the spit of pebbles to the path, I suppose to catch a boat. And I crept down from hiding to have a close look at his work.

The tide, far out, had turned. I came back later and watched by starlight till the waves, washing in from either side, had entered under the arch and it stood in them. Any big sea would have toppled it but that was a quiet night, the ripples worked as the man had, little by little, very gradually and as it were considerately turning air to water. I watched his work disappear. Back in my bed I thought of the two curves meeting, the keystone weighing them secure, the water flowing and swirling through and over and all around. And I got up early, before it was light, and found my way down there again, past the Pool with its lapping and its queer aquatic voices, past the hotel with its anxious manager, to see the stranger's arch, whether it still stood. And it did! It had withstood the reflux and stood there draggled with green weed under the flickering beginnings of an almost lightless day.

The arch survived two more tides, then the sea got rough and when I went next there was a heap of stones and only its maker or a witness of its making would believe that such a thing had ever been.

Sunday 20 December

Some foul weather, I've been confined, for work, in the hotel. Chris is trying to persuade Elaine not to bother with university—waste of time—but to continue round the world with him. At the end of March he will resume his plane ticket. He thinks he will skip the rest of Europe and head straight for Goa. She should come with him, he says. Elaine isn't sure. She might stay on here, she says, if Brian offered her work for the season or if there was anything going in the café or at the post office. Chris says she should think bigger than that. Europe's finished, he says. She should come along with him, he'll show her a different life. Sarah is furious with Chris. She has short black hair, very bright eyes. He tells me she's probably a lesbian. She tells me she knows for certain he's made the same offer—what exactly is he offering?—to a Polish girl who works in a bar on Halangy, a

Lithuanian girl helping at the school on St. Nicholas, and doubtless a few more. She tells Elaine she should go to university, get a degree, and consider his 'offer' after that, if she must. Elaine points out that Sarah, with her degree, is painting the hotel kitchen, same as her. That's for now, says Sarah. I've got better ideas than trailing round the world after a beach-bum. Chris denies he's a beach-bum. He's got a diploma in hotel management. Any woman coming along with him might do very well for herself, in Australia.

They have these discussions while we work or around the table at coffee time. I like all three of them. Sarah is very forthright, Chris is a bit afraid of her. He must be ten years older than Elaine but when Sarah is speaking neither he nor Elaine looks very self-confident. Chris tells me his mother came from Essex—Chelmsford, he thinks. She was in a home with her little brother and the home sent her, without her brother, to Australia, to another home, somewhere in the outback. She had a bad time, Chris says. She died when he was ten. He doesn't know who his father is. The Christian Brothers looked after him. He says in his opinion he did pretty well to survive all that and get to college and come out with a diploma in hotel management. I agree. All I say is Elaine needs some qualifications too, for her self-defence. Really I meant self-realization but I couldn't think how to put it. Anyway, self-defence isn't far wrong. Chris shrugs. Elaine tells me the holidays she had on Enys were the best times of her life. The family was happy then and she values the holidays even more now that it isn't. When she has an afternoon off she visits the old places again. They stayed in a house by the beach where the bonfire was. I asked her did she remember Eddie at all. Yes, she said, poor Eddie and his poor mother. The first time she saw him she screamed and ran away but after a while she got used to him. He was only a child, she said, although a grown man. Once he gave her a wedding-cake shell, the way a little boy might. I've still got it, she said.

Christmas Eve

Brian's passion is family history. One good thing about being closed, he says, is it gives him time to work at that. He spends hours online. Even when he opens the bar for an evening he'll go to his room after they've all gone home, switch on, and at once he's back in 1911 or 1901. Those censuses, he says, are a lifeline to him. He shakes his head over the superabundance they open up. Last a lifetime, he says. He is very anxious to get things right, but, of course, having worked at it for some years now, in fact since the children were born, he's well aware that absolute certainty is impossible. Before the censuses and all the other resources came online, when he and his wife were still living in Guildford, he'd go down to the National Archive and root around for hours, whenever he could. And he wrote to surviving relatives in Britain, Ireland, Australia, New Zealand, Canada and the USA, to get their stories. He has an impressive collection, still being added to, of wills, deeds, private correspondence and certificates of births, marriages and deaths. Mostly he researches his wife's side of the family, it is more interesting than his, he has got much further back on her side than on his own, to 1685, to be exact, and he expects in the end he'll be able to prove they came over with the Conquest. Herself, she wasn't a bit interested in her family's history and whenever he told her something he'd found that he found very interesting—for example, that her maternal great-grandfather, a carter in Lower Broughton, was illegitimate and very likely the son of a priest—she looked at him in a way he remembers vividly now she has gone. Still he carries on with her side of the family more than with his, he still wants to know where she came from, so to speak. Of course, when the censuses were put online and you could spend all the time you liked in your own bedroom studying them, you pretty soon had to face the fact that an awful lot of things just didn't tally. Family stories handed down as gospel were quite often flatly contradicted by those lists of people resident or visiting at a certain address on 31 March 1901 or 2 April 1911. A Thomas Huntley, for example, dealer in calico, on Brian's side, always said to have abandoned his wife, a Gracey, daughter of a clerk in a tram company, and to have fled to Ireland on the day of Queen Victoria's diamond jubilee, is recorded in 1901 at 14 Goole Road, Tadcaster as head of the household with his wife and four children, among them Brian's great-grandmother through whom, presumably, the story that he was the black sheep had come down. On the other hand, you couldn't always assume the official record was right and the family story wrong. Surely not everyone told the truth on census day (many told nothing at all) and as a hotel manager Brian knew perfectly well that what people said about themselves wasn't always the truth. It only started to look like the truth if you wrote it down. And of course, if it ever got on to an official record card or on to a police computer then it looked very true indeed, until somebody proved it false.

Now Brian thinks I'm interested in family history, and perhaps I am. He thinks I'm as interested in his family history and his wife's as he is himself. So he might say, for example, without any preliminary, By the way, their first house wasn't where I thought it was—11 Littleton Road, near the river, in that very insalubrious area—it was 311, one of the newest, out near the racecourse, almost in open country, so they must have been better off than I've been supposing—they being his wife's great-grandparents.

He is trying to forget it's Christmas. Well, that's not true. He's going to open the bar tomorrow and give everyone a drink and a mince pie who cares to come. That's typical of him, he does what he thinks he ought to. But for himself he's trying to forget it's Christmas.

I've been wondering would I have been quite useless as a father.

I counted thirteen swans on the Pool today. The water was very turbid, the wind blowing strongly. I saw them through the hotel window, I was painting the frames inside. It moved me to tears, how white they were on the turbid water and how they held steady against the wind, or tacked and steered into it, or let it drift them when they chose.

Elaine tells me that Sarah isn't in the least a lesbian, not that it would matter if she were. Men, especially men like Chris, always call women lesbians if they answer back. Sarah's degree is in marine biology. If *she* stayed, Elaine says, it would be to do some good.

A hedge of pittosporum when you've trimmed not just the tops but also the face of it there in a bright sun if the wind comes across, it shivers as though the shorn condition were hard to bear.

I've noticed that for some days after rough weather the sea may continue to be very troubled. The wind has lessened almost to nothing, but great rollers ride in from somewhere far far out. There might be no wind at all but a sea arrives that looks worked up by a tempest. I had taken to calling it the phenomenon of insufficient cause but that's not quite accurate. It's more a want of explanation. Such a sea and not a breath of wind. No apparent reason. That's closer. Of course there's an explanation, but far out, far deeper out, beyond my wits and senses.

Some nights you are as clear as the brightest and most definite among the many constellations. Other nights you look threadbare, the winds of space blow through you, your shape is still just about discernible but only by me and only because, even breaking up, it reminds me of something.

Mary tells me that before the war her father made the children's toys. She told me this when I told her I'd found an old treadle fretsaw and thought I could get it working again. He made a big dolls' house for the first two girls, all just right, very exact, with the proper furniture in every room, everything neatly and brightly painted. He made a monkey dangling on a wire between scissor sticks and when you pressed the bottom ends together the wire tightened and the monkey did acrobatics. And he made a yacht for the first boy, Joseph, with all the rigging perfect. He called her *Star of the Sea.* Mary remembers a day when Joseph—he's dead now—sailed that yacht on the Pool and the wind blew her right out among the swans and how upset Joseph was to see her out there in the middle among those big creatures. And Father said not to worry, and fetched the little punt up from the beach and launched it on the shallow Pool. That was the first time he gave Joseph an oar and said they should row back from the middle together, once they'd rescued the yacht. At first they went round and round like a leaf, not advancing at all, but then Joseph got the hang of it and they came in and was Joseph proud of himself! I said there were a couple of hulls I'd found in the workshop and also some rigging but that had perished. Mary said, You'll find all sorts in there. I found his marquetry knives, I said, and two or three packs of the veneers you need for marquetry. He made my mother some beautiful things, Mary said. One was his own boat heading out down the channel at dawn for the pots out near the lighthouse. We've still got that one. What became of the others I don't know. I don't suppose many do marquetry nowadays. He was often down here in his shed after the war, but he didn't make much, less and less in fact. Or he would go out in his boat but not really for the fishing.

I feel on edge, the least thing would do it. But also I feel something you'd hardly credit in me, an insouciance. Really I don't much care what happens next.

31 December

Quite a few came to Brian's Christmas party, thirty I should say. The men put on suits and ties and since I'd only ever seen them in work clothes before, they were very strange to me. I don't mean they looked in the least ridiculous or uncomfortable. On the contrary, it felt like manners: this is an occasion, this is how you look. But their hands and faces, especially the boatmen's, bare in their Sunday best, it brought the outdoors, the weather, the sea into the room, which Brian had gone to the trouble of decorating. The women had dressed up even more. They wore a good deal of makeup and jewellery. And the children, especially the girls, more children than I knew existed, they were also dressed for the occasion. I had no decent clothes to change into.

The first glass and the mince pies were on the house. Then Brian went behind the bar and Chris joined him.

I had a conversation with one of the boatmen—Matthew, I think his name was, he has a ginger beard—about the way things drift. I told him I'd found bits of charred wood here on the west side, bits of blue pallet, that I was pretty sure had come from the bonfire on the east side. He shrugged and said quite likely but I shouldn't make a rule of it, you never could tell. Tide, current, wind, you never know. People go in the water here and are never seen again. Perhaps they land up somewhere, perhaps they don't. Take Alf Lewis last summer, he went in the channel, drunk, so you can understand him drowning, but he's never come up again so far as anyone knows. I don't know about Alf Lewis, I said. Matthew shrugged. He blew in. Now he's gone. Good riddance, some say. I waited but he wouldn't say more. So instead I nodded towards the bar and said it was nice of Brian to give everyone a drink and a mince pie. Matthew nodded, but as though he'd have disagreed if I'd been somebody worth disagreeing with. Then I made a mistake. I asked did Lucy ever come to things like this. Matthew looked me in the eyes and slowly shook his head, which I took to mean, It's none of your business, and not, No, Lucy never comes to things like this. He's a big man, a big beard, with very small eyes. I asked would he like another drink. He said, No thanks, so I left him and went to the bar myself.

Later—I was already thinking of making my surreptitious exit—Sarah and Elaine came over to me in the window. I had noticed their transformation, among the other women, but close up it shocked me, they seemed sent in their beauty and gaiety to remind me of what I had never striven hard enough to possess and now never would and did not deserve. Their arms were bare, Elaine wore a necklace of pale jade, Sarah a bracelet of lapis lazuli, her dress was a dark blue and that colour and the colour of Elaine's dress, a blue-green, I had often watched travelling over the sea from the top of my ladder in Nathan's fields in the wind and the swishing to earth of the olive-grey loppings of pittosporum. They were tipsy and full of mirth, knowing their own attractiveness, knowing how their dresses and the occasion, the decorations, the light of the sky and the sea through the window, the wine, how it all worked to increase their youthfulness and beauty, the life in them, beyond what I could bear to contemplate. They were close together, I think of them now as having each an arm around the other's waist, and a glass in the outer hand, and like that they came up close and kissed me, one on each cheek, so that I was for a moment fully in their aura, the scent in their hair, the wine on their breath, all the gaiety. Then they stood back, close together, childish. Elaine said, We came to say Happy Christmas, and nudged Sarah with her shoulder. Sarah said, We don't know anything about you. You're our workmate and we don't know anything about you. We know everything about Chris and quite a bit about Brian, and Elaine and I are best mates but we don't know a thing about you. Is it true you were a monk? Chris says he's sure you were a monk. He says he can always tell a monk, because of his early life.

Eyes and smiles, dresses and stones of the sea, they were cajoling me and I felt what it would be like (would have been like) to be a person with companions, alive in an easy exchange with a dear friend or two, and if I'd been able to speak I should have tried to say so, perhaps as a preamble, on the threshold of candour: that their youth and gaiety and delight in themselves had opened me, a little at least, so that for a moment, for the duration of their waiting to hear what I might answer, I saw into a world so spacious and cheerful my own felt like the cramped cast-off shell some naked crab had squatted in and years later still peered out of and dared not leave. I was, I said. Chris is right. But it was years ago, I was his age—younger even—I was about your age. They didn't want to be serious. Had there been the least music they would have danced. They didn't want to be polite, considerate, sympathetic. They wanted everything to be funny for an hour or so. And in their careless good nature they wanted me to be like that too. I should have taken each by the hand, there and then, and summoned up a syrtaki from Ithaca or Samothrace and danced the lumbering graceless dance of my leaden soul, right there among the dressed-up islanders, between two girls, danced, and they would have hearkened either side of me and heard the tune in my head and taken it up, lifted and lightened it, and led me and I'd have followed, dancing, dancing, ugly bear of a soul, dancing, until I was changed. Were you chaste? Sarah asked. Was it hard, our age, being chaste? Were you obedient? Did you do as you were told? Will you obey Elaine and me if we ask you to do a thing? I can see you wouldn't mind being poor, I agree it is disgusting to be rich. But was it not hard, our age, being chaste? They wanted me to increase the laughter in them, they gave me the chance, but I could feel the shadow of me, of my seriousness, the stain, the leaden atmosphere of me, beginning to creep over them, like bad afterthoughts, like regret, like the sad obligation to apologize, and I knew I would defeat them and the whole occasion, the light dancing at the window, the sparkle and the fumes of wine, the will to gaiety, I would defeat it in them, so I said what I always say, Forgive me, and left.

I tell you this so that you will know, again, that you were right.

Leaving the hotel, I went to the church. There was a service Christmas Eve and another Christmas Morning. I didn't attend either. The first was the children's nativity play which they'd been rehearsing for weeks. The props—a crib in a stable made of blue pallets, the doll, the toy animals—were still there and the costumes (those of the Kings so scarlet, black, silver, gold and sparkling) were folded and laid to one side. All the church was decorated with greenery and the earliest narcissi and butcher's broom for holly. Six oil lamps hang from the ceiling on long chains, six beautiful brass bowls and the glass funnels of flame. Six windows: the two north illustrate the verses concerning the lily of the fields; the two east are without script or image, only light; the two south read, Let the waters bring forth abundantly the moving creature that hath life. And they show that life. The lights and colours of all six windows put me in mind of the dresses, the necklace and the bracelet of Sarah and Elaine.

Being with the monks soon killed even my desire to believe in God. But I love such houses as this one on Enys, so well built, so close to the quay where every day there is a busyness of boats and goods and people and the sea embraces equally the living worshippers and the dead. And the beautiful work in the house, the fitness of it, and the flowers and greenery of the island for decoration, the singing, the children's yearly acting out the old story, the light and the silence when everyone has left, how I love all that.

It was too early to go back to my shed. My nervousness and sadness were acute and I didn't think I'd be able to combat them well enough by any reading or by cleaning and sharpening the tools in Mary's workshop. Most days towards dusk it is like that. How will I secure the oblivion of sleep? I've often thought no sane and happy person could bear my life for even an hour if suddenly translated into it. Only because my life has *grown* to be like this, because it has habituated me to it, is it bearable. If it is bearable.

I climbed the hill that forms the southern headland of my little bay. All the six hills have their tumuli but here, nearest my shed, the remains are especially apparent. Many events of late have assumed a peculiar definiteness, like finality. They present themselves to me as though prepared—as though they are ready and they lie in wait. So on this hill I found that the best preserved of the tombs, which I last visited a couple of weeks ago, has been, so to speak, further clarified, made more compelling, by somebody outlining the shape of it with large clean ovoid pebbles through the gorse and heather. I supposed at once that the builder of the arch had returned and done this too. First because it was a labour. I counted two hundred and seven pebbles and they must have been carried, and surely not more than three or four at a time, up from the one beach under the headland where in all sizes the pebbles are smooth and egg-shaped. At his way into the zone of the tumulus he had placed two larger stones, each as much as you could carry from sea level. And the kist, where the corpse had huddled up small and which I had always seen empty, he had floored quite deeply with clean limpet shells. The pebbles lay around the sinuous circumference the way you might lay out a necklace on a surface, to see what shapes it was capable of when not determined by a woman's neck and throat. The pebbles are smoothed more or less finely according to the coarseness of the granite's crystals—which decide the colours also, the shades of grey, white, pink, almost black, to which, as he strung his chosen stones to enclose the grave, he had paid close attention. The kist at the heart, floored with limpet cones, was bone-white and bone-yellow.

I stood there until the sky became as bleached as bone and the light far out as sheer and pitiless and uninhabitable as a work of gold, silver and steel. I let myself get cold. I was thinking of the builder's exertions, how he must have sweated, the faster beating of his heart as he climbed with the weight of stones, how warm his hands were, handling them, the brief lingering of his warmth on their egg-shaped surfaces, their resumption of their natural cold. And remembering how he had appraised his arch that he intended to go underwater, how he had nodded in approval and farewell, I felt sure he had done the same when he had made apparent the skeletal shape of the tomb on the windy hill and tipped a dry libation of limpet shells into the small space where the human had gone into the earth.

I think these letters may still be a sort of courtship. Not pleading that you will love me, only hoping you will remember me. And then I think even that is asking too much.

Sunday 3 January

I was on Flagstaff Hill when the year turned. Halangy had fireworks. From my distance the rockets did not seem to reach very high. Orion, on the other hand, seemed to walk quite low. The moon was lessening. Mostly what you are aware of is the water, the large lagoon of it, the ocean all around, in varying degrees of restlessness but always everywhere restless. Lights on the water, the four or five boats, the beacons winking where there are rocks and shallows. Odd lights of a habitation, near and far. Very faint haze of the mainland. The red lights of the wireless mast on Halangy, so many conversations pass through there. The blue-green watery earth spinning and circling till it stops. Lights, the man-made, amount to nothing, the constellations are shapes only to us and not one moon or star or sun or planet acknowledges the beginning we celebrate with fireworks, song and drink.

This morning I had a visit from Mary. I was in the workshop, the light pouring through, the sea behind the dune sounding very near. I was cleaning and sharpening her father's chisels. Steel has a smell when you get the rust off it and shape the blade razor-sharp on an oiled whetstone. I touch the edge and sniff it. I've made a rack above the workbench and as each chisel is done I slot it where it belongs in the order of diminishing width of blade. I've oiled the wooden handles, they have a dull glow now and a good smell. The saws, all of them, all shapes and sizes for various kinds of wood, for logs, planks, plywood, dowling, balsa, also for metal, are restored and they hang in place. Likewise his hammers, planes, pliers, screwdrivers, bradawls... The wood he never used is stacked or laid down so you could easily distinguish the piece you want. In a dozen or more very beautiful old pale green jam jars I've sorted nails and screws into various sizes. I've rigged up better lighting, planed and proofed the two windows and the door. With the heater from my shed you could work all night in any weather if you wished. Yesterday, still clearing a far corner, I opened a sack and found the mallets, chisels, gouges, knives you need for woodcarving and a thick log of apple wood that he had begun to shape into a woman's head and shoulders, the rough tress of her hair coming over on the left side. Mary was surprised by that and surveying the whole place and how far I'd got with it, she said, in a tone I felt to be benevolent, You look set to carry on where he left off. I shrugged and asked her about Alf Lewis.

He came from the mainland, as they mostly do, and beached his leaky boat in Merrick Bay. It was late October. People said he was lucky he hadn't sunk. At the post office he bought a bottle of brandy and a frozen chicken. He asked might there be any work over the winter but nobody much liked the look of him and they were noncommittal. For a week he lived on his boat and waded ashore at low water for provisions and to ask again was there any work. Then came a gale and a high tide, he smashed up under the tamarisks, on the rocks, and that was the end of his boat. But a woman looking after her grandchildren, Betty Daniel, who lived down there took pity on him and said he could live in her boathouse and do odd jobs for rent. And that was more or less the way of it, for fifteen years. He never did many jobs but Mrs. Daniel never seemed to mind. The grandchildren loved him. He got down on his hands and knees and one rode on his back while the other led him by a rope around his neck. They called him Horsey, never anything else, even when they were too big to ride on him. He lived off social security and Mrs. Daniel's charity. She lent him an old punt and he rowed across the channel, bought a *Racing Post*, sat in the Dorrien Arms and bet more than he could afford on the horses. When the tides were big he liked to walk across at low water. He'd time it so he'd get there only paddling and after a few pints he'd wade back, holding his paper and any other bits of shopping above his head. He did that, summer and winter, for fifteen years. Then last August when he stood up to leave the pub a fog had come in, thick as a bag, everybody said, and they said he should wait a couple of hours, there was a boat going back, he could take the boat for once. But he wouldn't be told, he left the pub and vanished. Nobody missed him for a day or two, then the bookmaker phoned Mrs. Daniel and said to tell Alf his horse had won at 10 to 1 and was he coming over to collect his winnings. Afterwards that made people laugh, since he was never lucky with his bets. Mrs. Daniel and the grown-up grandchildren were very upset but nobody else was. Still, said Mary, it gave her a chill around the heart to think of anyone vanishing in the sea like that, in a fog.

6 January

An orange wellington boot (the right foot), cuttlefish, a
double sachet of emergency fresh water made by a firm in
Bergen, a net tangled with its rope and plastic floats, a doll's
head, the plastic handle of a knife, a packet of rusks from
Belgium, an orange starfish (dead and stiff), ribs and vertebrae of, I think, a dolphin, plastic bottles (milk, bleach,
shampoo, antifreeze, marmite), one trainer (left foot), one
green rubber glove (left), cotton buds, a gin bottle, a very
soft grapefruit, chunk of polystyrene, bamboo pole, twelve-
foot length of four-by-four, dogfish egg, cube of wood off
a pallet, plastic fish-crate from Coruna and another (a yard
away) from Goedereede, plastic clasp for a downspout, biro,
oiled-up guillemot, plastic tulip, lid off a funerary urn, a
cork, a condom, three cartidges, a black plastic bag, claws.

I had another visit from Eddie, earlier than last time, I was at
my table, breathing in the steam of my coffee, watching the
light becoming strong enough for a winter's day, and suddenly
there was his face again, in the glass, as though mirrored,
and again it shocked me to the heart and in a bad state some
moments passed until I understood that what he wanted was
my friendship. He tapped at the window, pointed to his face,
then at me, smiled—the smile of a clown—showed me his
palms, nodded his head, pressed his right hand on his heart,
again with the pointing finger indicated me, and raised all the
features of his face in a question. I let him in, and between glee
at that and wonder at the place he had been let into, he got
into a sort of ecstasy beyond the power of his hands and face
to express. I sat him down on my chair, gave him coffee in my
other cup, and cut him a slice of the cake that Mary had given
me the day before. He can't really speak. At least, he can't
make recognizable words. Instead he makes a great variety
of sounds such as infants do when they are used to the babble

of adult language all around them but can't or don't wish to imitate it yet—gurglings, pipings, chuckles, little runs of chirrups, squeals and cries, all in the timbre of a grown man's voice, wonderfully expressive. In a deep sense I at once knew what he meant. I've never been in the presence of such good nature and simple happiness before. Nothing in all his noises, gestures, bearing qualified in the least his joy and his goodwill. For that time he was absolutely good and joyful, unconditionally, without any safeguard, wholly open and delivered up in it. Everything about my shed delighted him. He gripped and stroked the plain chair, knelt at the bed (where I was sitting) and laid his hands flat on the rough blanket and on the cold white sheet folded back in a band across it. Fleetingly he laid his cheek on the pillow. Then he resumed his seat, crammed the cake into his mouth and gulped the coffee. His very pale eyes have the sags of idiocy under them, he drools, his hands are big, a stray white tress of hair falls over his eyes and he wipes it away. After a while he became quiet and fell to studying the objects in the room with a grave seriousness. My finds along the one shelf, arranged in a line next to the few books, attracted him, he rose, lifted up each in turn with extraordinary care, examined each, looked from it to me and back again to it, as though to understand the connection. So I watched myself being appraised in my finding, taking up, bringing home, setting down to live with: the long delicate skull of a gannet, the skull of a seal, three of its vertebrae, the severed and entirely desiccated wing of a tern, a fragment of wood honeycombed by shipworm... I could hear the wrens, the sparrows, the thrushes, the starlings, the blackbirds that with their various noises begin my every day. And the breeze in the tamarisks and the surf up under the dune. The light became strong and bright. Eddie stood at the shelf, his big hands were so considerate they could have cradled the skeleton of a shrew, and he looked at me and at the object in question and made the noises of his wondering and pondering.

He was there an hour, then Lucy came, anxious as ever, found him, scolded him and said she was sorry I had been intruded upon. I said he should visit whenever he liked, I'd be glad of his company and if he didn't find me in he should make himself at home and stay as long as he wished. And you'll know where to look for him, I said to her.

16 January

New moon. Brian has gone to the mainland to see his wife and children. He made an appointment. He is staying in a B&B just around the corner from the family home, though his wife said there was no need to go to such lengths, he could have slept in the spare bedroom. He says she wasn't unfriendly when he spoke to her, but quite definite that she doesn't want to live with him, not here, not over there, not anywhere. But she agrees it is only fair he should see the children now and then. She has emailed him some recent photographs of them (not of her) and promises to do that at regular intervals.

It is not just because he misses her and Amy and Zoë that he has arranged this interview (as he calls it). He also wants to ask her some questions for his family history, about her childhood in a village on the Lancashire coast. He spent his own childhood scarcely ten miles away, but inland, in a small town, and of course their experiences were very different. He admits her origins and her local habitation always did have, in his eyes, a romance quite lacking in his. The coast there is very flat. It is a queer zone of brackish water, salt grass, little channels, thousands of peewits, and the sheep graze, as it seems, far out on a terrain that belongs by rights to the Irish Sea. He and his wife went back there sometimes when they were courting and it has haunted him ever since. So now he has drawn up a list of questions—seventeen in all—which he hopes she will answer for him, before it is too late. He showed me the list. Among his questions are: What was her mother's Co-op number? What was the name of her Gran's farm where she used to look for eggs and where the pig burst out of its sty and scared her half to death? Which uncle was it who got stranded in his car—a Ford Popular?— on the dyke road during the 1953 flood? Were the toilets in her primary school outside in the yard? What was the name of the woman who walked seven miles to the nearest railway station and took the train to her mother's each time— nine times in all—she felt her baby was about to come?

I could remember the rest of Brian's questions if I lay on the bed under my army coat and thought. And not seventeen but seven times seventeen are the questions I could think of to put to you.

The tides are big. Brian left early, while there was still water for the launch, and we, his workforce, took the day off. Chris sat down at the office computer to plan the next few months of his life. He still tries for Elaine, but rather half-heartedly. Not that he's doing any better with anyone else. Sarah, Elaine and I went out on the Merrick Bay flats.

The islands make a broken rim around a sunken plain which floods on the incoming tide and empties on the ebb. At low water the walls of the lost fields continue downwards and out of sight under the sand. The maps still show the vanished causeways. There are obliterated hearths and wells. The tombs are on the surviving hills. And rammed up into the roots of the tamarisks, quite close to the boathouse that was his home for fifteen years, are the few remaining bits of Alf's boat, held down by the stones that smashed it.

Going out on the flats is like trespassing. You know you mustn't be found there when the owner returns. I've been out on my own, at Merrick Bay and elsewhere, several times, and always with that feeling of brief licence. In the two young women it excited a hilarity rather as the wine and the dressing up had done at Brian's party on Christmas Day. Poor

Brian was away, they had the day off, they were pleased with themselves, they said I shouldn't go working in the fields for Nathan but should come out with them, on the flats. The day was cold and very bright with a breeze that gave the look of hurry to the ebbing water and an edge to their elation. In fact I had already decided I wouldn't work for Nathan. I was intending to go out, but alone, to get some idea of where Alf had vanished, and I kept to that purpose, but kept it to myself, and in a way I should perhaps be ashamed of I cherished it all the more in the company of Sarah and Elaine.

Sarah, at least to begin with, had her own serious purpose for which she carried a chart, a notebook, an indelible pen, a dozen small plastic jars, a lens and a sharp knife in a hard leather satchel slung across her shoulder so that it rested on her hip. Her idea was to collect some specimen periwinkles, of the four species, from different tide zones, and also fronds of serrated wrack to study what grew on them. Elaine helped her for a while. The tide was still falling. I watched the birds— two spoonbills, a rare arrival; the more and more common egrets; the local heron and swans; the countless waders I don't have the knowledge to distinguish; all in their characteristic fashions going about the endless business of probing, uncovering, stabbing, scooping, an intense almost leisurely concentration on getting enough to eat, the sea having withdrawn its protection from millions of edible fellow-creatures. Such grace and menace. The birds moved away from us only as far as they judged necessary. They kept to their purpose, warily.

I watched, walked on, halted, watched. But really I was drifting towards the diminishing channel that still made two islands of Enys and St. Nicholas, I felt pulled as the waters were, so easy has it become to lapse out of human company. Then the girls called out, not my name, just a crying, not gull or tern or curlew or oystercatcher, but of that order of cry, not-human, fit for the bubbling and coursing of salt water and the stink of weed. I waited, they came over. Like me, they were barefoot, their boots on the laces around their necks, trousers rolled up. Sarah said, We've done enough work. Elaine said, We've had an idea. Her tone was like Sarah's when at the party she asked was I obedient, would I do what they asked, was I chaste? I nodded. Yes, a drink. There's time if we're quick.

The channel was a wide river, shallow and flowing fast. Odd, an ocean quaffing a lagoon. The girls let go of me—they had me by either arm—and paddled through at once, wetted no higher than the knees. From the other side they called across. But for an interlude I was going into myself, into the room in my imagination where Alf stumbled, went under, surfaced, struggled and the cold tide like a shark took hold of him and dragged him off, never to be seen again. The girls hallooed, they were as strange to me as selkies. I splashed through and gathered them against me. I was high on the thought of Alf as he began his afterlife. Drinks, I said. We've got an hour.

The Dorrien Arms is no distance. We went there barefoot with our boots around our necks. A brandy each, quickly. Then wine, with bread and smoked mackerel. Monk, said Sarah, we like you when you get us tipsy. Their faces burned, from the flats. I never knew such proximity of life. The two young women, they might decide anything for the good of their lives, they might turn their gaze in a sweet and predatory way on anything, and take it. And there I sat, close and opposite, in pure admiration. You and you, I said. I drink to you. And Alf, already dead, turned in the current and set with it out towards nowhere, towards never being apparent to anyone ever again, he turned with the acquiescence of the dead and headed away and in the solemnity of our bread and fish and wine I took their hands, felt their warmth, kissed their fingers, relinquished them. Monk, said Elaine, you're nice when you've had a drink or two. The hour passed. There was no fog but it was winter and the afternoon did not have long to live. Another half hour. Come on, I said. Drink up. Your mothers would not forgive me.

And so we left, barefoot, the light of outdoors, brilliant, chased with breeze, leapt at everything, jaunty and careless, and all the phenomena were flung into keen appearance and the light that did it to them shouted triumphantly. And we walked out through the coils and spurtings of lives that live under the sand, over popping wrack and the harsh debris of shells to the channel we had to wade. The tamarisks of Merrick Bay were clearly visible but at a distance that looked too great ever to traverse. The tide had turned, the current had reversed, but if you slipped it would not deposit you safe on an islet within the inhabited ring. The ring is broken, the gaps are large and many, the suction of deep water will take you out. I thought we were not where we had crossed. Almost certainly we were not at the shallowest fording place. Wait, I said. But the girls stepped in and went knee-deep at once. Sarah took off her satchel, held it high and proceeded, Elaine following. The water split in a briefly cresting wave around each in turn, rose to their breasts, then lapsed. They stood on the far side shrieking with laughter. I took off my coat, held it in a bundle above my head. I could not have imagined the cold and the force of the water, the two together as one embodiment, and now I can, it went into my stomach, so now I shall remember it and in the imagination feel it again. An army coat, if you let it get sodden through, would take you under at once. I've told nobody—till you—anything at all of what I learned.

We hurried. Elaine, who could hardly speak for shivering, said Sarah said I should come back with them and be warmed up. But I parted company when we were near the beach. In my shed among my papers on my table top there was a gift for me: a vase, I guessed from Eddie and from the tip. My coat was dry, I went to bed in it. The vase was more than a bit chipped around the rim, but none the less beautiful—like a gourd in shape, with red poppies on a black glaze. For some time I shook with cold and my mind ran as fast as the water in a delirium. I wanted to hold the vase, have its roundness between my hands, offer its darkness and its poppies to a beloved person. And in my fever of cold that seemed to me an entirely reasonable wish and I felt sure it would be granted. Then I must have slept and when I woke it was dark and I was warm, glad, hungry.

19 January

Brian has returned from the mainland disappointed. He did not advance at all in his dealings with his wife. On the contrary, she put him further off. She agrees that Amy and Zoë should visit him at Easter, if they want to, but he will have to fetch them and bring them back. She thinks if she came over herself it would put her in a false position, by which she means she doesn't want anybody here supposing their marriage might be on the mend. When he got nowhere 'in that department' Brian thought he could perhaps approach her through his seventeen questions. But there he was sorely mistaken. She refused point blank to answer a single one of them. And when—very gently, in his opinion—he suggested she owed him that at least, the questions being so important to him, she became quite hostile and told him straight her childhood was none of his business, which he found very hurtful because when they were courting he had believed she shared it with him. In the end she said, You don't own me, Brian, and after that all he could do was go back to his B&B. The girls were already in bed by then and he didn't dare call next morning and say goodbye to them as they left for school.

Now Brian hardly knows how he'll find the courage to start the new season and be cheerful with the guests. At the thought of it he feels very low indeed. He knows the rich man who owns the place will want to see a big improvement on last year, though money for most people, even the kind who stay in his hotel, is still quite tight. Brian panics when he thinks of the effort he will have to make. And he won't find much recreation in his family history. He feels almost prohibited from doing it by his wife's hurtful words.

Eddie came again. He brought me a fistful of white narcissi and nodded his heavy head in great delight and satisfaction towards the vase. They scent my room. But the best was that, having presented them to me and when I'd filled the vase with water from my can and set the flowers in and we had both admired them, then he sat down on my bed in complete stillness, all his usual small chunnering noises ceased, he became entirely quiet and calm. So much so that after a while I smiled at him and resumed the writing he had interrupted with his visit. And that is how his mother found us when after an hour or more she came looking for him. We were quiet. Eddie likes coming here, she said. He'll miss you when you leave.

Nests from last year, or from several years ago, held in the clasp of the new branches that sprout around the place where the tall upright was lopped. Once or twice I've found the skeletons of fledglings in them, delicate remains in the well-made and deeply protected home. Brambles that climb from the earth through twenty feet of dense euonymus or pittosporum, wriggling through and finally attaining what they were born always to seek: the light. My silver ladder stands in the grey-green fall of branches, twigs and leaves. The leaves quiver like a haul of fishes dying brightly in the sunlight on the net. And the wind, almost every day the wind, bustling through the unkempt crest that I will lop. I rob the wind of a resistance by which it makes the passage of itself felt.

21 January

I set the female bust on the workbench under the lamp and looked at it. A few more hours of work and she would have been there, manifest, come out of the wood, become real out of the idea of her. Even thus far emerged, with her roughed-out face and plait of hair and the swelling that would become her breasts, she has some force. I have sharpened all his cutting and gouging tools and wrapped them in an oily cloth that will keep then ready instantly for use. I sat to one side on a packing case and looked. I examined my hands. Really, I might have some chance of bringing her further out. She would never be wholly there, I don't have the gift for that. But some way, nonetheless, towards being there. And I'm not forbidden. Mary has said as much. Still I can't or shan't.

22 January

Most nights I sleep at once, then wake and see that hardly two hours have passed. Waking so soon, the night still to be got through, I fill up with disappointment and anxiety. I've slept worse and worse since I went away from you. In the night, lying awake, the night impossibly long, I undo all the good I did or that was done to me during the day. Every elation, I deflate. Every kindness, I convert to dust. Every insight, joy in a thing, hope of more such things, I worry soon to death. Truly, I can summon up a face that smiles at me and in whose eyes I see myself a welcome friend and I can turn that face and smile to deceit and mockery at once. Then I assemble all the arguments against me. I accumulate the proof that I'm not fit to live. Some nights the fear is such it drives me out of bed, out of the little warmth and comfort and homeliness I have assembled around me under a wooden roof and between four wooden walls, and I walk out through the lovely opening of my blessed horseshoe of tamarisks and climb the dune and huddle in a dead man's army greatcoat and stare at the sea and hearken to its noise. And after some time, under the pulsing stars, the lighthouse winking mechanically every fifteen seconds, it all feels like a foolishness, the despair itself not worth the candle, the thought of killing myself seems laughably self-important, and all I want is my bit of warmth and shelter under the blankets and some sleep.

23 January

An enlivening tempest, the winds rode in on the risen backs of the Atlantic and I went out among the tumuli and showed my face and opened my arms to them and tried to breathe their force into my lungs. Just north of here, in a cavernous hole, enough timber has lodged to build a log cabin with and live alone in, in a bee-loud glade. When will you ever, Peace, wild wooddove, shy wings shut…? When I came home, caked in brine, from discovering that cache and wondering was it worth my while to wait for low water and go and lug it in, there was Eddie with more narcissi in his massive fist and again once they were breathing in his gift, the vase, we sat in silence and quietness, he and I, utterly companionable, I did not turn my back on him and write, but there we sat, listening to the gale, till Lucy came through it looking for him.

24 January

Mary looked in at the workshop door. There's a cake for you on your table, she said. I was standing by the bench, contemplating the unfinished carving. I'll miss seeing you in Father's coat, she said. In fact, I'd rather you took it with you when you leave.

I'll send these last four days together. Even so, they're hardly worth a stamp.

28 January

I'll leave a note on my table under the black vase asking that
this pen, my notebooks, your photograph and a necklace
that was my mother's should be sent to you. And I'll leave
the postage. I'll take back to the tip the things I took from
the tip and the things I got from beachcombing I'll take
back to the beach. Elaine and Sarah can share the books and
Lucy should have the vase itself. I'll add that to my note.
And my rags and my camping stuff they can do what they
like with. The tip. Mary will collect the things she lent me.

I always wanted to give you the necklace and never quite
dared. The beads are of cherry amber. I've often imagined
how they would look on you.

My notebooks will be worse reading than these letters. At
least in the letters I was going out to somebody. If I say
these letters are my better self you will realize what a poor
thing I have been. And in my notebooks I say so, again
and again. I fought against my impoverishment and lost. I
had an eye for abundance, I could see it all around me, life
for the living, a proper joy, proper sorrows, deeply among
other people. I could see it but I couldn't do it. At least
believe me when I say I loved. But I could never have and
hold what I loved. Somehow I never had the knack. Or I
never had the courage. So I have lived in poverty knowing
all the while that life is rich, rich. And I have lived in obedience. I obeyed the orders that would harm me. Early on
it was God and the monks and when I was shot of them I
devised in myself even crueller, yet more nonsensical and
in the end even madder dictators. So I lived in obedience to
temptations and commands whose one purpose was to kill
the life in me. Now and again I was disobedient, I answered
back, I said no, joyously I transgressed. For a while I was a

passable imitation of a man claiming his right to live. But I always came to heel in the end, knuckled under, took the punishment for my revolt. In my notebooks I wrote all this—the mechanics of it. I did once think that if I could describe it very precisely I could fight it better. That was a mistake. I never understood *why* I was like I was, but I did see very clearly *how* I was, how it worked in me, the mechanism that sided with death against my life. I knew I didn't understand why but I hoped that if I saw how it worked, I might escape. Must one know why? Should it not be enough to see how? Well, it wasn't enough. The best I ever got from writing it all down was the bleak satisfaction of making clear sentences. I could analyze and differentiate and split fine hairs and set it all out clearly but it didn't help. Nothing helped. I saw that I did not have it in me to save myself. I wrote these letters, which have been—grant me that much—more about other people and about the earth's lovely phenomena than about myself, to keep myself in dealings with somebody else.

Full moon this weekend. The weather is very still. In the abandoned bulb fields the daffodils and the narcissi are in flower. They find their way up into the sunshine through dead bracken, gorse and brambles. In the fields most recently let go they appear in their regimented straight lines, in a continuing discipline though the forces of law and order have departed. But in the oldest ruins the flowers have split and spread and they come up where they like through all the dead stuff gloriously. The tides will be very big again this weekend.

Saturday 30 January

Forgive me, I changed my mind. I've thrown my mother's necklace into the sea and fed my notebooks and your photograph into the hotel's incinerator that we call Puffing Billy. So nobody from here will post you anything after this. I was ashamed of my notebooks and didn't want them lodging in your mind. And again I didn't quite dare give you the necklace of a woman you heard me talk about but never met.

Sometimes I have imagined you burning these letters as they arrive, burning them all unopened and unread. Only very rarely have I had the sudden conviction that you do read them and keep them. Lately I've told myself you don't open them but you lay them down in a safe place in order of arrival so that the last would be first to hand. And now I am hoping that when, after a few weeks, nothing further arrives, you'll take up this last one first, for an explanation. There is no explanation—but only this request. *Please* burn the rest unread. They were my effort and it failed. There's no reason now why you should read them.

When I posted Thursday's letter Mrs. Goddard said, You keep us in business, Mr. Smith. I don't know how we'll manage when you leave. She is very happy these last days because her daughter is coming home from New Zealand with a husband and a baby boy she has never seen. They plan to stay three months and, who knows, they might stay longer.

I'll take this letter to Mrs. Goddard and she'll say what she has always said when I've posted a letter to you on a Saturday: You know it won't go out till Monday now? I've always liked her for her tact. She has never said, You don't get answers, do you? I shan't tell her this letter will be the last.

Mary's workshop looks all shipshape. I'll walk through Nathan's fields. The hedges look very trim. I'll take my books to the community centre, except one each for Elaine and Sarah which I'll leave here. The rest, but for the vase which I want Eddie to give to his mother, is for the beach or the tip. I'll keep this heavy coat on. I'll keep this pen in its deep inside pocket.

Tea at the Midland

The wind blew steadily hard with frequent surges of greater ferocity that shook the vast plate glass behind which a woman and a man were having tea. The waters of the bay, quite shallow, came in slant at great speed from the southwest. They were breaking white on a turbid ground far out, tide and wind driving them, line after line, nothing opposing or impeding them so they came on and on until they were expended. The afternoon winter sky was torn and holed by the wind and a troubled golden light flung down at all angles, abiding nowhere, flashing out and vanishing. And under that ceaselessly riven sky, riding the furrows and ridges of the sea, were a score or more of surfers towed on boards by kites. You might have said they were showing off but in truth it was a self-delighting among others doing likewise. The woman behind plate glass could not have been in their thoughts, they were not performing to impress and entertain her. Far out, they rode on the waves or sheer or at an angle through them and always only to try what they could do. In the din of waves and wind under that ripped-open sky they were enjoying themselves, they felt the life in them to be entirely theirs, to deploy how they liked best. To the woman watching they looked like grace itself, the heart and soul of which is freedom. It pleased her particularly that they were attached by invisible strings to colourful curves of rapidly moving air. How clean and clever that was! You throw up something like a handkerchief, you tether it and by its headlong wish to fly away, you are towed along. And not in the straight line of *its* choosing, no: you tack and swerve as you please and swing out wide around at least a hemisphere of centrifugence. Beautiful, she thought. Such versatile autonomy among the strict determinants and all that coordination of mind and body, fitness, practice, confidence, skill and execution, all for fun!

The man had scarcely noticed the surf-riders. He was aware of the crazed light and the shocks of wind chiefly as irritations. All he saw was the woman, and that he had no presence in her thoughts. So he said again, A pedophile is a pedophile. That's all there is to it.

She suffered a jolt, hearing him. And that itself, her being startled, annoyed him more. She had been so intact and absent. Her eyes seemed to have to adjust to his different world.—That still, she said. I'm sorry. But can't you let it be?—He couldn't, he was thwarted and angered, knowing that he had not been able to force an adjustment in her thinking.—I thought you'd like the place, she said. I read up about it. I even thought we might come here one night, if you could manage it, and we'd have a room with a big curved window and in the morning look out over the bay.—He heard this as recrimination. She had left the particular argument and moved aside to his more general capacity for disappointing her. He, however, clung to the argument, but she knew, even if he didn't know or wouldn't admit it, that all he wanted was something which the antagonisms that swarmed in him could batten on for a while. Feeling very sure of that, she asked, malevolently, as though it were indeed only a question that any two rational people might debate, Would you have liked it if you hadn't known it was by Eric Gill? Or if you hadn't known Eric Gill was a pedophile?—That's not the point, he said. I know both those things so I can't like it. He had sex with his own daughters, for Christ's sake.—She answered, And with his sisters. And with the dog. Don't forget the dog. And quite possibly he thought it was for Christ's sake. Now suppose he'd done all that but also he made peace in the Middle East. Would you want them to start the killing again when they found out about his private life?—That's not the same, he said. Making peace is useful at least.—I agree, she said. And making beauty isn't. *Odysseus Welcomed from the Sea* isn't at all useful, though it is worth quite a lot of money, I believe.—Frankly, he said, I don't even think it's beautiful. Knowing what I know, the thought of him carving naked men and women makes me queasy.—And if there was a dog or a little girl in there, you'd vomit?

She turned away, looking at the waves, the light and the surfers again, but not watching them keenly, for which loss she hated him. He sat in a rage. Whenever she turned away and sat in silence he desired very violently to force her to attend and continue further and further in the thing that was harming them. But they were sitting at a table over afternoon tea in a place that had pretensions to style and decorum. So he was baffled and thwarted, he could do nothing, only knot himself tighter in his anger and hate her more.

Then she said in a soft and level voice, not placatory, not in the least appealing to him, only sad and without taking her eyes off the sea, If I heeded you I couldn't watch the surfers with any pleasure until I knew for certain none was a rapist or a member of the BNP. And perhaps I should even have to learn to hate the sea because just out there, where that beautiful golden light is, those poor cockle-pickers drowned when the tide came in on them faster than they could run. I should have to keep thinking of them phoning China on their mobile phones and telling their loved ones they were about to drown.—You turn everything wrongly, he said.—No, she answered, I'm trying to think the way you seem to want me to think, joining everything up, so that I don't concentrate on one thing without bringing in everything else. When we make love and I cry out for the joy and the pleasure of it I have to bear in mind that some woman somewhere at exactly that time is being abominably tortured and she is screaming in unbearable pain. That's what it would be like if all things were joined up.

She turned to him. What did you tell your wife this time, by the way? What lie did you tell her so we could have tea together? You should write it on your forehead so that I won't forget should you ever turn and look at me kindly.—I risk so much for you, he said.—And I risk nothing for you? I often think you think I've got nothing to lose.—I'm going, he said. You stay and look at the clouds. I'll pay on my way out.—Go if you like, she said. But please don't pay. This was my treat, remember.—She looked out to sea again.— Odysseus was a horrible man. He didn't deserve the courtesy he received from Nausikaa and her mother and father. I don't forget that when I see him coming out of hiding with the olive branch. I know what he has done already in the twenty years away. And I know the foul things he will do when he gets home. But at that moment, the one that Gill chose for his frieze, he is naked and helpless and the young woman is courteous to him and she knows for certain that her mother and father will welcome him at their hearth. Aren't we allowed to contemplate such moments?—I haven't read it, he said.—Well you could, she said. There's nothing to stop you. I even, I am such a fool, I even thought I would read the passages to you if we had one of those rooms with a view of the sea and of the mountains across the bay that would have snow on them.

She had tears in her eyes. He attended more closely. He felt she might be near to appealing to him, helping him out of it, so that they could get back to somewhere earlier and go a different way, leaving this latest stumbling block aside. There's another thing, she said.—What is it? he asked, softening, letting her see that he would be kind again, if she would let him.—On Scheria, she said, it was their custom to look after shipwrecked sailors and to row them home, however far away. That was their law and they were proud of it.—The tears in her eyes overflowed, her cheeks were wet with them. He waited, unsure, becoming suspicious.— So their best rowers, fifty-two young men, rowed Odysseus back to Ithaca overnight and lifted him ashore asleep and laid him gently down and piled all the gifts he had been given by Scheria around him on the sand. Isn't that beautiful? He wakes among their gifts and he is home. But on the way back, do you know, in sight of their own island, out of pique, to punish them for helping Odysseus, whom he hates, Poseidon turns them and their ship to stone. So Alcinous, the king, to placate Poseidon, a swine, a bully, a thug of a god, decrees they will never help shipwrecked sailors home again. Odysseus, who didn't deserve it, was the last.

He stood up. I don't know why you tell me that, he said.—She wiped her tears on the good linen serviette that had come with their tea and scones.—You never cry, he said. I don't think I've ever seen you cry. And here you are crying about this thing and these people in a book. What about me? I never see you crying about me and you.—And you won't, she said. I promise you, you won't.

He left. She turned again to watch the surfers. The sun was near to setting and golden light came through in floods from under the ragged cover of weltering cloud. The wind shook furiously at the glass. And the surfers skied like angels enjoying the feel of the waters of the earth, they skimmed, at times they lifted off and flew, they landed with a dash of spray. She watched till the light began to fail and one by one the strange black figures paddled ashore with their boards and sails packed small and weighing next to nothing.

She paid. At the frieze a tall man had knelt and, with an arm around her shoulders, was explaining to a little girl what was going on. It's about welcome, he said. Every stranger was sacred to the people of that island. They clothed him and fed him without even asking his name. It's a very good picture to have on a rough coast. The lady admitted she would have liked to marry him but he already had a wife at home. So they rowed him home.

STRONG ENOUGH TO HELP

But that Saturday morning, end of October, instead of trying to write a poem, he suddenly and without knowing why began to write out all he could remember of the sayings and turns of phrase his mother and her mother and her sister had reached for to colour and solemnify their speech. They came in a rush in no particular order, he heard them in the women's voices, distinct voices, but any of the three women might have spoken them out of the stock they held in common for the family down the generations on the female side. Listening, he wrote: little pigs have big ears, least said soonest mended, enough's as good as feast, face like a wet Whit Week, love locked out, like death warmed up, the ever-open door, black as the chimney back, better to be born lucky than rich, pots for rags, he had a good home and he left, like feeding a donkey strawberries, waste not want not, made up no grumbling, rise and shine, sooner keep you a week than a fortnight, I'll make one less, it's as cheap sitting as standing— And there he halted. At the back of his head, or behind him in the room pressing on his neck and shoulders, he felt the vast reservoir of the women's unspoilt language, he felt it would bow him flat on the table top if he sat there any longer listening to

those voices and transcribing what he heard. In the dining room
where every Saturday morning he cleared away his breakfast
things and folded back a certain measure of the cloth and seated
himself at the dark table with his pen and sheets of paper, in
that familiar room he was oppressed. Best stop, he said aloud.
Better go out now and do my shopping. Carry on this afternoon perhaps. But then he looked at the last thing he had written. He said it aloud in Gran Benson's voice: It's as cheap sitting
as standing. And he saw the old woman herself, white-haired,
skewed, shrunken in her scuffed armchair by a bit of fire, the
light behind her through the dirty windows from the yard, and
the dog, Sam, on her right side against her feet. But that wasn't
it. Her words were still in the air and he knew with a thrill of
something akin to fear that there was a gap before them, a space,
and into that space, before he could question it, with a shock
of cold, with a starting of tears, came the words that belonged
there: Sit thee down, lad. And that was it, her exact tone. The
white-haired old woman in a shawl, the friendly mongrel laying
its head across her feet, her left side faintly warmed by the few
coals, she looked up at him as he came in and he stood there and,
having kissed her on the cold smooth forehead, still stood there,
at a loss no doubt, seeming unsure, and looking up she said: Sit
thee down, lad. And added: It's as cheap sitting as standing.

So he sat at the polished black table in the dining room,
among furnishings he had not chosen but had merely gone
on living with, and loneliness, hopelessness, deep deep sadness possessed him utterly, froze him, the pen still in his
hand, and he seemed to be seeing the opposite wall and his
father's copied painting of a painting of Wastwater, not just
through tears but through ice.

Then the doorbell rang.

The bell frightened him, it made no sense. In his own
house he was elsewhere, facing something he did not feel
equal to. What had the bell to do with that? It frightened
him, he could not understand it ringing where he was.

The bell rang again. Merely obeying, he went to the front door.

There stood a black woman, wearing gold. Altogether her appearance was radiant. Mr. Barlow? she said.—Yes, he answered. I am.—Mr. Arthur Barlow?—Yes, he said.—Well my name is Gladys, she said, I'm from the DCMS and here— she lifted her lapel—is my Interviewer Identity Card, to prove it. I do hope I did not wake you, Mr. Barlow. You are my first port of call.—No, said Arthur Barlow, I get up at six every morning, weekends included, to read.—Gladys smiled very happily. You read, Mr. Barlow?—Yes, he said. Poetry. I read a lot of poetry. Who are you, if you don't mind me asking? You're not an estate agent, are you? You're not a religion?—No, no, said Gladys. Nothing like that. I'm from the Department of Culture, Media and Sport and I've come to ask you how you spend your time and what you think of the leisure activities and facilities available in this town. We sent you a letter about ten days ago, to tell you you were chosen.—Oh, said Arthur Barlow, perhaps I haven't opened it yet. When I'm very busy I tend not to open things like that at once.—It had a book of first-class stamps in, said Gladys, which was our little thank you to you, for agreeing to be chosen. Do you write letters, Mr. Barlow? The stamps will come in handy, if you do.—I send away for poetry books, said Arthur Barlow. So thank you very much, the stamps will come in handy for that.

Gladys opened her bright red folder, but said: Are you all right, Mr. Barlow? Would you rather I came back later, or another day?—No, no, said Arthur Barlow. Nothing to worry about. I've had a bit of a shock, that's all.—Oh dear, said Gladys. I'm so sorry. Some bad news? A bereavement?—You mean my suit? said Arthur Barlow. No, I always put this on when I read poetry, or try to write poety, which is what I always do on Saturday mornings only today something else happened and it gave me a shock. It's true I wore this suit to the funerals but when I apply myself to poetry I put it on because it's the best I've got and I do think a person should dress up when he reads poetry or even tries to write some of his own. Mother bought me this suit for my interview and of course I wore it for the funerals but the interview was years and years ago so, as you see, I haven't put on weight, there's that much can be said in my favour.—If anything you must have lost some weight, said Gladys. By the looks of it. So you think you could answer my few questions, Mr. Barlow, if the shock you've had hasn't upset you too much? And she opened her folder again and looked him full in the face.—If you've sent me a book of first-class stamps, said Arthur Barlow, I can surely answer your few questions.—Gladys smiled.

But then Arthur Barlow had a thought, his pale eyes bulged, his thin face, the wispy beard, the thinning colourless hair, all his physiognomy expressed unease. They're not private things you'll be asking, are they? he said. I'm not one for talking about private things.—Nothing of the sort, said Gladys emphatically. I would never take on a job like that. Only about activities and facilities. Your name and address will be kept separate from your answers. No individual will be identifiable from the results.— Then do you want to come in and ask me? Arthur Barlow asked. Or shall you ask me here on the doorstep?—Entirely as you wish, said Gladys.—Come in then, said Arthur Barlow.

But as soon as he had closed the door behind Gladys and led her into the dining room Arthur Barlow knew that the shock was still with him and if he'd been alone he would have said aloud, Oh dear, this is very serious. By mistake he motioned her to sit where he had been sitting, at the head of the table, facing the wall and the picture of Wastwater, so that he stood uncertainly for a moment and folded back another half yard of cloth before seating himself at her right hand, facing the window and the garden fence.—And these must be your poems, said Gladys, not liking to put her folder down on Arthur Barlow's fountain pen and papers. I've never sat at a poet's table before. Not so far as I know, at least.—Arthur Barlow removed his belongings. It's not exactly a poem, he said.

Now, said Gladys briskly. This won't take long. Your age, please, Mr. Barlow?—Fifty-five.—Single, married, widower, divorced?—Single.—And the ethnic group will be white British, will it?—I suppose it will, said Arthur Barlow.—And your occupation, Mr. Barlow?—Filing clerk at the hospital. Though not for much longer.—A career move, Mr. Barlow?— Not exactly, said Arthur Barlow. They're making me redundant after Christmas. There's less and less call for people like me.—Oh, I am sorry, said Gladys. But at least you'll have more time for your poetry.—That's what I tell myself, said Arthur Barlow.—Now, said Gladys: leisure. Are you more sport or culture?—I suppose I'm culture.—You don't watch football, you don't go swimming, you don't play golf or engage in any other physical competitive activity, you don't go to the gym, nothing like that?—Nothing like that.—Culture then, said Gladys. When was your last visit to the cinema, the theatre, opera, ballet, any kind of concert, an art gallery, a museum?—I don't do any of those, said Arthur Barlow. I go to poetry readings when there's one I can get to on a train or a bus.—And how many hours a week, on average, do you spend watching television?—I don't have a television. I have a wireless and a tape recorder. I listen to poetry programs and to tape recordings of poets reading their work.—Do you have access to the Internet?—No, said Arthur Barlow, nothing like that.

Gladys put down her biro and looked Arthur Barlow full in the face. It struck him that she was beautiful and radiant with life. Weakened by the vision (as it might be called) of Gran Benson in her scuffed armchair and now by Gladys's manifest sympathy, Arthur Barlow shrugged and said, There's not much to me, Gladys, I'm afraid. Only the poetry. Really, that's all there is to me, the poetry.—The public library, said Gladys. You surely belong to the public library, Mr. Barlow?— That I do, said Arthur Barlow, animated. Couldn't live without it. Especially the reference section. I use the dictionaries, you see, to try to follow the translations of foreign poets word by word. And from the lending library I borrow things that I can't afford or can't get hold of through the catalogues. And of course it's in the library I find out who's coming to read anywhere round here within striking distance. So at least you can put me down for that, Gladys. I'm a great user of the public library and the staff could not be nicer. They know me in there. They're very kind to me. It's a home from home. I've got my own library here, of course, but I couldn't live without the public library too. Once a week at the very least I walk there and back, whatever the weather, so that keeps me fit, you might say, as much as going swimming would or playing golf.

Gladys closed her folder and began to button up her golden coat. Thank you, Mr. Barlow, she said. I don't need to take up any more of your valuable time.—You'll see my books, won't you? said Arthur Barlow. Then you'll have a good idea how I occupy myself. There's some next door, in the parlour, as Mother used to call it.—Gladys followed him through. The parlour was cold; the books lined all its walls; a three-piece suite, a glass cabinet, a stand for a pot or vase, had been moved away from the walls to accommodate the books. This is the third room, Arthur Barlow said. Alphabetically, starting upstairs, my bedroom and the spare room are the first two, it begins with S down here, the anthologies are in that corner by the window.—And all poetry?—And things to do with poetry, the lives and the letters of poets and what they said about poetry.—And not much space for any more, by the looks of it.—No, said Arthur Barlow. And that's a big worry to me. I'm afraid I may have to use Mother's bedroom after all, which I hoped would never happen. And pardon my asking, Gladys, would I be right in thinking that you don't belong in these parts? Are you not from where I'm from, more or less?—Moss Side, where else? said Gladys. But I'd say you were more Ordsall way, across the river, more Seedley or Weaste?—Ordsall, said Arthur Barlow, but with the clearances we went to Pendleton. But the shock I referred to earlier came to me from Weaste. It was Gran Benson in her end-terrace house in Weaste.

When I was a boy the trains ran past her gable end, so near and fast they shook the house. But when I visited her just before we left, the line had gone and they were building a bit more motorway and they wanted where her house stood for the width of it. What a noise, day and night! And the dust and the lights! My real gran, Gran Nuttall, was dead by then and Gran Benson, her sister, wouldn't come down south with us. She said she wanted to die among her own people. Not that she had any by then, only Sam, the dog. Her daughter was dead long since and so was her son-in-law. And the grandsons went to Australia so there she was on her own with Sam. Mother kept calling in to see to her and trying to persuade her to come down south with us. But she was adamant. She might have gone into a council home only they wouldn't let her bring her dog. So she stayed put. Not that we wanted to be in the south, you understand. But Father thought we might be better off and the hospital said they'd move him down here if he liked, filing.—I must leave you, Mr. Barlow, said Gladys. I have another call on your street, at Number 97.—One last thing, said Arthur Barlow. Did your grandmother or your grandmother's sister ever say, 'Sit thee down, lass' or 'Nowt lost where pigs are kept' or 'I'll make one less'—and go slowly off to bed?—Gladys laughed, such a resplendent laugh. Bless you, Mr. Barlow, of course they never did. They said things like, 'Walk-good keeps good spirit,' 'Hungrybelly an Fullbelly dohn walk same pass' and 'When lonely man dead, grass come grow a him door.'—Oh Gladys, said Arthur Barlow, you could read me the Caribbeans! I've only got the one voice and it's very poor. If I could hear you read the Caribbeans, how those strong men and women would come off the page and be alive in the room with me!—But Gladys buttoned up her golden coat against the cold and shook Arthur Barlow's hand and left his house.

Arthur Barlow went into the kitchen. It was the time when he made his cup of coffee. He had been on the verge of asking Gladys would she join him, when she left. The place was neat and clean. His use of its facilities and utensils was regular and precise. Never an unnecessary pan or plate or spoon. The vision, still working, resumed in him, greatly intensified by all that Gladys had brought in, and he saw that he would no longer be able to decide for himself how much of his future life he would deal with at any one time. His rota henceforth would not be able to hold out the flood of loneliness of the years still needing to be lived. He might say I will read and write for two hours then make a cup of coffee, same for a further one and a half hours, then make some lunch, after which I will at once go shopping and visit the public library, he might say all that aloud in the empty house and raise it as a bulwark against the days and weeks and months and years to come, but he knew the tidal wave was building and might at any time break in and bring it home to him in the here and now what the life of unalterable loneliness would be like. He looked out at the garden. It was rather a dank day. A yellow rose, still going strong, blooming abundantly over the right-hand fence, was the one bright thing to see. The kettle clicked off. Top of the list of my New Year Resolutions, said Arthur Barlow, is: restore this garden to its former glory.

The doorbell rang. It was Gladys, smiling. Nobody in at 97, she said. So I've come back here.

Coffee. What a pretty rose, said Gladys.—Yes, said Arthur Barlow, I bought it for Mother on her seventieth birthday. It flowers late and well into November.—I'll have to leave in half an hour, said Gladys. My youngest is only looked after till one o'clock. We moved down here ten years ago. My husband thought it would improve our chances. He was an accountant, working for a charity. But three nights a week he drove a fork-lift in a warehouse and died in an accident, sadly. I thought of going back north but the children were settled here by then. My youngest is eleven but because of a problem she isn't quite that grown-up yet. My kind neighbour looks after her while I do my Saturday job. My boys are big and strong. I hope they will find work they can enjoy. Do you enjoy your work, Mr.

Barlow?—Arthur Barlow stood up abruptly and answered her staring into the garden. I used to enjoy it in a funny way but lately I've not enjoyed it even in that funny way. They moved me to the cull and destroy program and, to be honest, I have begun to find that particular job a bit depressing. I have to find the dead who have been dead eight years or more and dispatch them to the incinerator. You wouldn't believe it, Gladys, there are twelve miles of medical records just in the place I work.— He turned and sat down again.—It's very good of you, Gladys, to come back in for a few more minutes. Mostly when the bell rings it's the postman with a new volume of verse and I thought it might be him but I was more pleased it was you. Otherwise it's only the gas or the electric. And twice a year two lads come down all the way from North Shields selling fish. I generally buy from them though I don't like cooking fish. The worst are the estate agents. They come asking would I like to sell. They know I'm in this house all on my own. They've got clients on their books would kill to have my house, being where it is, and make bedsits of it.—My mam and dad, said Gladys, looking Arthur Barlow full in the face, when they got off the boat at Salford Docks they stayed in Seaton Street with my aunty and uncle who had come over three or four years before. Next morning they signed on at the Labour Exchange and by the end of the week she'd got a job in a Jewish gabardine factory in Ancoats and he had started on the buses though at home he'd been a studio photographer. After a while they moved to a place of their own in Darcy Street and that's where my two brothers and me were born. I went back looking for the houses before we left but Seaton Street and Darcy Street and all the other streets round there have gone. Good riddance, I say. There was no nice accommodation in those parts. It shocked my mam and dad to see how poor the locals were. And then the drizzle and the fog and never any music.

Arthur Barlow again went to the window. Gladys, he said, I'm very likely getting worse. My shock this morning said as much. I keep thinking of those estate agents, if that is what they are. One night last month the noise at Number 19 was worse than ever. It was late on a Friday and I wanted to sleep so as to be fit for my Saturday morning trying to write a poem. In the end I thought they'll surely not mind me asking them will they turn it down. And I put my shoes and dressing gown on and walked across. The door was open and I looked inside. I've never seen such a sight and it was as though they'd never seen anything like the sight of me there on the doorstep looking in. I asked them nicely would they mind turning it down or shutting the front door at least because I couldn't sleep. And everybody laughed. Such a din of youngsters laughing at me because I feared I wouldn't sleep. Then one of the lads said—forgive me, Gladys, this really is what he said—he said, Fuck off and die, granddad. Our sort live here now. I was very hurt by that—I mean, I'm not a granddad—and I suppose I must have stood there open-mouthed. And then a very big young man, very big and strong, walked over from among the girls and lifted me up. He lifted me up and held me in his arms as though the weight of me was nothing at all. And he said to the others, Where's he from? and when they answered, Number 2, across the road, he carried me across like that and set me down at my own front door, which I'd left open, and said, Sleep tight.— Arthur Barlow came back to the kitchen table. Gladys averted her eyes and said, And you a gentleman with all those books.

Gladys rose to leave. Arthur Barlow followed her towards his front door. But reaching the parlour, his downstairs library, she stepped inside.—So much poetry, she said. And the first two rooms of it upstairs. And the postman delivering more and more. And you yourself, Mr. Barlow, writing and writing. Tell me, have you shown what you write to any living soul?—I did once, said Arthur Barlow, in the year after Mother died. I was all at sea and I fell in love with a young woman in the hospital. I gave her the poems I wrote for her, every Monday morning I gave her a sheaf of them, I'm sorry to say.—Why sorry?— Because she did not want them, because it was bad manners, because she told me to lay off, because I let myself go, because nobody should let himself go the way I did with her. In the end she complained about me and the Supervisor gave me a warning. They moved me out soon after that, to the repository I spoke of where there are twelve miles of medical records.—I see, said Gladys. And when you read poetry, am I right in thinking, from something you said earlier, that you read it aloud?— Oh yes, said Arthur Barlow, it's best read aloud. That way it comes more alive in you, if you see what I mean. And only by reading it aloud can you get it by heart, of course.—You know some poetry by heart, Mr. Barlow?—Indeed I do. I suppose like most people I wonder how I'd manage if I were put in solitary confinement or if I ever have to leave this place and can't take my books with me, I ask myself how I'll manage if I don't have a store of poetry by heart.—Is there any for children here? Gladys asked. My Edith is a great one for poetry. You should see her face, Mr. Barlow, when she sings one of our songs or says a poem.—Over there, said Arthur Barlow, behind that armchair near the window, there's two or three yards of poems for children. I've always collected them specially, old and new, from all over the world.—And do you have any by heart?—For answer Arthur Barlow straightened his tie, clasped his hands, stood very upright, looked through the window at the ugly street and said:

The Forest of Tangle

Deep in the Forest of Tangle
The King of the Makers sat
With a faggot of stripes for the tiger
And a flitter of wings for the bat.

He'd teeth and he'd claws for the cayman
And barks for the foxes and seals,
He'd a grindstone for sharpening swordfish
And electrical charges for eels.

He'd hundreds of kangaroo-pouches
On bushes and creepers and vines,
He'd hoots for the owls, and for glow-worms
He'd goodness knows how many shines.

He'd bellows for bullfrogs in dozens
And rattles for snakes by the score,
He'd hums for the humming-birds, buzzes for bees,
And elephant trumpets galore.

He'd pectoral fins for sea-fishes
With which they might glide through the air,
He'd porcupine quills and a bevy of bills
And various furs for the bear.

It carries on, said Arthur Barlow, but I think I'd better stop
there.—Thank you, said Gladys. And now it's time I went.—
Again she shook his hand, again he led her to his front door.
He said goodbye, he watched her turn the corner, golden,
out of sight. He fiddled with the knot of his dark tie. Late
morning, dank.

At the far end of the street the postman was proceeding
slowly towards Number 2. Just as well stand here and wait
and see, said Arthur Barlow. So he went to the gate and stood
on the pavement watching the progress of Naz, the postman,
who was always glad for him when his post looked like a
book. Gladys, returning, got very close before he turned to
see whose the footsteps were. Arthur, she said, if I came back
here with my Edith on a day and at a time convenient to you,
would you be so kind as to say her a poem and read her one
or two out of your anthologies? And if you like, I'll read you
some of the Caribbeans in my voice from home so that they
come alive in your room, as you put it, those strong men and
women.—Naz came up. Good morning, Mr. Barlow, he said.
Looks like another book for you.

TRAINS

The approach of a train. Above their heads it whistles and the pretty glasses shiver. In the silence then they listen to the clank of trucks. The Widow's bosom heaves. I can't bear hearing 'em, she says. I was born and brought up under the railway line but since that young feller went and did what he did I can't hear a train without getting palpitations. There's hardly a night I don't start up in bed. Hook-nosed, white-powdered Mrs. Clack. Her podgy fingers fidget on the bar. Him with his wisp of beard and frightened eyes. He lay in bed. She thinks of him lying there listening to the trains, the north- and the southbound, the goods trains full and empty with their different beats. Who knew the trains and where they were coming from and where they were heading, and chose himself one, and having chosen it he chose a bit of track and went and watched his train go by. How many times? He turned away, back down the embankment and through the allotments where fathers of families were tending their leeks and dahlias. Kept turning away, until his courage was adequate, or his despair. The Widow remembers him coming for a room as though it were yesterday. Would you have a room? he asked, head on one side, standing in the gloaming in his thin clothes. They said you might have a room. How long for? she asked. He shrugged: For the foreseeable future. Those were his words, she says, I'll never forget those words. Well, she had a room in Holly Street, just round the corner from her public house, in her dead father's house, last one on the left, at the dead end, where the embankment blocks the street and where the trains go, fast or slow, after they've come over the viaduct or before they stretch themselves across it. Suited him fine, with his no possessions but a few funny books, under the trains, the windows rattling many times a day, many times also in the night. Whistle, and steadily approaching leap of devouring noise.

There was a girl in that house under the railway line, in Lilian's father's house in Holly Street where the lad lived with the wisp of beard and the collection of funny books, there was a girl in there, Louise by name, but it did no good. The trains went to and fro, they shook the house, and one of them one morning, the 6:05 London to Edinburgh that doesn't stop here but goes for the viaduct like a beast leaping, the 6:05, running ten minutes late and angry no doubt, went over his funny head. Nothing Louise could do. In Lilian's view men ask too much of womankind. To hear you talk, she says, a woman's to blame every time a man gives up the ghost. We need a lot of looking after, Mrs. Clack, says Joe. You can say that again, she says, from the cradle to the grave it never stops, you're always round our skirts wanting your noses wiped. A woman never has time to do anything else. That's in the nature of things, says Bowles. Men have all the worries, they have to answer the big questions of life. It's only right and proper that women should get their tea and try and cheer 'em up a bit. He shoves his pot across. Dumbly the men watch Lilian work the handle of the pump. Down and down and down she depresses it.

Of Louise it was widely known that she loved nothing better than to synchronize the climax of her sexual pleasure with the coming of an express train. She was a dab hand at this, she didn't mind admitting it. Her young men got used to the idea, and only the stupidest among them took offence. Some, of course, after the conceited nature of the male, imagined her shudders were due to them themselves; but they were at best a vessel the god locomotive briefly filled. She loved all the trains, even the ancient puffing billies that pottered by in slack periods, trundling a few empty wagons; also the local couple of carriages that never got up steam; and the long, sometimes as it seemed never-ending march of clanking coal trucks. But she loved the through trains best, the terrific expresses hurtling north or south, and they were the ones she rode into her finale. It was said she could hear them crossing the Tees or the Tyne, that she was attuned to the first vibration of the miles and miles of track and could feel it beginning to throb and could hear the iron beginning to sing long before anyone else could. But that is very likely lies.

Louise often came knocking on our friend's door. Often? Well, if she had no company or if she woke up too late to get to work. His room was upstairs at the back of the house, over the yard. You're nearer the trains than I am, Louise said. Lucky you. The worst room in the house in every other respect: never any sunshine, distemper flaking off, a rattling sash that wouldn't shut, a cracked pane, a boarded-up hearth and soot coming down behind it and bits of brick and birds. But it's true about the trains. The first thing to start and the last to finish was a big glass lampshade dead in the middle of the ceiling. It started like a tickling under the belly button. Nothing wrong with that room, says Lilian, nor with any other room in Father's house, and no sense throwing away money on decorations when people aren't stopping. She dabs her diamanté eyes: the one for Father who drank himself to death, the other for the waif who laid down his head and died. She can't forget the day he turned up on her doorstep asking did she have a room to let for the foreseeable future.

Louise cried when she heard what had happened, and she broke her heart crying when she saw our friend's funny books. She moved out next day and married a signalman. Now she travels where she pleases on his special pass.

But what was she like, this Louise? What were her chief qualities? A creamy white skin; a triangle of maidenhair of an astonishing blackness and copiousness; a kind heart. Plump? She was rounded, her curves were firm. She was said to be very careless in her dress. The postman and the milkman always knocked, Jehovah's Witnesses and men selling encyclopedias called there oftener than elsewhere and once a quarter when they left home to visit 39 Holly Street officials of the Gas Board and the Electricity Board whistled and sang and polished the peaks of their caps. Some say she never noticed what she had on and what she didn't have on. Lilian: Don't give me that. She's answered the door stark naked to my certain knowledge. Still half-asleep, Mrs. Clack, it could happen to anyone. Rat-a-tat-tat, here comes the postman, she's nearest the door, she stands there rubbing her eyes and yawning in his face.

Late in the evening if there was nobody with her or late in the morning if she had overslept she might come up and pay our friend a visit. Either time he'd be in bed. The door was never locked, she knocked, he never answered, she opened it and said can I come in? He never answered, he'd be sitting propped up against the greasy wall with his hands outside the covers, flat, he had lovely hands, she said, except his nails were dirty. Their conversations, such as they were, took place mostly across the gap from the door to the bed. I'm out of sugar, she began, or have you got a slice of bread? It was remarkable, she observed, how little he seemed to occupy the room. Apart from the few books there was little sign that anybody lived there. He had a kettle and a cup and a few other bits and pieces for catering, and perhaps there was another shirt or something in the wardrobe. She was comparing the place with her own room, where human occupation was obvious in a big way.

It was Slim who said that about the whiteness of her skin and the blackness of her burning bush. He knew a man in town called Peg who knew a lad called Ike who had known Louise. Slim said it as though he had known Louise himself. She leaned in the open doorway with her dressing gown coming undone and asked our unhappy friend for the loan of a spoonful of sugar or a slice of bread and when he said help yourself, she still stood there and after a silence tried something else. It seems she had none of the ordinary womanly designs on him, but the thought of him up there all on his own in the back room overlooking the dustbins preyed on her mind or at least it occurred to her and gave her a funny feeling if she woke up with nobody to have breakfast with or if it was late in the evening and there was going to be nobody in her bed. None of the other lodgers interested her, though she interested them; anyway, it is not known that she ever went knocking at their doors on the scrounge.

How you feeling today then? she asked, and a conversation might follow on from that. He had a posh voice, slightly squeaky; the sight of his lips moving in their bits of beard gave her the creeps. Certainly there was something of the insect about him. Stetson, for instance, was of the opinion that squashing was what he wanted. He said this at the bar, whenever the subject came up. Louise thought otherwise, she was not appalled by spiders (fortunately in that house) and would go to some trouble to save them from drowning in her bath. Those lodgers who were interested in Louise but in whom she was not interested opened their doors a crack when she went for a bath, since it was always on the cards that she might walk past a minute later naked and carrying a spider in her gently clenched fist. Our friend smiled a lot, but always in a sneering way or as if his lips were being pulled by a spasm. His teeth, alas, were in a poor condition. He wore spectacles—Jesus, says Joe, do we have to think of these things?—which he often removed as he spoke or as she spoke, and rubbed his eyes, the lids of which were sometimes as red as cockscombs. His hair was like his beard, nothing much.

To her enquiry after his health he replied: Better, thank you, how kind of you to ask. If it were evening and she enquired what sort of a day he'd spent he raised his hands and let them fall and said words failed him, he must be very blessed, he doubted whether many people ever had days like his. He had sat under the broken statue of Apollo, he said, in Wharton Park, and had watched the trains, it was an excellent place to watch them from, you could see them coming, out of the north and out of the south, at a great distance.

When he mentioned the trains she glanced at him searchingly to see if he knew her open secret, and there was indeed a look of insinuation in his eyes; but what he was alluding to was his own business, of course, and he was darting her glances to see if she had guessed it. Finally, since one insinuating look looks much like another, she could not be sure, but said in an even and friendly voice: I'll come along with you one of these days, I like trains too, you know. The motioning of his hands was courtesy itself, but his lips twitched like a devil's and what he emitted was a high giggle which soon faltered and broke.

Do you know, he said, you are the only person I have spoken to since a week last Friday. Louise was horrified. But in the shop? she said. He served himself, there was no need to speak, the woman told him what it cost and he gave her the money. The Chinkies do the same, they never speak, I've been observing them. And at the NAB? I nod my head, he said, or shake it, as the case may be. I sign on the dotted line and go away again. I shouldn't come bothering you, says Louise. You mebbe like not talking. Once in a while, he says, can't do much harm. And listening? You'd mebbe rather not listen to human speech? Mostly I don't, he says, I overhear a few things, but on your average day no one addresses me.

The next step, obviously, was to ask him what he thought about all day then, sitting up there under the statue of Apollo or down in the square under Lord Londonderry and not speaking to anybody and not listening and never being spoken to, and our friend had maybe hoped she'd go that far; but her instinct warned her off. If Louise wasn't afraid of spiders she was terrified by the thought of a spider swirling down the plughole and drowning in the drains, and the thought of what he filled his skull with day after day seemed to her very like a plughole and a long long fall and a drowning in the dark.

There must have been a silence then, our suicidal friend a trifle peeved perhaps that Louise had not asked to be shown the contents of his head, and Louise herself backing away in her thoughts from the horror of him and moving on to the safer ground of a general pity for the lonely and the beginnings of an uneasiness on her own account. Then, in the silence, she felt the first still very distant vibrations of an approaching train, one from the south, an express certainly. She looked towards the bed again, and for perhaps ten seconds was able to study its occupant's face without his knowing. The features had lapsed into an expression of complete sadness, without sarcasm. Then he too, still before the lampshade on the ceiling, picked up the tremor of the train, and his eyes turned to hers. They frightened her, there was a gleam of wicked hope in them. She continued to stare at him, ever more fixedly, as the train approached and as her famous sensations intensified she set them against his.

Hard to quite locate the agonies a shivering lampshade causes in a man. Sometimes it seems to start in the core of the heart and go down through into his cock and not come out of there but course up and down the lengthening innermost capillary with shock after shock; and sometimes from the back of the head and down the spine with a terrible quick tickling into his vestigial tail; and always under the belly there's an itch that can't be scratched. If that were the only noise the room

would have been unlivable in and a man in bed there would
have expired if it had gone on for very long; but pretty soon it
was lost in the general din. Louise, no doubt, could hear that
lampshade, or some similar thrilling and tickling, under all the
ensuing racket, running through it like an exquisitely thin reed.
The sash started rattling, the gas fire buzzed; the noise came on
at a steady gallop, its wheels pounding the track, which whined
like ice. The whole room shook, you felt it seized and battered
by the noise, you lay in bed and felt broken apart.

When the train came overhead they both closed their eyes.
When they reopened them, when the long tail of carriages
had been drawn away and the room little by little and each
part after its particular tone (the lampshade last, lingering and
lingering) had ceased to tremble, when they opened their
eyes, our friend the first to, only Louise was smiling. It's good
in here, she said, you're lucky. Sometimes they hoot, I like it
when they hoot. His hair was damp, his face was the colour of
the wall, he was biting on bits of his Fu Manchu moustache.

Louise began to talk. He nodded for her to continue, so she
did, but his eyes were away on the far wall, staring and desperate. He wore a white shirt in bed with a filthy collar, down
which he pushed a finger from time to time. He was damp
throughout. Louise talked, not looking at him. She wondered
aloud whether she shouldn't just chuck up her job—if she
missed many more days they would sack her anyway—and
go down to London for a few months. She had a friend down
there she thought would let her stay. She wondered sometimes why anyone stuck around in this dump. What she liked
about the trains, she said, was that they were always going
somewhere, even the slow ones, even the little local ones, and
if you got one you could change and catch another, the lines
went everywhere, like veins, so she believed, like the veins
and arteries that went all over your body.

Slim had it from Peg who had it from Ike that Louise
if ever she went rambling on and nobody was paying much

attention would absent-mindedly start feeling herself through the gaps where buttons were undone (or missing more like) in her slatternly dressing gown. That is, she liked the feel of her own skin, for which nobody can blame her, so while she talked she gently rubbed with the flat of her hand or searched over herself with her fingertips or scratched with her nails and pushed down naturally off her creamy tummy into her abundant curly private hair and went on talking about getting out of this place and moved her hand up feelingly over her ribs and tickled herself in the armpit and felt the heartside of her lovely bosom and stood in the open doorway leaning back on the doorpost, one foot in a shoddy slipper and with the other, bare, feeling the length of her leg from the knee to the ankle.

On the late evening before the day in question she came up after closing time with a bottle of Bull's Blood and her Mickey Mouse mug. Sunny Jim was in bed, sitting upright. Mind if I come in? she asked. He didn't say no. For once she shut the door. Mind if I light the fire? she asked. I've had a bath. He didn't say no. She had: the skin under her open dressing gown was rosy and damp, blotched here and there with talc. Her black hair, where it lay on her neck, was wet. She knelt and lit the fire. Mind if I open my bottle? she asked. It's my birthday. He didn't say no. He said: There's a knife in there with a thing on it. In the drawer under his books. The knife was the sort a jolly old scoutmaster might wear, dangling from a leather belt on a clip on his hip, a big black jackknife, rough to clasp and having for parts: one blade, one gouge, one corkscrew, sprung like sharks. You do it, she said.

Fastidious fingers with dirty nails—he picked the spiral out—handed the knife back with the tool protrudent. You do it, he said. Louise sat down on the bedside chair, she bored the cork, she screwed, she gripped the bottle between her slippered feet, oh lovely view of her rosy breasts, the folds of her tum, her hairy lair, intensely foreshortened. Our friend had closed his eyes.

The cork coming out made her laugh. You got a cup? she asked. Never mind, we'll share. Glug, glug, glug, glug—you first, say Happy Birthday. When he smiled it occurred to her that perhaps there was something wrong with his mouth, perhaps there always had been and he had tried to hide it with his bits of hair. When he smiled his mouth looked like something a surgeon had made for him. He smiled and smiled and toasted her with the Bull's Blood, cocking his funny head to the right. He handed her the cup and she drank from the other side.

I'm going away, she said, I've made my mind up, no sense rotting in this hole anymore. Did you get any presents? he asked, did you get any birthday cards? That's usual, isn't it? People send things, the postman comes. I was still in bed, Louise replied, I had to get up and answer him. Our friend reached for the mug and drank it off. Thin throat, she thought. He took off his glasses whilst she poured some more. Her nipples, both on show, were pink as rosebuds; his eyes looked like bits of old foreskin. He looked eyeless when he sat there with his eyelids down, as though he were left with two red holes. How have you been? she asked. Oh better, he cried, oh better and better—isn't it obvious? And what have you done all day? I watched the trains. From up on the hill? No, from another place, close to.

She drank. You're a funny boy, she said, I've not met many like you. I'd be surprised if there were any, he said. She shrugged. A train, a slow one. They sat and watched one another through the noise. It's behind his eyes, she thought, behind his red eyelids mid somewhere at the back of his eyeballs. The train was interminable, a laborious clanking. I quite like the slow ones, Louise said. I don't, he said and nor would you if you were me. If you were me you couldn't imagine anything worse than a slow train, and the slower the worse.

They drank in turns, passing the cup. Soon she was careless of which side she drank from. She sat on the chair by his bed, her breasts came out, she covered them when it occurred to her to, her knees poked through, the length of her leg showed as far as the black shadow. It's as though you're poorly sick, she said, and I'm here visiting you. I'm incurable, he said, I'm beyond the reach of medical science. You look like Jesus, Louise said, at least you do when you take your glasses off. He took them off, he lolled his head against the dirty wall. It's the beard, I suppose, she said.

But it's your *birthday*, he said, and you're giving me this Bull's Blood to encourage me, I ought to give you something, oughtn't I? What's he got in this den he could give a girl? she wondered. Not his horrible knife, I hope. In here, he said, patting the breast pocket of his dirty white shirt. Do you want it now? Yes please, she said.

He slid in two fingers, the middle one and the one nearest the thumb, to be exact, and brought out, gripped between them, a flattened ha'penny, held it, turned it this way and that. Have it, he said, my dearest possession, have it and Happy Birthday. Louise took his present in the palm of her hand. It was very thin, no longer quite round, rather pear-shaped. Thanks, she said, are you sure? Wear it there, he said, extending his dirty pointing finger close to her bosom, on a chain if you can get one fine enough, or in a pocket on the left side. I will, she said, copper's supposed to be good for you. The eye of faith, he said, peering very closely, can still discern one of our kings, the bald one, this way up, and tails is a galleon, a ship of hope. But they are flattened and ghostly. It's been under a train, she said. It has indeed, he said, it's been under a great black locomotive of the Duchess class, 46229 Duchess of Hamilton, weight 105 tons. I've had it since I was ten, I kept it for good luck.

There's a place not very far from here, the kids get down the embankment. One way, south, the line is clear, but from the north it comes suddenly out of a tunnel. He was on his own when he did it, of course. He watched the others doing it from the bridge, then when they'd gone he went down himself with his ha'penny in his hand. He watched them listening on the line, they kneeled in a row and all put their ears down. When they'd gone he went and did the same. It was late afternoon, winter. At the age of ten he had no idea why things were like they were and why he was like he was. At the age of twenty he had none either. At the age of ten he was already beginning to doubt whether things would ever get much better. He got down on his knees, bare knees, took off his glasses, laid his ear on the cold rail. There was nothing but silence, the stones dug into his knees, the cold went into his cheek and the side of his head. It was some time before he heard the singing in the track. Ever since then he has heard it coming nearer, the thing that is between a feeling and a sound, a certain terrible frequency, like a light bulb before it goes. He withdrew in good time; as soon as the singing had acquired the definite undertone of wheels, as soon as the track had begun to yelp and whang. He placed his ha'penny and climbed to safety up the bank. The train burst out of the tunnel, he was thrown back by the noise, but clutched with his eyes at the name and number and saw the fire. Then he went down, searched for the coin, and was lucky to find it in the growing dark. Thereafter he wore that copper wafer nearest his heart.

Right, said Louise, I'll be off then and thank you very much. The gas had gone out, there was no point asking him for a shilling. Wait, he said, and touched his watch that lay on the counterpane. Do me a favour will you and wait seven minutes. The sleeper's due and it's generally on time. She didn't say no. She took the mug off him, took up the empty bottle from the floor, put the knife away. Alright, she said, and then I'll go. When she was seated again, facing our poor friend, she clasped her hands in her exposed lap and waited. She heard it first, and seeing her face he saw that her apprehension of the trains was finer then his. It came steadily, she did not close her eyes. She lay back in the chair, the room began to sway. She opened her hands and pressed them outwards between her thighs, she rocked and swayed as though she were travelling. She stared at him, she fixed him, she held him to her eyes and would not let him look away, she watched him through, his eyes never closed, they fixed hers like an insect's, he was seeing the visored head of Death approaching but she held on and smiled her smile and he smiled his and over them both together the noise of iron went and after that, in one long plume, a scream.

That was lucky, she said, he hooted. And now I'm off. Sweet dreams.

Louise had a bad name, no doubt. Very good of the signalman to marry her, Lilian says. If he has seen the tear-shaped ha'penny, and surely he must have, he'll have read her the riot act about the foolishness of children and how he hopes to God none of theirs'll ever do anything of the sort. He'd be bound to come down heavy on such larks. Ike said, according to Peg according to Slim, that the sight of Louise with her tits coming out revolted him. He said she was only fit to honk on, nothing more. You men are all alike, says Lilian, and a woman has no defence but her good name. You have your way and treat us common as dirt. Mind you, some ask for it. She hopes no daughter of hers would carry on like that. If she'd had one, that is, which she hasn't. But why they think that girl might have done any good is beyond her. Anyone could see he was too far gone and it would take more than a chit of a girl to bring him back. An experienced woman might have managed it, of course, but not that little slut. Still, it is very sad. She'll never forget him standing there asking if she had a room for the foreseeable future, by any chance. An educated voice. What is the point of education if that's what it does to you? The Marquis agrees. Besides, it's not at all certain she made any effort to save him. Her and her Bull's Blood. I don't recollect, says

Lilian, you ever saying she pleaded with him. Any normal girl would have pleaded with him. There's some might say she even drove him to it, by flaunting herself, I mean. I mean if he was religious. You said she said he looked like Jesus when he took his glasses off. Touch me not, says the Marquis, in an educated voice. He is about to say he will have another of the same but everyone has paused, everyone falls silent, nobody moves, the Widow clasps her hands on her lurex bosom and above her the tremor starts, among the fairy lights, along the row of pretty glasses, a shiver, a subtle tune, it finds the frequency of everybody's fears, the men at the bar and Lilian who serves them, they bow their heads, wishing the noise itself would come, come quickly, the real noise, come quickly over them while they are silent and thinking only of their terrors.

The Necessary Strength

That horse makes me nervous, Judith said. I don't like him being here. He's all right, said Max. We can do them a favour, I suppose. Judith said nothing, but in silence took issue with both 'we' and 'them'. It was early evening, Max's time for being with his family—a pity, as he said himself, to spoil it by quarrelling. They were in the living room, and against the large west window, full up against it in the teeming sun, the white horse pressed his face. The girls thought him funny; Max said that such a white long head with blinding sun behind it was a wonderful phenomenon; but it made Judith nervous, there was a quite deep gap between the house wall and where the horse stood lunging at the windowpane, and she feared he might fall in there and come through with a smash and a great deal of blood; and besides, his orange tongue and the slaver he made on the window disgusted her.

Megan asked could she ride the horse. Max said he didn't see why not, he would ask Ellie when he saw her next; but Judith said no she couldn't, the horse was too big and being on his own all the time made him peculiar and dangerous. Then the sunny room, with its western view of a bay of the silver sea, was crossed with strains and bitternesses, everyone fell silent and the horse stared in at them.

Judith stood up, with her book. She would go and read at the other side of the house, as far away from the horse as possible, though there was no sun in that room, it would be cold and to read she would need a light on. Max and the girls looked at her. She could wring their hearts merely by standing up, for then her smallness of stature was apparent and, if she took a step, her crippling at the hips. Stay, said Max. It's nicer in here. All three looked at her. The sun was merciless: it showed the cavernous darkness around her eyes. But her eyes were a sapphire blue, shockingly beautiful however familiar they might become to anybody. The alignment of her husband and her daughters, though one of pity, was still an alliance against her, she felt; and standing there she forgot her intention and felt merely apart and sad.

The horse turned, and chased away. Judith sat down again with the girls, and drew them in close, to look at their paintings. Esther's was of a house, any house, with flowers, a welcoming path, a curl of smoke; Megan's was of a loch, its blue surface almost snowed over with water lilies. What a sight! said Max at the window. The horse was by the far fence, where the ground fell away to the rocky beach. A white horse, and the sun getting more and more red. In him, like a reflex, whenever Judith had moved him to love and pity, came concern for himself. Soon then, rather sooner than usual, he said he must work and the girls went to kiss him good night. That done, he climbed the aluminium ladder out of the living room into the loft above it, where he worked. He took very little time to settle, they heard his movements on the floor, their ceiling; then nothing. He was working.

Judith sat on, with the children. She loved that room and was glad not to have left it. It was where she taught the children in the mornings while their father slept. There were charts on the walls and posters and work the girls had done;

vases of flowers and grasses on the windowsills; and in a corner, almost too small now even for Esther, stood an ancient cramped school desk. She took Esther against her and sang softly in Yiddish. The girls were hard to get to bed in summer. Even gone midnight it was never properly dark. Megan left off painting and went to the window. That horse is crazy, she said. Esther was asleep. Had Judith been stronger she would have carried her away to bed. As it was, she sat there, dozing herself, and the ancient songs continued in her head. She wanted strength, she was dozing, soodling, and worrying at the question of the necessary strength when suddenly—a shock to her—she heard Max cross the floor above and saw his feet coming down out of the hole that was the entry into his own space. It was a shock, she could not remember when he had last broken off work and come back down into the living room while his wife and children were still there. Megan at the window turned his way in amazement. What's the matter? Judith asked. Esther woke up. The sunset is extraordinary, said Max. We must go out and look at it.

Judith was angry. All the sunsets at Acha were extraordinary. Why come down for this one? But because he had, the children were excited. If he came down, as he never had before, it was an occasion and they must all go out. Esther was wide awake. Megan felt curious, thrilled, apprehensive.

They all went out. The house stood in its own field, that sloped away to the fence and a gate above the beach. The ground was rough, the children ran ahead, Max came after with Judith whose progress was slow. Halfway down she halted. This will do, she said, and contemplated the sky. There was a bar of luminous cloud across the whole view, but no sun visible, so that for a moment she thought Max must have been mistaken and the show was finished. No, wait, said Max. It's just beginning. And he laid an arm around her shoulders and so ushered her into a proper contemplation of the phenomenon. The sun drooped like something melting, all out of shape, down from the band of cloud. Slowly it eased itself into the gap between the cloud and the line of the sea, and there recovered its roundness and intensified its colour. The rays came over the water, over the fence, over the field almost horizontally, a queer orange light. The children were at the fence, on the low ferny cliff above the sea, and into the light, from nowhere as it seemed, approaching them, flushed by the sun, came the white horse. Judith started forward but Max held her back. He's all right. Only look at the sun on him. There was a breeze off the sea and in thin clothes Judith was shivering. The sun seemed to have halted. The horse, leaving the children, walked towards her and Max in a very measured way. Phenomenal, said Max. The creature was aureoled around by an orange golden light, but Judith said: I'm cold. It would be twenty minutes before the sun, and all its extraordinary after-effects, finally vanished. See, said Max, it goes down on a slope. It would dip for only a couple of hours below the rim, and in its descent was dragged off the vertical by the pull of the north. So beautiful, said Max. I'm going in, said Judith. Night after night was beautiful. Why come down for this? Why bring everyone out? Why excite the children so late? Keep them away from the horse, she said. And you put them to bed. She limped in. Max turned to watch. She was too small for such large effects, and the tufted ground threw her from side to side. But her thin white blouse took colour like the horse's coat, and the house's windows blazed.

She lay in bed, angry, brooding on Max's descent into the living room out of his upstairs lair. How he could do as he pleased, to trouble her; and all the old griefs revived. There had never been any discussion over whose the new room should be. The girls could have had a room each. It was wonderfully light, a skylight, a west and a south window. Now she never went up there, the ladder hurt her, it was too steep, as he must have known it would be. For months, her hips worsening, she had not been up there, not even climbed high enough to poke her head in and see what work he was doing in that place apart, that den all his to climb up to and climb down from above the living room in the family house. She heard him come in and put the girls to bed—or heard him instruct Megan to put Esther to bed. Then heard him go downstairs again, not looking in on her; heard him in the kitchen making coffee; heard him go through to his aluminium ladder. Slowly the room darkened, but never completely. There was a cuckoo, all night; and worse, blundering in among her dreams, she heard the horse in the gap or trench behind the house, rubbing and banging against the outside wall. He had all the field under a vast summer sky, but chose instead to shove and snuffle around their dwelling where it was darkest and where he did not belong.

Max was working. In very fine pencil he was drawing bones. He might spend a whole night on a couple of sheep's vertebrae, or on the mechanics of its upper leg, the jointing. On a skull, on the wriggling script where the segments fitted, on the accommodation for the eyeballs, teeth and spinal cord, on the chambers, passages, apartments, all the housing, easily he could expend a month of silent nights. He learned the precise form and fit of these components, but also their texture on the surface and inside, healthy and in the pitting and delicate honeycombing and filigree of decay, clean as a whistle or stained in peat, bracken, weed. Nearly all his sorties from the house were in search of bones or bone-like things. On the beach he got dry claws and carapaces and the ridged and stippled casings of sea urchins. In summer, more restless, at three or four in the morning, in the queer light with the sleepless crying birds he went out foraging, he crossed the thin pale road and entered the pathless wasteland of mauve rock, black peat, every shade of boggy green, and tumbling white water. Up there he found antlers, some still bloody at the base where they had left the living head, others cast years ago and shortened by corrosion. He found pebbles of quartz, like fossilized eyeballs, and lichens that are the dryest and least ample life there is. Up there the roots of the old Caledonian pines shone in the golden bog-water like giant starfish. Wood like that he approved of: hard and pale as bone. There was a particular river which, disregarding its Gaelic name, he called the Bone River. High up in it a carcass had lodged, and over months, by water with the help of a few crows, all the weight and stink and fleshly substantiality was got away and the animal disarticulated and passed downstream and Max collected it in pieces for his work.

Once he found the skull of a horse, came home with it under his arm, re-entered the sleeping house, climbed out of the living room into his working space and there and then, until the children woke and it was time for him to go to bed, he began to draw the find that was as long, large, intricate and fascinating as many an animal entire.

In winter he made almost no excursions but kept to his upper room, and the dead but brilliant moon shone in at him through the skylight. He worked, on a high stool at a draughtsman's tilted desk, clamping the bones at the angle he wanted them, lighting them as he liked, and transferring them as exactly as his eye and hand and the fine tip of a pencil could do it, to paper. And when he had got them exactly, on scores of white sheets, then out of them in colours that were barely colours, using brushes sometimes as fine as a nerve end, he composed the pictures that were his speciality. He took bone, precisely observed, as his base and real material, and lifted out from it into beautiful chilly abstractions.

Now and then, while he was sleeping, the girls climbed up into his space. Megan fingered and weighed the white objects—they were all around, on every shelf and surface—and looked through the folders thoughtfully. Esther made a cosy home in the corner, with her dolls. But Judith never came up, and he knew she did not. Her crippled hips would have made it very difficult; and besides, as he knew, she had grown to loathe his work.

Ellie came down to ride her horse. Judith watched her return, along the sea's edge at a canter. Yes, she was fit to be looked at. She was the image of freedom and well-being. On impulse, when she had stowed away her gear in the shed as Max had said she could, Judith invited her in. It was early evening. Max was still sitting with his family in the sunny living room. Here's Ellie, Judith said. Suddenly she took an interest in this girl and began to question her, gently but to the point. Why had she given up university? What did she think she would do in Acha, where there was no work, nobody her age, nothing to stimulate her intelligence? Ellie was not averse to trying to answer, but in the course of every attempt she glanced repeatedly towards Max, to see how she was doing. How beautiful she is, said Judith to herself, and she is in love with him. Ellie had found university harsh and cynical. There was no one you could talk to about things that really mattered, the boys only wanted sex and her teachers were always making fun. In the end it upset her, she stopped eating, she had come home, she was still not better from it. Sitting there in the beams of the sun, continually pushing back her heavy dark hair, she looked, Judith thought, too beautiful for her own good. Her face, flushed from riding when she came in, was pale as the moon now, luminously pale, her skin of an almost transparent purity. Still without vehemence Judith pressed her. Women needed their independence, they had to be competent, get qualifications, be always able to take their own lives in hand. Ellie shrugged, was lost for words, looked to Max. Ellie loves this place, he said. Don't you have to work? Judith asked him, and when he said no, not for a little while, she stood up and with a decisiveness that quite outweighed her lameness she left the room and came back with whisky and three glasses. She poured out, and said: If you're not working, I'll play. I don't

137

like to when you work. You could, he said. It would help me. Well I don't, she said, but now sat down at the piano close to the foot of the aluminium ladder, and began to play.

Max saw how thin her hair had become, how dark with fatigue and pain her face, how slight her wrists. Ellie, when Judith turned, saw the shocking brilliance of her blue eyes and the bright chic clothes she had made herself, and when she began to sing that was the sense of her entirely: brightness, energy, a lively force, in her rapid fingers, in the lift of her head, in her more and more confident voice as it remembered the songs of her mother tongue and gave them out. Pour another, Max, she said, and get your violin. He did as he was bid, poured another three glasses, nimbly went up the ladder behind her and was down in a trice and tuning his instrument to her playing. Now Ellie, wholly of the audience with the two children, watched husband and wife revive their old unison. Judith led, but Max was quick on the uptake and adept at developing what she began. They filled the living room with the peculiar gaiety that comes when a sociable skill is practised recklessly. Outside, another extraordinary sunset was under way, and against it the white horse came and stood at the window peering in. Judith raised her voice and sang at him. Max skipped across and serenaded him. They did not lessen his solemnity. He twitched at the shoulder, the flies teased his eyes, but he stared in steadily from under his fringe and his hot breath misted the pane. Judith sang and played, the children clapped and joined in, and under Judith's quick tuition Ellie was enabled also. They drank more. Ellie looked from Max to Judith in a rather breathless admiration. She was seeing them in a new light, but Judith especially: Judith seemed inexhaustible, and was indeed, as she sang, marvelling at how rich she and Max had been. Things she had composed herself, years ago, he remembered, and when she brought them back he worked up a new accompaniment. In build and appearance he was like her: slight, quick, with a girlish mouth, his good looks were as fine as a girl's. Over the violin, while he played, he watched her keenly, with a touch of fear. Her blue eyes disconcerted him, he felt mocked by them. At last, sensitive to what she wanted, he fell away into the audience, and, facing the wall, showing them her back, she sang something he did not know, something none of her audience knew, but he knew the tone and sense of it, and the three girls, in their different fashions, comprehended it too, it came up out of her in a dialect stranger and more ancient then hers at home, bitter, inconsolable, mocking its own beauty, harshly insisting that beauty is no redress, and yet still beautiful, but sadder, more stricken, more outraged than it was beautiful. Then briskly she said: You will be wanting to work, Max. And to Ellie: You are a fool if you stick around in Acha. And she limped to the children, took one by each hand, and swayed and stumbled like something smitten across the backbone, out of the living room.

Max woke her. His hand, come in under her nightdress, rested on her left hip. Waking she struggled fearfully to recompose a world. It was their routine to meet in the kitchen, as his waking hours ended and hers began, and they might have a cup of tea together, before he went for his sleep in their bed. Why go against his habit now? Very gently, very tenderly he stroked her hip and a length of her thigh. The room was already light. Her eyes filled with tears of shame. Don't, Max, she said. Please don't. He desisted, and they lay side by side, looking up at the ceiling. Why aren't you working? she asked. I thought... he began, I wanted... You were wrong, she said. I'm leaving you. I'm taking the girls. I shall need some money. We must sell the house. He wept. She let him. Then he said: You don't know how I love you. She answered: When I thought it might be cancer and I drove ninety miles to have my tests you wouldn't come with me, you said you'd be too upset, you said you wouldn't be able to work.

—I couldn't work. All the time you were away I sat up there crying and couldn't do a thing.—You like that kind of pain. I don't like any kind. It hurt me to press the pedals in the car. The girls were sick—not once, half a dozen times—I had to keep stopping, getting out, cleaning them up. There are different kinds of suffering, said Max. You can't drive, she said. You won't learn. I hate the road, he said. I wish they'd never built it. Both saw only reiteration ahead, and were silent. Max had an apprehension of his future loneliness. He dwelled on it, his heart beat faster. He came back again, more tempted by it than ever, to the notion that in misery, guilt, icy loneliness, he might do better work. I have to suffer, he said aloud. I have to. Then I'll do good work. Your suffering stinks, she said. All suffering stinks and is a waste of time. No, he said, becoming excited, we'll sell, I'll get a cottage on my own, I'll get one further up the coast where there is no road. He saw, as something beautifully clean and purposeful, the reduction of his life to loneliness and work. His eyes shone. He sat up in the exhilaration of the idea.

Judith got out of bed and, turning away from him, dressed quickly. You are beautiful, he said. The line of your back is beautiful. And now you won't let me touch you. I'm lame, she said, and it is getting worse. Then when she was dressed she turned to him sitting up naked in their bed. He was thin and strong, fit, smooth-skinned. His face was alert and lit with the idea of loneliness and productive suffering. You'll get Ellie in, said Judith. Ellie will keep house for you and sweeten the early mornings when you coincide in bed. At least I can talk to her about my work, said Max.

The girls were still sleeping, Judith went out. Cloudless early morning, paradisal. The little bay was brimful, quiet, shining. A couple of seals had come in close. Slowly, tried by every unevenness, Judith went down to the fence. The girls got to the sand in leaps and bounds, and through the bracken, on a rough path bearing left, Ellie could lead down her horse;

but for Judith the fence was the limit. There had once been a way that she could manage, with everybody helping, but a storm, magnificent to watch through their southern and western windows, had rolled the boulders differently and spoiled it. She watched the seals. In the full water, their element, they rose together, necked, vanished, and reappeared apart. It seemed pure delight, in the water and the sunny air, that sinuous rolling together at the head and the neck, and diving vertically down and levelling again through the clear blue-green, like dancing. Max swam some mornings, she knew that. They met at the kitchen table, there was salt on his skin, his hair was wet, he drank a cup of tea with her and went to bed.

She turned away. The house in the one green field was sunlit. The first romantic adventure of the place, their work at it together, always with music and sharp thirsts and hungers, their love and mutual aid, woke in her now like temptation. The field had sprouted its pale and magenta orchids. The others, the common little flowers, Judith said them aloud as though teaching the children: eyebright, bedstraw, milkwort, tormentil. Visible south of the house was the road which Max detested. It was narrow, pale, insignificant, but seemed to Judith a brave idea, a brave undertaking, getting away south around a difficult coast. Behind the road, east, was the moor—moor and bog and mountain, that she could as easily have flown over as walked. But she knew: there were lichens in it with red and lively tips, there was cotton grass as soft as the children's hair when she cut it the first time and kept two curls of it among her jewellry; and in places where the shielings had once been, in spring the bracken unfurled more sweetly than she could bear to remember. At the back of everything were the high mountains, scraped raw, grey as ash in certain lights, pinkish, violet or red in others.

And so on and so on. Stars and the frozen waterfalls in winter, the sunsets all year round. Was she to live off beautiful phenomena, and bring the girls up addicted to them? Like nausea, always like nausea however often she felt it, there rose in her again the need for the necessary strength. She clenched her fists and set off up the rough slope back to the sleeping house. Then the white horse came.

In a wide arc, around the perimeter of the field, from hiding behind the house, he came down at full tilt, the rough ground never hindering him. Admiration, her instant first feeling, ran over rapidly into terror at his mastery and power, as he came down the slope and between her and the fence, through that small gap, passed with a streaming mane, and mounted again, and again went behind the house. She was left trembling at the rush, the din, the smell of the horse that had circled her, doing as it liked. Get home, was her only thought, get in and lock the door. If she was small against the mountains and the magnificent sunsets of Acha, that smallness was philosophical, an attitude of mind; but against the horse in common reality she was as fragile as a sparrow's skull. She made for the house, sobbing with fear, cursing her hips, and the horse came down again, set at her, as it seemed, full on, and swerved and passed and gathered himself up the slope, with all the lazy energy in creation to dispose of. A reasoning voice in Judith said: he is the image of strength, he is showing you what he can do, he can pass to right or left as he pleases, swish you with his tail for fun, without malice, he is young, he means nothing bad. But she tried to run, feeling she would break apart in terror if he came again, she tried and failed, she fell, her left hip came out.

Fainting on the pain, even as she went under she said: this has happened before, I know what to do; but when she came up again, out of a drowning sickness of pain, when she came up without any strength of voice to call for help from the sleeping house, the horse stood over her. He was the bodily apparition of every dread: the dread of utter weakness, of total disability, of the shame and helplessness of being lame, the dread of dependence, the dread of a cancer in a length of bone, and other terrors too, even deeper, in her blood, in the family, in the generations, in her race, the dread of them coming back; and on these she went under again, in more terror than pain, as the long white head of the horse, his swelling eyes, the black shafts in his nose, pushed down at her. One hoof raised gently on her chest would have crushed the life out of her, but it was the face, the orange tongue, the froth on the black lips, all her terror was concentrated there, on the steady face, she saw its strangeness as an utter difference, as a thing incomprehensible, a gap made in her apprehension of the world, and into that gap, as into a rent in nature, came nothing but blank terror that would never end. So she saw the horse, lying crippled under him.

Then not so. Then suddenly not so. On her back in a field as helpless as a flung sheep under the hooded crows, suddenly, and increasingly, it was not so. She saw that his liquid eyes were beset by insects, a vein in his left shoulder pulsed and twitched, and he dipped his long head down and with a clumsy gentleness knocked at her cheek, knocked and snorted softly, nuzzled and knocked, insisting. He trailed his fringe and sticky mane across her face, and raised his head in a long upward indication of how she might rise, and down again, nudging at her face and trailing the coarse hair until she understood and fastened a hand in it and gently, backing and lifting, he drew her up and she sat, tilting off her useless hip. So far so good. An inkling of triumph was in her now. She had a basis. She had done it before. Again the horse bowed his head. She twisted in both hands now, into the sticky, coarse, grey-white hair and hauled and he lifted and she rose and held against him in a queer *déhanchement*, all on the right. Last time it was the car, last time she had dragged herself ten yards up the rutted uncarriageable track, from among her spilled shopping back to the car, and heaved herself up bodily against its warm bonnet, and had then done there what she did now, pressing her face against the horse's throbbing flank, against her pain, did it again, shoved in the hip, ball into socket back where it belonged, and clung on to him patiently standing still, against the nausea and the pain.

Clinging to his mane, one step at a time, feeling the working of his near leg at the shoulder, its power held in to walk with her, she got home up the hill. At the door he left her, and resumed his lunatic courses down and around the field.

Judith opened the door. Megan was in the kitchen making tea. Her look was adult and officious. Dad's upset, she said. I'm making him some tea. Yes, said Judith, do that. And from the door to a chair, from chair to table, from table to a corner of the stove she got through to the sofa in the living room, and lay down. She saw before her, stacked like mountains, great but not unprecedented trials of her strength.

THE SHIELING

They invented a place. It was far away from here, indeed from anywhere, high up, at the limits, like a shieling. He particularly liked the word 'shieling'. A bare place, as far up the valley as you could go and the house itself very simple. In reality such dwellings, the shielings, are only for habitation in the summer, the brief summer; but theirs they allowed themselves to proof almost snugly against the winter months. In winter, the long winter, this place of their invention would be needed most. So he fitted a chimney that drew remarkably well and built a hearth out of the rough stones that were lying around. There was little fuel, of course—a few almost petrified roots very hard to saw—so when they climbed to this place at the top of the valley they always carried a billet or two of firewood in their packs. He liked the word 'billet', in that usage.

Not that they ever did climb to it, not in the flesh. It was a place for our thoughts and dreams to go to, she said. A sort of safe house for them. Not for us in the flesh. Why the need for such a place? She asked me did I understand the word 'dejection'? I replied that I did. Well, she said, when he saw me in my state of dejection, or more especially when he had to leave me in that state, he begged me to try to lift my spirits by imagining a place where it would be easier to breathe and where my voice, which in the dejected state seemed to sink far into my chest, might revive and come forth again. Will you be there too? she asked. Will we be quiet? He said he would, of course he would, sometimes at least they would be there together and, yes, they would be quiet. He said it would do her good to imagine herself in a high and remote place where the air was a joy to breathe and him there with her, sometimes at least, quietly. In fact he was the least restful of men, could never sit still, must always be anxiously ordering things, in a pre-emptive sort of way. You don't trust your life, do you? she said. Which means you don't trust us. Often, when I think of you, of your anxiety, I get so nervous, for you, for us both, I would almost rather be in the state of dejection, where I don't feel anything much. This hurt him, like a reproach, and he answered back, to hurt her too, that whenever he dreamed of her it did him more harm than good. When he told me how he dreamed of me, she said, what night dreams and day dreams he had of me, I was very hurt. He saw me taking somebody else's arm and turning away. He saw himself coming to my house and getting no answer and standing there on the step like any hawker. It hurt me terribly, she said. I was all the more dejected. Why could we never be a reassuring place for our thoughts and dreams of one another?

In the shieling, she said, we had only the necessary things: a bed, a table, two chairs, the few things wanted for living there a while. Even books, we had very few, nine at the most, that was the rule, if we added one, we must take one away. In truth the shieling was a sparsely furnished place. And it seems they were never there for long, not even in thinking and dreaming did they absent themselves for long. Nor did they allow themselves to be there together very often. I said I'd have thought it would do them most good to imagine climbing to the shieling, opening it up, making it homely again, together. She blushed like a girl, agreeing. Nonetheless, she said, the times when they dreamed or thought themselves there together were few, mostly each went alone, the long and arduous climb, the opening up, the settling in, was solitary. And I wondered how that could help, did it not rather make things worse, to climb in thoughts and dreams to their shared invention, and be solitary in it? But she said no, certainly not for her and she truly believed not for him either, did being in the shieling alone, she without him, he without her, make their situation worse.

The virtue of the place lay in its being their invention, in their having made it so clear on all the senses, everything so solid, necessary, useful and to hand. Therein lay the virtue of the place, she said. And she added that she loved the word 'virtue', when it had that sense. How she smiled, how her face lit up when she confessed to me in a rush of words that even in the busy city where they were obliged to meet, in all the noise and trample of other people and in all the anxiety of clocks and timetables, if they began to dwell on the exact shape and colouring of a particular hearth stone in their shieling, on the wooden handle of a knife and its cheerful mismatch with the bone handle of a fork, dwelling on those and any dozen other concrete facts, they could abstract themselves completely and were as happy as children in the details of their invention. 'Dwelling on' is a lovely expression, don't you think? Dwelling on and in: the indwelling virtue of the place.

So either might sit down at the table with or without a fire and sleep alone and wake in the bed alone, and still there was virtue in it, great power to help. And at the table, moving aside the plate and the glass, he wrote a note or quite a long letter for her, or she for him, to find, having climbed alone, pushed open the door and paused, before stepping in. Or laid a book on the table from the frugal library (whose contents changed according to mood and need) and put a slip of paper in it, to mark a particular page, and a scribbled word: Read this. Tell me what you think.

Sometimes instead of a note or a book she left him a picture, either on the table or stuck above the hearth. She was good at art and might have drawn and painted him an abode as complex and intriguing as the castles and palaces on hilltops in the background of Renaissance paintings: delightful winding roads that climbed to safety on snow or blue sky, distracting the mind from the foreground martyrdoms, allowing it rest and peace. But all she ever did for him, knowing his mind and his desires, was the place of their shared invention, each time with some alteration that she knew he would notice and trusted he would approve: a rowan by the front door instead of a hawthorn; harebells in the window, not heather. Once she added a small knoll, to one side and a little forward of the shieling, on land they thought of as theirs, and laid steps up it, so they would have a vantage point. He was glad of that and wondered how they had ever managed without.

From that invented hillock in warm weather either might watch for the other coming, she explained, such a clear view they had down the long valley, and there she stood, or he stood, watching for the friend. How slow the approach was, how long a time elapsed between the first sighting and the first embrace; but that interlude, though the feelings lifted as the climber inch by inch drew near, that long space of time had no anxiety in it, not the least, it was all sureness, confidence, step by step, minute by minute, becoming ever more precisely flesh and blood and bone, a confirmed familiarity, the person as trustworthy as the place itself. And there again, she said, looking at me very closely to be sure I had understood, in that too the virtue of our invention was proven. I was helped alone and I was helped when I thought of myself on our vantage point watching his slow arrival.

When they were together in the shieling—only ever for two or three days at the very most—then of course they made love; but when she told me this she said how much she, and he too, for that matter, preferred to say 'we slept together.' She was pedantically anxious that I should understand her in this and that I should not deduce anything false out of her distinctions. I understood that she wanted me to know that the pleasure they had given one another, the love they had made, was intense, and her body and soul would never forget it; but I also understood that in the whole invention their thinking and dreaming of sleeping together had even greater virtue, was even better able to help. That was what she dwelled on in her dejections, and what she urged him to dwell on in his constant anxiety and restlessness. She said to him: I am someone you can go to sleep with. And if you wake in the night you will hear me breathing quietly in my sleep. Think of that. Your hand will be on my breast. You will feel how contented my heart is. Dwell on that.

There was more, much more. You must remember that their shieling was an invented place; and an invention, even one confined to simplicity, austerity, necessity, might be elaborated forever by two people who have a vital interest in it. She spoke of the deep contentment there was in sitting face to face at the table, writing. How one looked up for a word and with a shock saw the other likewise listening and waiting. And this happened alone in the place, she said, as often and as easily as when they thought or dreamed themselves there together. Then the subject took hold of her, the words came tumbling forth from her like the stream they had to climb to reach the shieling of their invention. More and more she found to say—and how I encouraged her!—on the subject of a place so simple, so bare in its appointment and decoration, so frugal in its amenities. All her girlhood awoke in her when she told me what was there, what might have been there, how free they were, within the strict forms

149

laid on their desires, to add and subtract, to change and to innovate, and all their doing, saying, sleeping and dreaming in that place I felt it binding me to her, as her listener, forever. For example, she said, there was a window at the back of the house. Through it we could see the stony ground, the screes either side, the lingering snow, the gap, the col, the windy exit from our valley over into the next.

Their place reminded me of many places, needless to say. I located it easily in three or four different lands; felt I had been there; felt I might go there again; but on the one occasion when I asked her would she name the place, her looks froze against me, as against an indecency. I blushed in shame, I begged her forgiveness. After a while she forgave me by resuming her voice. Forgiveness was a part of the place, she said. 'Forgive and Forget' might have been an inscription over our door. I believe it was for a while. We imagined several, and swapped them. My favourite was 'Let be.' I don't like forgetting. I like to think we could remember and forgive. But I especially love the words 'Let be.' The gesture of the shieling was that, therein lay its great good. I mean, she said, the hand raised in greeting, open to show peace and welcome, but also, because of who we were, because of what we were like, it was the hand and the fingers that will be raised and extended to touch the lips of the friend when he or she is full of doubt and fear and the words better never said, not needing to be said, are rushing into utterance and the hand very gently stops them: There is no need, let be.

I think she could see that my indecent asking after a name for the place still grieved me, because of her own accord she added something more (and other) than I had asked for. Once I did come to such a place, she said. By accident really, by folly and passive drifting and failure to watch my step. I was with somebody who was very fond of me and I liked him well enough or I should never have been there with him, I suppose. We were walking, it was his idea, he said he knew a place he was sure I would like, it would lift my spirits, he said. I doubted it, I very much doubted it, but I had no energy in me to say no. I had lost the cure of my own soul. We were climbing and came out of a forest and quite suddenly—I had not paid attention—there was a wide valley stretching away and above us, narrowing to a col. I seemed to be dreaming, I let myself trek in a dream by waterfalls and by rowan trees, a long long climb, in silence, like the wraith of myself following a man I liked well enough and who I knew was very fond of me. She paused, she looked at me with more trouble in her face than I could bear to witness. I put up my hand, I extended my fingers, gently, gently to stop her voice. Then she shrugged and said, I'm sure you can guess the rest. We came to the ruins of a shieling, the stones of it were tumbled down and all around. It was a shieling at the very limit of tractable land, where the bare rock began. How I wept to see it. I turned away. I left him standing there in his poor ignorance. I made back down the valley on my own. I was inconsolable. Still am in fact.

GOAT

That Christmas, the coldest in living memory and his last, Goat skippered in the old Bluecoats School. Long before winter the lads had ripped out all the lead and copper they could reach and when Goat moved in the place ran nearly everywhere with water. The main staircase was a cascade. But he set up home in the headmaster's study and even when the freeze came, since he had a fire in there, he thought himself well off.

The Canon never forgot his one and only meeting with Goat. During the dismal endgame of his life, in the home his family chose for him near the M25, he would talk of Goat and that famous Christmas Eve to anybody who would listen or indeed to nobody. Yes, he said, I was crossing the marketplace on my way to the midnight service, when close by the equestrian statue of Lord Londonderry, under the Christmas tree, I met a young woman called Fay. Where are you going? she asked. To the cathedral, I answered. She wore hiking boots, jeans, a navy-blue pea jacket, red mittens, red scarf, red Phrygian cap. Then just as well come with me, she said. I'm doing my soup run and my next and last is Goat. So the Canon accompanied Fay back up the hill he had just come down. A few people who knew him, hurrying to divine service through the cold, raised their frosty eyebrows as they passed.

I'm sure you've seen me around, said Fay. I've seen *you* around. I've often wondered what you think about when you're shaving. I mean that face of yours in the mirror must surely make you think.

Halfway up the hill, which the Canon had climbed and descended several thousand times during his long residence in that northern town, Fay halted between a cobbler's and an auction room at a pair of iron gates whose existence he had overlooked and which she pushed open now and tugged him through under a ruinous apartment straddling the gap. Here we are, she said. Having quitted the street, their light was starlight, glittering frost and the dull gleams of broken glass and broken ice. Iron, concrete and the smashings of bricks and wood were furred in a delicate culture of bright grey frost. This was their yard, she said. Those are the old toilets. Little Harry gets in there some nights but it's too cold at present. Goat won't let him share the warm. The school with its scores of shattered panes, its dangling gutters, keeling drainpipes and desquamated roof, bulked up enormously before them. From one of her deep pockets Fay took out a torch. Careful, she said. The ice. I needed wellies when I first came here. Now we need crampons.

Far south, till the end, the Canon would speak of the ice as a sort of Xanadu. He recalled the mouth of the old Bluecoats School, a charitable foundation awaiting demolition, as the gob of a hellish paradise, fangs either side and a long hard undulation tempting him up like the best, most forbidden, entertainment at a fair. The seven steps were perilous, he said. We clung to the stumps of what had been a wrought-iron handrail and reached the great doors which were busted open.

In the large vestibule Fay and the Canon stood together for a moment's silence. She played the beam of her torch over the high ceiling through which—through shattered laths and clinging plaster—hung swords of ice. The parquet floor below them, unevenly glazed with ice, was nubbed and bumped with the beginnings of stalagmites. Here and there lay the corpses of rats and pigeons, more or less gnawed or decomposed, in the fixative of ice. And bottles, cans, syringes, magazines and condoms, set fast in the glistering cold. The Canon, remembering his own school days, was most moved by the rolls of honour high on the walls: the captains, sportsmen and the dead in wars, their names in letters of gold under a patina of frost. Stillness, not a whisper of the water whose present form was ice. You would have loved the water, Fay said. This main stairs was like a stream you'd climb in Wales to a cwm and a lake, springs bubbled up wherever you trod and your head was wetted with sprinklers. Present in the ice, the Canon felt himself rapt by Fay's words into visions of the waters of life unleashed, in spate, unstoppable. I thought you'd look like that if I brought you here, she said. Goat's upstairs. Be careful. Why do you call him Goat? the Canon asked. That's his name, said Fay. Just right. He's got two bumps on his forehead that look as though they might be horns. Also he's very randy. He suffers from priapism. Suffers? said the Canon. But Fay had begun the climb.

Of the banister here only the brackets had survived, and by these, step by step, very slowly Fay and the Canon climbed the glacier stairs. Often she turned round to him, shone the lamp, urged extreme caution. Perhaps I'll fit up a rope next time, she said. The Canon, never a mountaineer, was amazed how little fear he felt. My shoes are quite unsuitable, he said to himself. And she's got boots on. She appraised him coolly. You're doing okay, she said. I'm doing okay, he muttered. I should get her to stencil that across my forehead.

They reached the landing. There was less ice. But watch your step, said Fay. Some floorboards had been ripped out, to get at the pipes or wiring or for fuel. Don't fall through.

Goat's along here. They passed a couple of classrooms and
the art room. Much breakage everywhere, nothing system-
atic, more an exuberance of beginnings, desks and chairs
with only a lid or a couple of legs missing, skirting wrenched
off intact. You might pillage for years in this place, the
Canon thought. Fuel in plenty till the ice retreats. Around
three walls of the art room, quite high up under the broken windows, ran a cast of the Elgin Marbles, scarcely more
damaged than they were by the robber baron himself. The
Canon stood looking up, the frost light was spectral, the
horses, men, women, sacrificial beasts, trooping like ghosts.
He stood so long Fay came back for him. The tears on his
cheeks had begun to freeze. It's warm at Goat's, she said,
having stood with him a while.

Goat's quarters were at the far end of the corridor behind
a barricade. He doesn't like visitors, said Fay. Except me.
Will he mind me? the Canon asked. No he won't mind
you, she answered. I've already mentioned you. More
floorboards were missing in this corner but a couple had
been laid back loose across the joists. That's his gangway,
said Fay. He'll pull it up when we've gone. They crossed,
and climbed over the barricade. That's the toilet, said Fay,
shining the torch. The door had been torn off and added to
Goat's defences. Of the thing itself not only the seat, burn-
able, but also much of the bowl had gone. Wash basin likewise. Sledgehammer work, by the looks of it. This room
with running water was an ice cave now except for some
damping on the wall against the study. At least the shit's all
in one place, said Fay, illuminating the ruined bowl. And
in the ice it doesn't smell. Admirable, said the Canon. In
bouts of coprophilia in his final years he would talk for
hours, if let, about Goat's convenience, that had once been
a headmaster's. Next door is cosier, said Fay.

She knocked, and she and the Canon laid an ear, her
right, his left, against the door. Their frost breaths mingled.

Fuck off! they heard loudly. Then softly, Unless it's you. It's me, said Fay. Enter, said Goat. They entered. The room was lit with fire and a couple of candle-ends. Goat sat barefooted (and the feet were black) in baggy trousers, a cherry-red shirt and the headmaster's gown, leaning back against the wall, his tobacco and a bottle in reach and a sheaf of paper propped in his lap. He had a broken nose, crinkled and soiled grey hair, some teeth and, yes, knobs on his forehead that might once have been or might be striving to become, horns. His mattress, and on it an overcoat and a stack of papers, lay along the far wall. Happy Christmas, Goat, said Fay. I've brought you some soup. Happy Christmas to you, sweetheart, said Goat. And to you too, Vicar. Peace on earth and God rest the slaughtered innocents. He's a canon, said Fay, taking a thermos, a cup, a bottle of wine and a penny whistle out of her rucksack, I told you. Ex, said the Canon, suddenly driven to say so. Ex, former, erstwhile canon. Ex-man-of-God. I'm going before they unfrock me, later today perhaps. I may announce it publicly later today. Meanwhile, dear Fay, dear Goat, be the first to know. And address me how you like. Once a canon, always a canon maybe. After this speech he rummaged under his greatcoat for the hip flask which—he told them—he could never get through divine service without. Drink with me, friends, he said, stooping first to Goat.

The room was hot. The frost flowers on its unbroken panes could not survive. Goat was burning the headmaster's desk, a good mahogany thing, all smashed and ready on the hearth, burning it as though there were no tomorrow. And see what I found in his bottom drawer, he said, handing the Canon a wad of photographs. Confiscated, no doubt, said Fay. Give them to me. They curled and blackened and vanished in the flames. Here's soup instead. Here's the blood-red wine. Here's bread. She took off her pea jacket. Goat folded his gown over the papers in his lap. Pardon me, he said. My old complaint. Very embarrassing. And how's family life for you, Father? Very poor, said the Canon. And it may end completely this afternoon. There may be an announcement. Herself had enough, has she? She has, said the Canon. My son and daughter married south, they board their children in expensive penitentiaries and with their spouses toil in the Golden Mile to raise the necessary cash. My wife has told me candidly she prefers them to me.

Goat took out his papers, propping them as before, and began to write. The hip flask circulated clockwise, the red bottle anticlockwise. Soup, bread; then from a sack, quite absently, continuing to scribble, Goat fetched out a tin of mince pies. The Canon took off his greatcoat and cardigan to reveal, below his snow-white collar, a shimmering purple front. It's a bishop's, he said. I bought it for fancy dress. Suits you, said Fay. Goat looked up and, eyeing her, threw on more splintered mahogany. Fay pulled off her sweater. And that's it, Goat, she said. Heat the room as hot as hell, that's as far as I go. But I will play you both a tune.

She moved to a corner, sat with her knees up and began to play. The flames, already dancing, lit her flickeringly, they moved on her face and bare arms like the ghosts of caresses, released, disembodied, become elemental, living forever. The Canon saw this at once and might have stared all night. But the reed pipe would not let him be still. Again, as when Fay had described the time before the ice, he heard water. Her playing attuned him immediately to all the hidden ways and energies of water. He felt those biding their time in the frozen pipework of the abandoned school, felt them keenly, from the deep municipal mains up to the stray ends in Goat's own privy, all of them waiting for warmth so that they could whisper, murmur, chuckle and exult in anarchy once more. That intricate life in waiting was made palpable to him as Fay played. But so too was the river under its casing of ice, he felt the sluggish flood still moving underneath over the ooze, the mud and all the deposits of bikes and trolleys, bottles, knives, angry women's rings and bombs from the last war. All that and more, but not just that, also the gnarled streams in the frozen hills to the west, hardened, silenced, clamped into inertia, set there waiting under the sheer ice of the milky way and billions of sharp points of unimaginable cold. That too, but also—the reed was very insidious—he felt in that hot room every highway and finer and finer branching, every thinnest ramification of the liquids of his body, all flowing in him in a sanctuary of warmth in a wrecked colossal palace seized and held fast by ice. He felt himself watered through and through and sensations shot electrically down all the moist conductors in his frame.

Fay slowed, she simplified her playing to half a dozen repeated notes, rising in interrogation, like a bird call, again and again, asking, summoning, her black eyes smiling at the men over her pipe and clever fingers. Goat set down his papers and pencil. With the ball of his left hand he rubbed his bumps. The Canon removed his Oxford shoes. Goat began to chortle. Eh, Bishop, he cackled, give us a turn, Holy Father. The Canon began to dance, in a slow twirling at first, his hands raised as though in surrender above his craggy head. Fay's whistle insisted. Goat began to clap, her bird call and his clapping marking time. Then the Canon was launched. Down came his arms, fists on his nipples, elbows out like residual wings, he tilted back his head and began to stamp and yodel. Now *he* made the beat, Goat and Fay, clapping and piping, had to catch him, and pretty soon, flapping like a dodo, knees up and crooning, he raised the grinning Goat to join him in the firelight. Fay whistled faster, she seemed able to keep both men in mind, to be playing for both, getting to the pit of the belly of each. They linked arms, they turned with time and against time, they parted, bowed, went solo, lumbering like grizzlies.

Goat fluttered like a bat in the headmaster's gown, up and out through his flies burst his cheerful affliction, dark as a donkey's, so witless, clownish, helpless, Goat and the Canon laughed to see it. Ghost in the machine, cried the Canon, popping out in flesh. There shall I be in the midst of you, cried Goat. And Fay raised her pipe and with slant notes climbing, with a spiralling and rifling of notes, faster and faster, higher and higher, she led. Then the Canon unbuttoned his immaculate collar, his collar of office, removed it, buttoned it again and with unrepeatable sureness of aim, with the skill suddenly given you in dreams, he hoopla-ed it over the risen vicar of Goat.

Fay ceased. Time, gentlemen, she said. Goat covered himself and sprawled with the Canon on the floor. Fay dressed. Time to go, Canon, she said. Obediently he found his cardigan, his heavy coat, his shoes. Goat sat up, looking sad. You coming again, girl? And you, boss, you coming again? The Canon nodded and shook him by the hand. Very soon, he said. I think I'll be a free man by tomorrow. Fay stowed away the flask and pipe and took out a package. Your Christmas present, Goat. She bent and kissed him on the forehead. He unwrapped his present at once. It was a notebook with black moleskin covers, he opened its white pages in his lap. Write me something, she said. Heart and soul, said Goat, the best I can.

On the corridor, like the cold itself, it struck the Canon into the heart that he must on no account fall and be crippled. I have to dance, he said to himself. From now on I have to be able to dance. He concentrated hard: over the missing floorboards, step by step down the escalade of ice, through the litter of hurtful debris in the yard. Fay watched for him, lighting where his hands and feet must go.

On the street what they heard first was a yowling of drunks from the marketplace, then sirens, some hastening away, others hastening near. The stars pulsed as though cold were their breath and sustenance, they throbbed like a power, like the dynamo of the remotest orders of life. You go that way, said Fay, pointing up the hill. And you? Through there, she answered, pointing across the street down towards the river. I'll see you around, she said. Yes, he answered. I'll be looking out for you.

That evening, having written a letter to his bishop and made an announcement to his wife, the Canon, unbearably restless, found a torch and his most suitable shoes and went out. At the iron gates he skulked till no passerby was near, then slipped quickly through into the yard. He was in a hurry, he tripped and skidded, till he mastered himself and concentrated on the guiding thought of the night before. He climbed the first steps very slowly, exulting that he had it in him to re-enter the dream alone. In the vestibule, standing below the hanging swords of ice, he took time to follow some sportsmen and captains by name from school to war, from one roll of honour to the next. This fortified him in his determination to stay alive. With pedantic caution, step by step, gripping the brackets, he climbed to the landing and the corridor. And there was the barricade—but with no gangway. He stepped from joist to joist, then over the desks, chairs and the toilet door. Only now did he wonder why he had come to find Goat. Why had he not roamed the streets in the hope of finding Fay? He knocked, no answer, he entered. There in the hearth squatted a dwarfish man with long arms and very bright eyes. The fire was blazing. He was feeding it pages and pages of pencilled script. Goat's gone, he said. It's my place now. You Little Harry? the Canon asked. A nod. And where has he gone? Dunno. To hell, I hope. Those pages, the Canon said, they his? They was, said Little Harry. They're for my fire now. Faster and faster he dealt them into the flames. The writing sped up the chimney like black butterflies. Give me the rest, will you? the Canon said. Little Harry shook his head. Silly fucker was always scribbling. I'll pay you, said the Canon. Too late, said Little Harry. They were all gone. His book, the Canon asked, he had a new black book. This here? said Little Harry, fetching it out from under him. That there, said the Canon. A tenner? Fifteen, said Little Harry. Hail Mary, the fucker's gone to hell. Tell his tart to visit me, will you?

It was a week before the Canon saw Fay. He sat in a café in the marketplace, watching. When they closed he sat on the steps under the horse. Then very late and the cold no less she came up unseen and sat beside him and took his hand. Goat's gone, he said. I know, she said. I got you his book, he said. See how much he wrote that night. I haven't read them of course. They'll be for you. She opened the book and closed it again at once. Little Harry hopes he fell through a hole. He laughed like the devil when he told me that.

Between then and Easter Fay and the Canon were often seen together in the marketplace café, in one or two of the rougher pubs or on the street just walking along. She still did her soup run. She even visited Little Harry. I can't pick and choose, she said. Walking on the streets with the Canon she would usually take his arm and he, everybody said, looked rather lost without her. Whenever he sat reading or doing a crossword or stood or walked, he looked always to be waiting for her. They were an odd couple; but that northern town had more than a few eccentrics and, had they been let, Fay and the Canon would have done okay. Were their relations carnal? Some said certainly yes, others certainly no, and both camps said you could tell at a glance was it yes or no. All agreed that when Fay and the Canon sat together in a café or a pub they had plenty to discuss. Plotting something, so it looked. In fact Fay had an idea for a piece of agitprop or a happening, she was unsure what to call it but if it were carried through it could not fail to make a difference. Her idea was to gather together five thousand of the county's deserving and undeserving poor, the feckless and the unlucky, the hundreds thrown on skid row by the wars, the rationalizations and the closures. And she, accompanied by the Canon, would play them into the cathedral with her pipe, interrupting choral evensong and occupying the place. Once settled in, they would dance, sing, recite poetry, tell stories, stage plays—and paint banners under which to march out in their own good time and carry the movement into all the cathedral cities. But even as they discussed this venture in ever-greater detail the absence of Goat became so palpable their spirits lapsed and they sat and looked at one another dejectedly. I often think he'll pop up again, said the Canon.

The Canon's wife had gone south; he had been evicted from his church house but was living comfortably enough in a bedsit with a view of the railway line.

The cold ended, the river flooded, great trees and dead sheep jostled with floes of dirty ice in the town's lower streets. Bluecoats is a wonder, said Fay, but he hadn't the heart to go and look. Easter was early, so sweetly persuasive with its mildness, snowdrops and blackthorn. Demolition began, the school was trucked away. The Canon found Fay wandering in tears among the market stalls. Goat, his poor remains, had been found in the basement. He had fallen through two floors. In a shroud, they said, curled in a black shroud, otherwise naked. After that Fay and the Canon pooled their funds and began living together but it didn't last long.

In the home just inside the halo of the M25 when anyone knocked at the Canon's door, they heard first, very loudly, Fuck off! Then, very softly, Unless it's you. They went in anyway and it was never you. But he told whoever it was, a doctor, a vicar, a Filipino nurse, that his family, hearing he intended to remarry, fearing he would father better children and anxious to secure for themselves his small estate, had kidnapped him and locked him in a room in hell. And at any least flicker of human interest he would tell the whole story of Goat and Fay, the fabulous cold, the rust- and copper-coloured falls of ice, the dance, the unleashing of the waters. The story was an ever-increasing wonder to him. I shake my head at myself when I'm shaving and I think of it, he said.

MEMORIAL

Caradoc's memorial service was a poor thing. In the little church there were more empty spaces than people. No one still studying at the College had known him. His surviving colleagues had never much liked him. He had published very little and on subjects they found distasteful. His rooms were in a separate house—a *petite maison*, the scurrilous called it—in the College grounds, and there was bitter wrangling over who should have them now. But the Master, new to the place and wishing to say something kind about him, ascertained that, by general agreement, he had been a good teacher; though even this, by the tone of voice in which it was conceded, sounded a rather louche achievement. Still the Master felt able to say publicly that Caradoc would be remembered with affection and gratitude by generations of undergraduates of the College.

There was tea in the refectory afterwards, but few wanted it. Most hurried away through the graveyard to their own affairs.

Odd among those attending were a man and a woman, obviously foreign, perhaps in their late fifties. They stood arm in arm at the very back of the church, the woman entirely in black, the man in a black suit and tie with a dazzlingly white shirt. They looked to be honouring an old code of conduct. Both were on the stout side with round and candid faces. They were weeping, their faces shone with tears. They stood arm in arm and, perhaps out of deference, let all the congregation leave before them. All saw their helpless faces, and looked away quickly.

It was warmer outside. The graveyard had leafed and flowered; it wore the scents of hawthorn and roses; in its silence there was birdsong. The foreigners stood in the porch. The man dried his wife's cheeks with a large white handkerchief, then dried his own. They stood there, at a loss.

From opposite ends of the graveyard, walking very deliberately, ignoring or not even noticing one another, two men approached them. Met on the flagged path, and faced them. They were perhaps in their late forties. Gino? said one. Lucia? said the other. The fair pronunciation of the names gave Gino and Lucia more hope than the two Englishmen, who introduced themselves as old pupils of Caradoc, could fulfill. But the four went out of the graveyard, turned left and in a café on the corner had tea and did their best to have a conversation.

Gino and Lucia spoke as if by force of wishing it they must be understood. They spoke in turn, a duet it sounded like, melodious, abundant, each heartening the other to remember and utter more. Their faces were so open, eyes and hands so expressive, it felt that in the transaction very little was being lost. Both Englishmen were thinking, How it comes back to you! Their stock, being revived, becoming more copious and useful.

Then quite suddenly it was over. Lucia began to weep again. Gino took out his large white handkerchief. The gist was easy to grasp: she had wanted him to die in her house, she had wanted to look after him to the end, she had wanted him in the little graveyard from where the snow, the fume and sometimes the creeping fires of Etna were to be seen by anyone looking up from tending a grave.

They waited together for the London bus. Lucia had a sister in Hillingdon. They would stay there the night. Then go home. Caradoc's old pupils waved them goodbye.

Then what? Neither asked. Heads down, side by side, they returned to the graveyard and found a seat against the far wall in a mild sunlight.

The taller of the two men began: It *was* you that night, wasn't it? But for answer he got a question: It *is* Jay, isn't it?

It was. I took a new name years ago. Thought it might change things.

Did it?

No. So just as well call me Jay. And you're Daniel, or you were then, and it was you that night. You and a girl called Merryn.

Yes, I still am. And it was us. We sat on this wall—nodding behind him—and looked out over there—nodding forwards—at his room where the lights were burning.

Thus introduced, they glanced sideways at one another, for a glimpse of the old faces. Then resumed, hands in their dark-suit pockets, staring forwards to the opposite wall of the grave-yard, the five yew trees along it, the little gate in it, the College behind it, and the house and the room that had been Caradoc's.

Yes, said Daniel, we were out most nights, so it seems to me now, getting locked in, getting locked out, climbing over walls and fences, wading the rivers. The rules being what they were back then, we kept off the empty streets and browsed through the parks and gardens. The rules in those days being so ridiculous, if you fell in love and meant it, you went feral, there was no other way, you spent your days sleepwalking and at nights you trespassed. How we trespassed! And to get together in my narrow bed, under the maps that papered the sloped ceiling, what routes we had to negotiate quiet as mice through the grown-ups' private pleasaunces. And what risks to share an innocent black coffee on a roof under Orion who had seen many such as us but liked us specially, we fancied.

I didn't much like you when you arrived that night.

It was her idea, not mine. Back there—again the nod—they were pulling the Gothic mansions down to raise up blocks of science and we got in through the ruins, into the gardens, to steal their stocks and roses. We had armfuls, lupines too, and peonies and hollyhocks, and though we lost some climbing we still had enough for a wedding and a funeral when we got ourselves comfortable on that wall and she made me tell her again about Caradoc and Italy. I had told her before, but it was in bed and she fell asleep. I carried on. She slept and woke and slept and my voice went babbling on. It was then that I learned you don't need the whole story. Falling asleep and missing some, coming in later, forgetting where you were, loveliest is the voice, the bits and pieces of the story running on and on. But wide awake that night on the wall and staring at his lighted window she insisted I tell it to her again, at least an episode.

Tell some now, said Jay.

Did he never tell you?

Maybe. But tell some again. It's different, his telling it and yours. And different down the years.

He said he'd be passing through Florence at the end of June. Let's say the 30th, he said. Be there, he said, and I'll pick you up. Be there waiting at let's say nine in the morning under Michelangelo's *David* (though I much prefer Donatello's) and I'll pick you up and take you as far as Rome. So there I was, and there he came, as the clocks struck nine, strolling across the square, smiling and looking very relaxed.

Yet here, said Jay, the buildings are as beautiful, the great domes and spires, the warm stone, the lanterns waiting for darkness, but did you ever see Caradoc in this place strolling and looking relaxed? Scarcely ever on the street at all.

I saw him once, said Daniel, soon after he had become my tutor, walking very quickly, almost scurrying, along the Broad and into the Turl. How strange he looked, out of place. I said to Merryn that it was like seeing a god, come down and managing the best he could. That was one of the first things I told her about him and it made her curious. Like a god, so out of place. But now I suppose I'd have to say he looked more like a man with a phobia, who couldn't bear daylight, traffic, the touch of people. I guess he was dashing to the indoor market, to the couple of familiar stalls, for a small shoulder of lamb, some cheeses, some fruit, to entertain a guest. I didn't accost him then or follow him, only watched, strangely intrigued and moved. It took me years to see that in the generosity of his entertaining must be included the effort it cost him to go out on the street and make a few purchases like any normal citizen.

But that night I sat on the wall here with Merryn and I tried to tell her what it felt like walking the streets of Florence with him, my teacher, my friend, become almost strange to me again because we were abroad and he was in his element and knew so much and imparted it in abundance, lightly. I didn't think of it then, it comes to me now, only now that he's dead and I'm sitting here looking at his room with you and the wall is behind me where I sat with her, this minute here and now it comes to me clearly what I felt that morning then. It was the rush of learning. It was the gathering force of the pentecost of learning blowing through me body and soul. Things he showed me then, enabled me to see and to go on seeing and see more and more elsewhere and down the years when he would not be there to show them. It was the continuation of his teaching in that room, his asking me questions, his clever inducing me to answer back, his getting me to ask and answer better, and his own questions and answers that would never let me rest. And the bottle of wine he bought, swelling in its straw basket, the cheese, the bread, the olives, the black grapes, his easy manners, how they liked him at the market stalls, how amiable he was and fluent in the language I had a few poor phrases of. I stood aside bashful, wanting one day to do likewise. I wanted his knowledge. Somewhere, nowhere, some remnant of the land of pastoral, we pulled off the road and picnicked under an olive tree. And that night in a restaurant in Orvieto he asked the waiter—yes, a very pretty boy—to tell him exactly how the little fish were cooked. And said pears were the fruit to eat with that particular pecorino cheese.

Yes, yes, said Jay. And eating pears and pecorino is like reading let's say Ronsard or Montaigne.

You ingest something. And being with a man at ease is a great gift in itself. He was bounteous to me.

So Merryn sitting up there with you and hearing all this and more thought she must meet the man and see for herself the way he worked.

She saw the light on. I said that was his room.

I was at the window. Perhaps you didn't see me. Certainly I had no wish to be seen. But I saw you two in the moonlight on the other side of these tombs up there sitting on the wall with your armfuls of flowers. I was thinking how unlike me you were. Caradoc was in his armchair behind my back. We were listening to Farantouri though neither of us knew a word of Greek. Listen, he had said, how she holds the lines— so steady. And I couldn't understand a word but I was listening well, if you know what I mean, truly in the heart, and looking at you two out there on the wall. And my loneliness welled up in me again and I could not see you for tears. Then came a knock at the door. I glanced at Caradoc. He raised his eyebrows. It was gone midnight. But he went and opened and there you were, like children with your silly flowers.

There was more, you see. I had told her more. In the end she could not bear not to know the man. I had told her that when we got to Rome and into the hotel and when he had

gone out for a while, I don't know why, I began to be afraid.
There were two beds, you see, but they were pushed together
to be almost like one. In Orvieto they were far apart. But
seeing the situation in that hotel in Rome I began to feel
afraid that he would want to make love to me—though until
then, and I don't just mean on the journey, I mean in all
the months of my getting to know him, in the tutorials and
going back later, quite late at nights, to his room up there,
to carry on talking and drink a glass or two, in all that time
and on all those private occasions, not once did he touch me
unlawfully, as you might say, nor even make any suggestion,
though, if I'm honest, I did quite often think he would. But in
that room in Rome I was suddenly afraid, seeing the beds so
close they looked like one, and I did a very bad thing: I pulled
them apart, I made a gap between them, they were heavy to
move, I felt very ashamed and foolish. And no sooner was I
finished than Caradoc came back in and saw at once what I
had done and a look went over his face, very hurt but then
at once forgiving. And all he said was, Time for bed, I think.
Would you like to use the bathroom first? When I came in
again, carrying my few clothes in a bundle, he was reading
a newspaper and didn't look out. And I was in my bed and
turned away when he came back to his. We lay in the dark
side by side with that ridiculous gap between us. He said good
night to me and I said good night to him. Then after a little while, as though talking to nobody, he began telling me
about Gino, how they had met in a bar in Naples where the
conscripts hung out, Gino was working there, and how he
had loved him at once and that same night they had found
a place they could stay together. More and more, about the
family in a village near Catania, the mother and father whom
Gino soon very proudly introduced him to, their poverty,
the struggle, their hopes in Gino, who was studying to be an
engineer. And it was like with Merryn when I made up stories for her or when I told her the picaresque tale of Caradoc

171

and the student engineer from a mafia village under Etna, I fell asleep listening, woke half-listening, slept again and he was still talking in the dark to me or to the ceiling. Next morning it was late and sunny before I woke and Caradoc had gone. I went down to the desk and they told me *il professore* had left an hour ago. They were gentle, they thought their thoughts, he was a familiar guest. They spoke slowly to me, they seemed to fear I would be sad. He was gone and had paid for two more nights in the room, so I should stay and get to know the city. And it was then that Merryn threw down her flowers, down into the graveyard, close by this seat, and took mine from my arms and threw them down after. And I did as she told me to: hung by my hands and dropped and stood below reaching up for her in her sandals, her bit of a skirt, her schoolgirly knickers, because she said the flowers had to be for him and for no one else, this teacher of mine, this faithful lover. I'm sorry now for intruding on you. But it had to be.

Jay rose abruptly, walked across to the far wall, passed between two very black and shapely yews, tried the little gate, found it locked, stepped back and looked up at the window that had been Caradoc's. After a while he returned and stood with his hands in his pockets looking down on Daniel. His hair was a tousled mop, boyish, but more grey than black. I don't mind about the intrusion, he said. But I do mind about the beds. On several counts. However, what's done is done and what's not done is not done. As to that night, I forgave you long before you left. What good was it doing me staring through the window at the pair of you on the wall? Does she still sing, by the way?

Yes, she still sings. I couldn't judge that night what the matter was, between you and Caradoc or in you yourself. But he was very courteous, as always. He gave us sambuca, do you remember?

All that palaver. The thin glass, the floating of the coffee beans, the setting fire to the spirit, the aroma, the bitter taste.

It was a wonder to Merryn. She's never forgotten it. The ceremony of it, the little dancing flames, she called him courtly lover and magician in one person.

Well, when you turned up like strays out of Arden I was on the run from the asylum, and Caradoc, while we were listening to Farantouri, was debating what to do with me.

And why had they locked you up?

Because I was mad. The College was going to send me down and I think that would have been the end of me, all the struggle my mother and father had to get me there, I'd have jumped under a train rather than go home that way and have to look them in the face. But after some discussion the College deemed me mad and had me locked away.

Were you mad?

Well, a bit like you or not at all like you, I had a passion for climbing: cranes and scaffolding, but trees best of all. How I loved climbing trees! Caradoc said I was like the baron in Calvino's story, *Il barone rampante*, and he bought me a copy and indeed I was, somewhat. My favourite tree was the beech in the College garden. Was there ever a tree like that before or since? I went back earlier today, just before that frightful service, and would you believe it, there is no tree—all gone, and only a ring on the lawn, a vast ring which was the shadow of its bulk, like the mark of a fort or camp as seen from the air in a drought when the present becomes transparent and you can see what was. I got up there most nights, doing nobody any harm. And I never hurt the tree, I loved it more than people, oh by far! Vast copper beech with long extending soughing and sway-ing limbs. Copper-black on a hot day, a heavy blackness, copper-red when you got to know the heart of it. Even in daylight there was always an opening on darkness for me in that garden and a darkening of the darkness in the night. And that is where I loved to be. High up, where the foliage broke like a sea monster surfacing and it was dappled with moon and stars. Doing no harm, not to man nor beast nor any living thing. Certainly not to the tree. But somebody must have betrayed me. And one night the Dean, damned time-server, damned slave in a living hell of his own making, stood there on the lawn with a flashlamp and a couple of porters, calling me in his castrated drawl to come down at once. Of course, I stayed where I was. That night, all the following day, all the following night. Then the Dean lost patience. He said he was fetching the police and the fire brigade. And I was tired and sadder than I'd ever been in my life before, sad as the tree was copious and dark, sad as its copper black was heavy, I was sad through and through, I had no heart for it anymore. And I leaned down till I could see his white face looking up, his pasty face, his hateful, chinless, spineless, gutless, feckless, witless, ugly mug looking up at me, and I said: Fuck off, Dean, fuck off. Absent thee from this pleasant place a while and I'll climb slowly down. But stand there five minutes longer and I'll jump. And off he toddled. He was out of his depth. I heard he wanted me sent down, mad or not, madness was no excuse for rudeness, so he said. But kinder counsels prevailed and I was transported to the nuthouse.

And that night you escaped?

It was child's play. Walls you and Merryn would have scaled in a twinkling and run along the copings of like squirrels. I was frightened. They were eyeing me up for ECT. They were saying I was a suitable case for treatment. So that evening I went through a toilet window and into the grounds and over a wall into some decent citizen's back garden and out past his bicycle and his coal bunker into the parks, for Caradoc's.

The graveyard was a warm place still, and lively. The two men in their suits were, with the yew trees, by far the darkest presences. Here and there, sitting against, lying upon,

strolling among the tombs were the College's current gen-
eration of students, reading, dozing, talking animatedly. A
couple quite speechlessly absorbed in one another; a young
woman with an open notebook looking round at everyone
else, at Jay and Daniel in particular perhaps.

Remembering the Dean, Jay continued, reminds me
how much less I liked Caradoc when I saw him with his colleagues. He took me into dinner once or twice, I don't quite
know why. Perhaps he thought I should witness these things.
Perhaps he was testing me. If so, I don't know whether I
passed or failed. I suffered, he must have seen that. I wished
he would be more different, I wished some original local
tone would surface in his voice, against their voices. But no,
he fitted, his speech was theirs, his subjects and opinions
were only theirs. And I watched—then as much as now—
and my view was that they didn't quite believe him, they
suspected him of dissembling, I even thought they must be
leading him on, to see how well or badly he would do. And
two or three times, until I told him I couldn't bear it, he
took me along to watch him playing his part.

I went on a pilgrimage to Bardsey once. I thought it
might help. I went on foot, I set off from here. And coming
to the Lleyn, that pushes out into the sea like Italy, I saw I
was very near Carmel, where he was born and grew up, and
I made the little detour, to understand him better. Terrace
houses, many ruinous, many for sale. The mines long abandoned, the sunlight slanting on the wet slate heaps, like the
glances you see off a crow's wings. The chapels too grand
for the few surviving streets. And looking back, the mountains. Did you ever see Caradoc's climbing books? Shelves
of them. Did he ever describe to you Joe Brown's routes up
Clogwyn? He was like a boy, a hero-worshipper, swearing
he would do such things himself when he was a man.

By then I knew about Gino and had begun my researches,
to try to find out more. And I had decided that Caradoc

loved him especially because of his family, the hardship, the determination to fight back by intelligence and education, his loyalty, his passionate desire to help. And that during the talk at High Table and in the Common Room Caradoc must perhaps be saying to himself, It's all right, I have to do this, I'll get by, I'll get through, it's not for much longer and I'll load up my car with my books and my presents and head off out of this place, all that long way south.

You know more than I do, said Daniel.

I found out, said Jay. From Caradoc some things: about the Mafia, the bandits, the fear; about Gino's work with the Communists, his classes for children, the demonstrations, the fights. I found a photograph of a Communist Party march, Gino and Caradoc together under the banner in a crowd of men wearing caps, Caradoc in his suit and without a tie. He worshipped Dolci. That was a life, he said, a life you wouldn't mind people looking at. But I got little out of Caradoc about his own generosity: his arrangements, his regular payments, really his funding of Gino in the struggle. I had to go elsewhere for that. I went down there once. Not with him, on my own. I was on the edge anyway, out on the borders, and I think now that gave me a sort of innocence and perhaps protected me. For a while I think I was almost a Fool, with the privileges of that office. Terrible those villages under Etna, so ruinous and fearful. I'd arrive and see no one and knew that everyone was seeing me. I stood in that little cemetery Lucia wanted him home in. There were anemones and much of the bulk of Etna was white with snow. I'm glad she never saw our crematorium. I hope no one told her he dropped dead on the street.

Again he stood up, and did a tour among the graves. He looked odd and ill-dressed, his suit hung on him slackly, as if he had worn it for years and lost weight in it. Daniel surveyed the young men and women, looking for the types, the recurrent patterns of being young. The church was built in the twelfth century, the oldest surviving graves are of the late seventeenth, there are a couple of memorial trees in the far corner, for the first deaths from AIDS. The yews are as shapely as steady flames.

Jay came back, sat down again, stared up at the overlooking window and said: That night before you two arrived Caradoc had been persuading me not to kill myself. I know for certain that he did this with others too. I was round there one night, very late, when he got a phone call and said he must go and I could sleep on the sofa if I wished, he wouldn't be back. And I learned later it was a boy on the top floor in a big house up the Woodstock Road, on the window ledge with a razor—and Caradoc talked him in again, and out of the idea.

What did he say to you?

That although I was free to do it, my true imperative was not to. That my responsibility was to stay alive so long as I might be useful. That although I was free to do it, I would harm other people—people who loved me—by doing it. I denied that I might be useful. I denied that anyone loved me. He said that I couldn't see clearly at present and that I had to trust somebody else's judgment until I could. He denied that nobody loved me. He denied I would never be useful. He took me in his arms and said that he for one would miss me sorely. Was that not reason enough to wait a while? I suppose you were already sitting on the wall by then. Soon afterwards I looked out and saw you. And then you arrived with your armfuls of flowers. I was weak and lachrymose and didn't want anyone but Caradoc knowing.

Merryn knew. I mean she knew you were weepy, but more that you wished no one but Caradoc to witness it. That was why she sang.

When the Farantouri came to an end there was a silence and Caradoc still hadn't decided what to do with his flowers but was standing with them in his arms rather gauchely and

Merryn was sitting on the carpet with her knees up leaning back against the sofa.

My eyes were sharpened by sadness, I was weak and keen-sighted because I wanted to be persuaded not to kill myself. She had a scratch on her right leg, just below the knee, from all your climbing, I suppose, the blood had trickled down and dried in a brown line. There were seeds of some sort in her hair.

Elmseeds.

There were elmseeds in her black hair. Legs like a boychild's, scuffed sandals. Then she sang. It was like the Farantouri, I understood not a word, a different voice and a girl not much younger than me sitting there somewhere familiar in England but her singing was strange, so foreign, from long ago elsewhere. I half-thought I knew some words, but none either singly or in a phrase made any usual sense. But it was like the Farantouri, I felt its fingers clutching at my heart, but not so wistful, not tragic, it wanted something, it had energy, it was younger in spirit, it saw difficulties but no reason not to go out and fight them. And the sadness—there was some sadness—was more like an imagined possibility, what the cost would be, what your loss and regret would be, if you didn't fight bravely and win through to where you desired and believed you deserved to be. I discerned, perhaps more than you did, that Caradoc too was greatly moved. I like to think it reminded him of his own first language, that he had forgotten or suppressed. Even now I don't know what she sang. I've heard nothing like it since. What was it?

A troubadour song. Occitan, I suppose.

She knew songs like that?

Still does. And I'll tell you how. You're like me, you need icons, I give you this. She had classes with Mrs. Delanty—another who never published, another every pupil revered—and one late afternoon it wasn't going very well, they weren't concentrating, perhaps they hadn't prepared it, the class was drifting into pieces. Then Mrs. Delanty closed her book and told them quietly to close theirs. Listen, she said. And she stood up, put her arms by her sides—like a little girl at a party, Merryn said—closed her eyes, lifted up her face, and sang. A white-haired lady, her girlish beauty showing through the many years. She sang a troubadour song, though it certainly wasn't the troubadours that the failing class had been about. She sang. It was a dawn song, Merryn said: two lovers having to part after their stolen and risky night together. So Merryn learned later. When the song was finished Mrs. Delanty opened her eyes, smiled at the class, said they should go now, she would see them at the same time next week and they would carry on from where they had left off. But that evening Merryn went to Mrs. Delanty's rooms and knocked. Quite late, nobody did such a thing. Called in, closing the door behind her, she stood there. What is it, child? Mrs. Delanty asked. And Merryn answered: Please, Mrs. Delanty, will you teach me that language? I want to be able to sing that song you sang. Of course you do, said Mrs. Delanty. And of course I will. We'll make a start tomorrow evening. Are you free at 8:30?

Jay stood up again. Paced around. Daniel observed his agitation, then looked away, over the yew trees and the wall, to what had been Caradoc's room. Somebody was standing at the window, looking down. Daniel had no idea who he might be, no interest either, except in the idea of a person, and years later another person, looking out and down over a graveyard in which the generations strolled, sat, lolled, conversed, made love.

Then Jay blocked his view and his thinking. So that was Merryn, he said. Caradoc was moved by her singing. He freely admitted that he found it hard to like the girlfriends of his young men but I could see that he did like her. As for you, I must say I like you better now. I thought then that you deserved neither Caradoc nor her. I didn't, said Daniel. I don't. You talked about Rimbaud, Jay said. You had just written on him and he was on your mind. You said it was a pity he let himself go. You said he should have bided his time. You said the *dérèglement de tous les sens* was an abdication of responsibility, he would have written better, more, for longer, for more people, to better effect, had he held on. And he should have known that, he was clever enough. You said it was a waste, it was all too rushed, the later poems already were a solipsistic cul-de-sac. I thought you very bourgeois.

I am. Petty bourgeois. Or you could say I want to stay alive, as lively as possible for as long as possible.

Sort of *bateau ivre* with life jackets and the coast guard standing by?

Sort of. And here's a funny thing. That essay I wrote for Caradoc on Rimbaud, it was far too long, by the end of the tutorial I had hardly finished reading it. He said I should come back, come back that evening at ten, and we'd discuss it then. And that's when I began to get to know him. That was the beginning of what made him say he would meet me in Florence under Michelangelo's *David* and take me to Rome. I think he was intrigued that a boy of twenty wrote in favour of a sort of common sense. And this is the funny thing. I wrote at that essay all of the previous night and to stay awake I got myself something off somebody in College who supplied such things. I was high, my heart and my brain were racing, I had more ideas than I could get out through the nib of my pen, the one and only time I've taken any such thing, and I wrote in favour of not letting go, of holding back, of biding your time, of not giving in to the pull of unrestraint.

Jay sat down, patted Daniel's arm, left his hand lying there for a moment. Then he said: I never took anything, though you might think I would. I was always going up very high, and it frightened me, and down very low, and I grovelled there in terror. I never wanted any drugs. All I ever took was what they force-fed me in the hospitals. So perhaps we are more alike than I thought that night. Here I am still, large as life, all skin and bone but by no means dead. Plenty are. Plenty fell off along the way. Back then and since. I was with that boy who jumped off the crane in Parks Road. He thought he could fly, or didn't care if he couldn't. It was back where your ruined gardens had been. He landed on the scientific concrete. I was up there with him, not very tempted. I climbed down, saw the mess, crept into the parks and lay by the river vomiting. And several since, if not so dramatic equally fatal. The needle, the bottle, the blade. Gone, gone, the damage done. And somehow I didn't. I must have believed what he said: I might love, I might be loved, I might be asked to help and be able to. I drifted this way quite often. He always took me in. Make yourself at home, he said. I did, I had nowhere else. When did you see him last?

Daniel blushed. He was ashamed. Not long before he died, he said. I hadn't told him I was coming here. I had some business of my own. Then I met him by accident in the Lane. He was at the back gate, you remember that door in the wall, he had his own key to it. He let me in there once or twice, as I'm sure he did you, he always made some comment and giggled. But when I saw him last I came on him suddenly and we were both embarrassed. He was fatter, his face had coarsened. Neither of us knew what to say to the other. There was some sunlight and he looked very ill in it, the flesh of his face all pocked and slack. I might say the eyes were still bright, very dark and bright, but they had withdrawn and were staring out as if from a hiding place, backing away almost to where his thoughts were. And his thoughts, like mine, were a long way from the speaking lips.

I was thinking how much better he had looked in Italy, the
sun was brighter there, he was on streets among people full
in the public view, but he was fit to be looked at. Was it only
because he had aged? I don't think so. After a little while I
left him and walked away quickly. It occurred to me at once
that I couldn't be sure whether he was about to go in at the
gate or had just come out of it. If the latter, then we should
at least have walked into town together; and he would be
waiting there now, in the Lane, until he could be sure of not
catching me up. Perhaps he was hurrying to the market, to
buy the few things to be hospitable to a visitor, as he had
been, often, to me.

I saw the same, said Jay, his loneliness, the wrecking of his
face, but I swore not to let it matter. I would see through it
to the spirit, as Troilus did through poor Cresseid's leprosy.
And mostly I saw him indoors. He looked okay indoors.
He embraced me, he welcomed me, he opened a bottle. I
never saw him in Italy, though I hitchhiked the route he
took every summer through France, all the long way down.
I mooched around Florence where he picked you up. I can
well imagine what you looked like under the statue, waiting. Be sure he saw you first. Be sure he was somewhere
spying to see you first. And it rejoiced his heart to see you so
burned with travelling, so lightly clad. And in his own good
time he strolled across the square, to claim you, his waif and
stray. And I know which hotel it was in Rome, near the
Spanish Steps, close to Keats's lodgings, he recommended
it, should I ever be passing. I was passing, penniless, I saw it
from the outside. I went on my way, all the long way down.
And when I saw that graveyard under Etna I wished him
safely home there when the time should come. For that was
always the plan. When Gino met Lucia and when it came to
marrying, he told her and her family as he had already told
his own that his love for Caradoc might change but would
never lessen and was a fact and a certainty and nobody could

be bound to him who did not honour that. And they did. Gladly, simply, thoroughly they honoured it. He had a flat in their house. And every year, in his seasons, he would arrive with his reading and his gifts and made provision for the family and was godfather to the three children and when the first, a little boy, died he grieved with them and for a year wore a ribbon of mourning during all his teaching and all his College duties and nobody all that time once saw him smile. You have children, do you?

Daniel nodded. Two weeks after that night it was the end of term and I was very anxious. I didn't know what I dared ask of her. I was fearful. We were out at nights in the gardens and the parks, often by the river, following the tributaries to the big Thames, thinking of it leaving. And we were on the roof high above the streets and watched aeroplanes and shooting stars and the constellations travelling. And we lay under the maps on the sloped ceiling, they showed the possibilities, but I never dared say, We'll go there, shan't we, promise? She seemed free as a bird to me, by choice still lingering where I happened to be. I saw Caradoc several times, but never with her, and when he asked me what my summer was looking like, I shrugged and turned away. The term finished and she hadn't said even goodbye. But back home there was a note for me, waiting. It said: If you want me, I'll be in the Tuileries, by Maillol's *La Nymphe*, 9 July at three in the afternoon. And if you find me we'll go looking for castles in Spain. There's a particular troubadour I'm interested in.

Jay's smile was only faintly sardonic.

Then came again, said Daniel, again and more, the rush of learning. These hands—he raised them—these eyes—he looked into Jay's—and whatever and wherever the soul is, how they learned. I came into my own. Into earthly happiness. And you?

Jay shrugged, stood up abruptly. Time I was off, he said. The evening had lingered but was ending. The girl closed her notebook and with both hands rubbed her bare shoulders. At the gate Jay said, Some days I think there was only him. Others, I think he directed me into plenitude and it's up to me to grasp it, bear it, say how it was and is.

THE MERMAID

J ack woke, Ev was snoring, but above that sound he could hear the sea, the wind had got up, there was a big sea, the sound of it made his heart beat faster. Gently, gently, he slid out from beside her, crept to the window, parted the curtains a fraction, enough for one eye: no rain, only the wind, a sliver of draught, the sash was trembling and across the street, across the field, there was the sea coming nearer and higher, the white sea. He thought: There'll be some wreck, the breakers coming in like friendly hounds with timbers in their mouths. Glancing down Jack saw that his John Thomas was out, up and out, sticking its head out of his pyjamas into the cold room, stiff as a chair leg. Always the same when a man wakes, especially in the middle of the night if he wakes then, he mentioned it to Stan one day when they were sitting in the Folly Field watching the visitors, and Stan said his was the same whenever he woke, especially if he woke in the night, like a table leg, so that you wondered what was going on down there when you were sleeping, all night long, something must be going on, in the mind at least, but you never remembered it, worse luck. Gently, gently Jack slid in again. The sea. He might get a nice piece of wood. What time was it? Ev had the clock on her side and her teeth, in a glass of water, guarded it, she knew the time and what time to get up and when the alarm went off Jack went downstairs and made the tea, at a quarter to eight. Ev wore a mobcap in her sleep, lay on her back and snored, her sharp little fingers gripping the eiderdown. Jack did the trick he had learned from Stan (it seemed to work): lifted and let fall back his head six times onto the pillow, to wake at six and be on the beach before anyone else, after the wood. Funny how the brain works. Jack was listening to the sea and going down nicely to where the mind whatever it thinks is not to blame, when Ev hit him suddenly on the nose with her hard elbow. The shock was frightful, his eyes wept, he felt at his upper lip whether blood were coming out. Ev snored, the clock was smiling faintly. Marvellous how a woman knows, deep down, even in her sleep, she always knows what's going on in her loved ones.

Jack went out the back way, down the garden, past his shed, into the back lane and round. It was still dark, there was nobody about. A car came by very slowly. He stood on the little street like a malefactor; then crossed, entered the field, hurried to the beach. The sea had withdrawn, the waves were milky white in a dozen layers where they spilled and ended, the widening beach was empty. Jack got to the tide line and struck along it into the wind, shingle and dunes on his right hand, the lights of town far ahead of him on the bay's long curve. The sky, lightening, was enough to see by, and new wood always showed up. He soon spotted a nice length of six-by-four, tugged it out of the slippy dead weight of thong and wrack, dragged it into hiding in the dunes. So he went on—a fishbox, a wicker chair, a useful pole—making caches in the dunes. Nothing like it, nothing else in his life was like getting up early after a wind in the night and scouring along a mile or so for what the sea had left. Everything pleased him, even the plastic bottles and tubes, the women's things in different languages. You never know. He had found a bed once,

without its bedding, of course, but a bed all the same, thick
with barnacles and weed, he couldn't budge it, there it stayed,
for weeks, he felt sorry for it in the daylight and was glad
when a gale took it away again, a bed on the sea, all rough and
slippery and stinking. At the seawall, that would have taken
him as far as the railway station, Jack turned back. Ev would
be waking and wanting her cup of tea. It was light. The first
masters and mistresses were coming along the wall, out of
town, and along the beach, out of the village, with their dogs.
Jack took up his best piece, a plank, and shouldered it. Later
he would get Stan to come down with the car and fetch the
rest. The wet plank under his steadying hand, its rasping sand,
its smell of brine and tar, he nestled it into his neck. He would
have liked to find some wood he could carve, but mostly it
was cheap timber used for packing, or it had been in the water
too long. Once he had found a log he thought he might do
something with, four or five feet long and about nine inches
thick, very smooth, he carried it home, it was surprisingly
light. The worms were in it, shipworm, he split it and all the
naked creatures, as squelchy as oysters, were brought to light
in their honeycomb. Soon the two lengths, leaning against
the wall, began to stink, and Ev made him take them back to
the beach. He went to the trouble of throwing them back into
the water at high tide, but by then, needless to say, the worms
in their wooden cells were dead.

Stan said he would get Jack a nice piece of wood to carve.
His neighbour had cut down a cherry tree, it was blocking
the light. He cut it down one Sunday while it was flowering. Stan said the neighbour's wife was heartbroken. She was
a very handsome woman, he visited her sometimes with little presents from the garden, her husband was away, driving
around upcountry on financial business. Stan and Jack met
in the Folly Field and sat on a bench watching the visitors.
In summer they liked to watch the girls going into the sea
and coming out again. Stan had a word for the very short

skirts they wore: he called them fanny-pelmets. Jack said the word to himself as he walked home and while he was doing woodwork in the shed. The next time he came into the Folly Field Stan was already sitting there with a fat log of cherry-wood between his knees. Mrs. Wilberforce's compliments, he said. Most of the visitors had gone, there was nobody much to look at. Here, said Stan, take a look at this. And he slid a pair of nutcrackers from his inside pocket, a carved black woman, naked, as a pair of nutcrackers. The nut goes in between her legs and when you squeeze, it cracks. Ethel won 'em at the Chapel ladies' whistdrive.

Jack came in the back way but Ev was at the kitchen window looking out. Jack had the log on his shoulder. It was a weight. He smiled, and pointed at it. Ev came into the garden, wiping her hands. That friend of yours, she said. He had it off a neighbour, Jack replied. They chopped it down, it was taking up too much light. Ev liked the look of the cherry-wood. Make a nice something, she said. Take that filthy coat off before you come in. Jack laid the log on his workbench in the shed. Its bark was red and smooth. Such a beautiful length of tree. Jack stroked it, sniffed it, laid his cheek on it. Time you finished me that stool, said Ev when he came in. Nearly done, he said, one of the legs was wrong.

Next day Jack went out early picking mushrooms. They grew in the field across the street. Must have been horses in there years ago, he said to Stan. Funny to think of them nearly on the beach. Jack had a secretive way of picking mushrooms. He was sure he was the only one who knew they were growing in that field. He was out early, but other people might be out as well walking their dogs. He held a plastic bag under his old raincoat. He held on to it with his left hand through a big hole in the pocket. That way he could slip the mushrooms in and nobody noticed. Sometimes he had to stand over one and pretend to be looking out to sea. The Minister's wife was passing with her alsatian. She said: Good morning, Mr. Little.

Good morning, Mrs. Blunt, said Jack. He picked a good lot and sorted out the best of them in his shed. They were for Mrs. Wilberforce. The rest he took in for himself and Ev, to breakfast on. Not so many this morning, he said, I dunno why. Your eyesight's going, I shouldn't wonder, said Ev. She was partial to mushrooms with a bit of crispy bacon. When the tea was made and they sat down in the little kitchen by the fire she would become quite jovial and holding up a mouthful of mushroom on her fork would say, for a joke, that she hoped he wasn't poisoning her. How black the morsel looked when she held it up. No danger of that, said Jack, eating his own with relish. He was so fond of the feel and smell of mushrooms when he was picking them and of their taste when he was eating them that he could scarcely believe they were not forbidden him. And what a strange thing to come of horse-piss! It was a miracle you could eat one and not die.

After breakfast Jack went out into his shed. To finish that stool, I hope, said Ev. Later he slipped out to the Folly Field with the mushrooms for Mrs. Wilberforce in a little wicker basket. Give her these, he said to Stan. And thank her very much. She can keep the basket too. I found it on the beach. Stan set off at once. Always glad of an excuse to call on Mrs. Wilberforce, he said.

Jack came in at dinnertime with the stool. It was a four-legged one, quite low. I put a bit of decoration on it, he said, to brighten it up. Yes, he had carved the seat into the likeness of a smiling face. It's the sun, he said. Uncomfortable to sit on, I should think, said Ev. Still, I can always cover it with a cushion, and it will be handy for standing on, to reach the Christmas pudding down.

There was not much doing in the Folly Field; most of the visitors had gone. The little fair had shut, all but the round-about. She's having her morning, said Jack. The house is full. I can tell you what they'll be talking about, said Stan. You heard the news? Jack hadn't. Councillor Rabbit exposing himself in Chapel. Jack shook his head. There's something wrong with us, he said. They were singing 'Love divine, all loves excelling' when Betty Creeble looked across the aisle and there he was with it out. Of course, when she'd seen it he hung his hat on it. But by then she was hysterical. He'd just been round for the collection too. Jack shook his head. Whatever's wrong with us? The Minister's having a word with him, said Stan. Stan's daughter was coming across the Folly Field with her boy and girl. Down for a week or so, said Stan. She got a husband yet? Jack asked. She was eating an ice cream cornet. Seems not, said Stan, doesn't seem to want one either. The children ran to the roundabout and climbed into a fire engine together. They were the only customers. The girl began ringing the bell. Then they were off. Stan kept up with them and did the circuit several times, prancing and neighing like a little horse. Jack was glad their mother was not wearing a very short skirt, but her jacket was open on a pretty blouse. Dad'll give himself a heart attack, she said. Your ice cream's coming out the bottom, said Jack, if you don't mind my saying so. He felt for a handkerchief to wipe her blouse, but dared not bring it out. Never mind, she said, and put her mouth under the cone where it was leaking. Jack paid for the children to have another ride. Stan went on hands and knees in the opposite direction. The boy looked as dark as a southern Italian, the girl was as blonde as corn. Then the owner gave them a ride for nothing. Jack tugged his beret and said he'd better be off. Not going in, are you? said Stan. You must be mad. I'll be in my shed, said Jack, doing my carving. Tell Mrs. W I'm doing a mermaid.

When he was carving Jack always thought of school. It was in the country, the boys came in from the farms. They were slow at words and figures, but it had happened every year that a boy in one or other of Jack's classes discovered he could use his hands. Never knew I had it in me, they used to say. They did some lovely work, Jack had some in the attic still, it was better than his own, and when they outdid him he was proud of them, he had shown them they could do it, that was his part and he was proud of that. They made serviceable things, he guessed there must be hundreds of useful household things still being used in that region of the country in the homes and perhaps taken elsewhere by now as families moved, perhaps even abroad. And if a boy ever asked him specially and they could get the wood Jack let him carve whatever he liked, a bird or an animal, for a present. During the war there was a camp near the school, for prisoners of war, Italians, they were marvellously good with their hands. Jack slipped them pieces of wood whenever he dared and they gave him back what they had made of it with their clasp knives, in exchange for cigarettes. Once he had a crib given him at Christmas: an ox, an ass, the manger, the baby Jesus, Mother Mary and Joseph and a couple of shepherds, all simple, warm and true, they were lovely to feel in the hands. They must be still in the house somewhere, Ev had never liked them much, he thought every Christmas of giving them to somebody with children.

Jack knew that his own hands were not especially skilful. Mrs. Wilberforce's log of cherry was too good for him. But he had an idea, he knew what he was trying to do. It was common knowledge what a mermaid looked like. She must have long hair and a fishy lower half and be carrying a comb and mirror. Jack thought he could do the fish scales pretty well, like leaves, like a low long skirt, and it was there that he had begun, below the waist, and she was taking shape. Time passed him quietly by. When Ev called him in for dinner he started like a guilty man and hid his carving under a pile of potato sacks.

I hear the illegits are down again, said Ev as they ate their cod. Jack admitted that he had seen them on the Folly Field. The man gave 'em a free ride, he said. I wonder she shows her face down here, said Ev. I wonder Ethel gives 'em house

191

room. Seem nice enough to me, said Jack. They would to you, said Ev. But it's the mother I blame. Poor illegits, how'll they ever manage, I'd like to know. I wonder Ethel can look me in the face. Jack finished up his cod. He was thinking of the children on the roundabout, one blonde, one dark, and of the young woman's blouse and how she had stood next to him and given him a friendly smile. Then he wondered what Mrs. Wilberforce would have to say about the illegits, and whether she was really interested in his carving. I see you put a cushion on my sun, he said. Looks better, said Ev. Behind her, on the wall, was a piece of marquetry he had done when they were married. It showed the church they were married in. He felt a crumpling sadness at the sight of it, and a sort of pity for them both. He rose. I'll see to these, he said, taking the plates, which were green and in the shape of obese fish. You'll want a nap after your morning with the ladies. There's pudding, said Ev. You know very well I always do a pudding. When she came in again—it was spotted dick—Jack said, wishing to smooth her: Bad business at the Chapel, so I hear. No woman's safe, said Ev, not even when she's singing hymns. Who told you anyway? That Stan, I suppose. I'll see to these, said Jack, as soon as he could. You'll be wanting a nap after your ladies.

Jack sent another gift of mushrooms to Mrs. Wilberforce. Tell her she can keep the little box, he said. I found it on the beach. She says thank you very much, said Stan, and how's the mermaid coming on? Tell her she's coming on very well, said Jack. Her tail was done, he had even managed to give a flourish to the extremity. Then he dug out a little hole for her belly button and that was it, all of the bottom half of her was done. Now for the rest. He admitted to Stan that he was going to find the upper half more difficult. I mean, he said, everyone knows what a fish looks like. He knew as soon as he came up to her hips and when he was making the hole and the little bulge (like half a cherry) for her belly button that the rest of her was going to be difficult. The sea was quiet,

the roundabout and every other amusement in the Folly Field
had closed, on the beach the Minister's wife was unleashing
her alsatian. No wreck, said Stan. Nothing, said Jack. What's
Ethel say about you visiting Mrs. W? Nothing, said Stan. I go
in through the garden, behind the bonfire, she never misses
me. You mean you do your visiting in your gardening coat?
Doesn't bother her, said Stan. And what d'you do up there?
Stan had the face of a childish devil when he grinned, and his
hands, when he rubbed them together, sounded as though
they felt like bark. Have a chat, he said, have a cup of tea.
Nothing else besides? A saffron bun maybe, if I touch lucky.
Jack did not know where Mrs. Wilberforce lived exactly.
Some days he might have gone that far and called on Stan,
but his usual walk was along the beach as far as the seawall or
along the front as far as the Folly Field. That way Ev knew
where he was. What's she like? he asked. I've maybe seen her
on Thursdays in the post office. Fullish, said Stan, and blonde.

The ladies Ev had when it was her turn to entertain were
mostly grey, grey or white, but not an old colour, more like
a frost and snow scene on a Christmas card. They came in
talking and when they were in they began to shout. When
it was over they shouted at the door, and went away again
talking. They often wore blue, and jewellery, their mouths
were done in red, and certainly one or two of them were fullish. Sometimes the noise they were making suddenly grew
louder and Jack was worried in his shed that they might be
coming out to visit him, to do him a serious mischief in a
friendly sort of way. Mrs. Blunt had a face which was massive
and immensely powerful around the jaws, her tongue was
like a steak. Betty Creeble (the lady whom Councillor Rabbit
had offended) seemed to have fractured as a flint does, rather
than to have worn as will, for example, chalk. Jack thought
Ev's ladies fiercer than buffalo. Must be very nice, he said,
at Mrs. W's, I mean. Some conversation with a well-spoken
woman must be very nice. Stan offered to take him along

next time he went—Come up the ditch, he said, and meet me by the bonfire—or next time Ev had her ladies, to be on the safe side; but Jack declined. He was gazing at his hands. Using the chisels and the hammer so much had made them sore.

Halfway. Jack decided to start at the top and work down to her middle. He gave her a round face, like the moon, but left it blank for the time being and did her hair, which he imagined a golden blonde, he took it right down her back to where her fishy half began. She was lying face down, her front was unspoiled trunk of cherry tree, and he did her hair, spreading it so that her bare back was covered, streams of hair, plaited, in long knots, a semblance of wrack and thong, as was fitting. Then he hid her under the sacks and went in to wash his hands.

By the way, said Ev, as they ate their haddock, I've thought what you can do me with that nice piece of wood. The haddock was yellower than usual. Funny how very unlike a fish it looked. I'll have a lighthouse that lights up. That would be very unusual, don't you think? You mean with a flashing light? Jack asked. Yes, flashing, said Ev. And if we stand it in the corner no one'll see the wires. And do some waves around the bottom to make it look more real. I see what you mean, said Jack. But I think you'll need a longer piece, and not so fat. It's long enough, said Ev, and you can shave it if it's fat.

The bare light bulb, the steam of his tea, the smells of wood and of the seashore. Jack lifted the mermaid out in her sacks and uncovered her. She was face up, a blank round face, her arms were still encased in the unquarried wood. He had decided she would be empty-handed after all. He had decided she would be hugging herself as though she were cold. The hair came down her shoulders as far as her waist like a cloak, but open, entirely open, at the front, so she was cold. Used to the sea, and cold? The air was colder. He gave her an open face, her smile was innocent and broad, but her eyes were so wide open it was shock her looks expressed. He roughed out her arms the way he wanted them. It was time to begin dividing and shaping her breasts. Happy valley, as Stan said. But the time was a quarter to eight and Ev had woken and would be expecting her cup of tea. Mushrooms, she said when he came in with the tray and wished her good morning. You haven't been out, I don't suppose. Just off, he said. But they're getting to the end, you know.

Soon there were no more mushrooms, neither for Ev nor for Mrs. Wilberforce, the nights drew in, the mornings were darker. Jack walked on the beach as far as the seawall or sat with Stan in the deserted Folly Field. I'm doing her bust, he said. Get me some oil, will you, next time you're in town. And he gave him the money out of the pocket without a hole. Ev wants a lighthouse, he added, one that flashes.

Her bust, her breasts. Jack was doing them after an idea he had of a woman's breasts in perfection in his head. By her slim arms, vertical and horizontal, they were enclosed and given a lovely and entirely natural prominence. Day after day, in the early mornings as it grew light and in the late afternoons as it grew dark, Jack was working on the mermaid's breasts with a love and patience that were a wonder to him afterwards. He was glad to have finished with the necessary chisels and the knives. Now he eased the finer and finer sandpapers with oil to induce the wood to become as smooth as skin. Her hair was rough, as it should be, and all of her fishy half, and even her face he was happy to leave like a doll's with broad features, but on her huddled shoulders, her hugging arms, and on her breasts that were like young creatures in a nest or fold, he worked, in the sweet wood, for the perfect smoothness of a human and living form. He was in a trance of work, under the bare bulb, his mug of tea absent-mindedly to hand, the sky outside either lightening or darkening. It put him in mind of the best work ever done by the most gifted boys (surprising themselves) in all his years at school, and of the animals reached out through the wire by the prisoners of war in exchange for a couple of Woodbines or a twist of tea. The memory—the association—filled him with pride.

After such work he came into his own house like a stranger.

There was a big sea. Jack lay awake, listening. He would wake himself early, but not to go looking for wood. His time before Ev woke was for the mermaid. He lay awake in the night, thinking. The sea came nearer. Jack was thinking of the illegits, and of their mother, Stan's daughter, who had stood beside him carelessly in the Folly Field.

Next morning after breakfast Jack climbed into the loft and found the nativity carvings. They were in a shoebox wrapped in brown paper. When he unwrapped them on the dining-room table they gave him a shock, it was years since he had had them out, and when he took the animals and the human figures one by one into his sore hands he felt a joy and a grief that bewildered him. He fitted the baby into the crib, set father and mother at the head, and crowded the shepherds and the ox and the ass around as though their curiosity were greater even than their reverence. The carving was rough, but every figure had its own liveliness, its dignity and an almost comical manifest good nature. Jack was entranced, like a child, he sat at the table staring, reached now and then for the ox or for Joseph or for the mother herself, as though by pressing them in his grip he could get a little way further into the feelings that were troubling him. He felt regret, but also a sort of gladness and gratitude that he was coming nearer to the source of his regret. Then Ev's voice said: What d'you want getting them out for? She startled him, she stood facing him across the table and her face had slipped, he had never seen such a look on her before, she looked momentarily disfigured as though a stroke had halted her and set her oddly in relation to the world. Well? she said. Well? Her voice had gone strange. Jack was balancing Joseph and Mary in either hand. Thought I'd give 'em to the illegits, he said. Thought they'd look nice where there's a

Christmas tree. Ev screamed, once, then again, it was a sound that seemed to have in it nothing at all of personal volition, as though she were ripped. Then she sat at the table and began to weep. Jack put the figures back into the shoebox and the brown paper around it easily resumed its folds. It was paper of a kind no longer ever seen, thick and with an oily texture. Written on it in Ev's big capitals, in purple copy pencil, was the one word NATIVITY. I'll have to get some more string, said Jack.

As he stood up with the box in his hands Ev uncovered her face. And where's my lighthouse? she asked. That would have been nice for Christmas in the corner. It was an ordinary morning in November, a Thursday. Shan't I be going to the post office? said Jack. Don't change the subject, Ev replied. I want my lighthouse. Jack set down the nativity box again, went down the garden to his shed, took up the mermaid in her sacks and carried her thus into the living room. There he unwrapped her on the table, turned on the standard lamp and set her upright on the orange floral chair. I made this instead, he said. Ev stared, said nothing, only stared at the mermaid standing on her fishy tail and smiling foolishly and hugging her breasts as though she were very cold. Ev said: So that's what you've been down there doing. Yes, said Jack. What do you think? Nice, said Ev, very nice. A mermaid will be very unusual. Her voice was quiet, Jack was beginning to smile. So you don't mind then? Stan says he'll get me another log. He tells me Mrs. W's got one left. Mrs. W, eh? said Ev. So that's where you get your pieces of wood from, is it? Just the one, said Jack. But she'll very likely give me another, for your lighthouse.

Very nice, Ev said again. She was standing in the lamplight next to the floral chair on which the mermaid was standing. Only one little thing, she said: Her tits will have to come off. Pardon me? said Jack. Cut 'em off, said Ev. I have my ladies round. They can't be expected to look at things like that. It isn't fit. You'll cut 'em off. Then she'll be very nice. Quite unusual really. Jack was looking at his hands. They were calloused and sore from the work he had done on the mermaid. Ev, he said. Her face was remarkable for its infinite creases and wrinkles, but her hair was newly permed. She was smiling, she seemed on the verge of a sort of hilarity. It wouldn't be natural, said Jack. Who ever saw a mermaid without a bust? That's not the point, said Ev. You'll do as I say. Jack got to his feet. He found that his hands were trembling He took up the mermaid and was wrapping her safely in the potato sacks. Ev said: And don't think I'm having her down there in your shed. She belongs in my front room. I'm having her on show. Jack backed away, hugging his burden.

When he came in again the table was laid for dinner. The nativity box was lying on the hearth empty. The fire was burning very fiercely. Ev set before him the pale-green fish-shaped plate. I've done you a nice piece of sole, she said.

Jack sat in the Folly Field with Stan. He was cold. She wants me to cut her bust off, he said. Hell hath no fury, said Stan. I don't follow, said Jack. I told her it wouldn't look natural, but she's adamant. He did not tell Stan about the nativity figures. He was ashamed. Stan finished his cigarette and tossed it away towards the empty beach. I'll tell you what, he said. Why don't you give her to Mrs. Wilberforce? She's always asking how you're getting on. Jack was tempted, he was very tempted. His heart raced at the proposal. Though he could not be certain that he had ever seen Mrs. Wilberforce, the idea of her, the idea in his head, which came not only when he sat with Stan in the Folly Field, was luminous and detailed. In spirit at least he often sat alongside Stan on the comfortable sofa in her parlour drinking tea and, on the luckiest days, eating one of her buns whilst the winter evening drew in. She lit the lamp, but left the big curtains open to watch the starlings hurtle past on a livid sky. And she might ask Stan would he mind throwing another log on the fire, and there they sat, making conversation without any difficulty, and she was indeed, as Stan had often said, a handsome woman. No doubt about it, the mermaid would look very well in that room. The sea was not so far distant (you could hear it when the wind was right), and the noise the big trees made when there was a wind in them was very like the sea. And didn't the mermaid belong there after all, to make up for the flowering cherry tree which Mrs. W had been so sorry to lose? She'd murder me, he said. She'd never know, said Stan. She would, said Jack. She finds out everything when her ladies come. Pity, said Stan. Would have made a nice present. Jack wondered whether his friend were deceiving him. Perhaps Mrs. Wilberforce never asked after him, perhaps she had never heard he was making a mermaid, perhaps Stan would present it to her one evening as the work of his own hands. Suddenly Jack even doubted whether he had been given any credit for the mushrooms. Stan could be very sly. Jack recalled numerous instances of his slyness in the course of their long friendship. Jack had become very downhearted by the time he said goodbye.

Jack switched the light on and unwrapped the mermaid. She lay on her back, her face as round as the moon, a helpless smile, hugging herself for cold. He was amazed at his achievement; or call it luck, a once in a lifetime abundance of good luck. The way her breasts were was exactly how the idea of them was in his head. He laid his cheek on them, closed his eyes, took into the blood of his heart her scent of oil and wood. Then he left her uncovered on the workbench, under the bare bulb.

Ev was getting the tea ready, a nice salad. Well? she said, chopping a cucumber. What if I made 'em a bit smaller? said Jack.

Ev put a hardboiled egg in the egg slicer. Cut 'em off, she said.

Next day, in the afternoon, Ev had her ladies. Jack took an unusual walk, away from the Folly Field. He walked through the village to the cemetery, and sat there for an hour or so looking out to sea. When it got dark he came home again, though he knew that the ladies would only just be having their tea. He could hear them from the kitchen, they were in the front room and the door was closed, their noise seemed greater than he had ever heard it. Were they more numerous? Had every lady in the Chapel come? He went a little way into the hall. The ladies were in the highest spirits. They beat at one another with their voices. Jack went a little nearer, applied his ear. But nothing very distinct was audible. He bowed himself, he knelt, he applied his eye. He saw his mermaid. She had been brought out of the corner and was standing on her tail in an easy chair. She smiled her smile, without any hope of pleasing. It seemed to Jack that the space within her arms was cavernous. Then she was obscured by a welter of blue and silver and gold. The hairdos of the ladies fitted their heads like shining helmets, their mouths, open for an enormous hilarity, were as red as jam. Jack rose very slowly and out of habit made towards the back door and the garden—but bethought himself and turned and climbed the stairs to bed.

Jack woke in the night, there was a high wind, Ev was snoring by his side, but above that sound he could hear the sound of the sea, the sea had risen, he imagined it foaming white and slung across the bay from point to point. There'll be some wreck, he thought, and did the trick with his head he had learned from Stan. Rose secretly before first light and taking his old coat from the garden shed was soon on the beach along the high-water mark. The tide had turned and was beginning to withdraw, it dragged down the shingle like a death rattle. The weed was a yard high, packed solid. The wind had scarcely lessened and there was rain on it. Jack's small exaltation left him at once. He could see no wood, nor anything else worth picking up. The lights of the railway station and the town looked infinitely beyond his strength, even the seawall was too far, he skidded and stumbled in the weed and on the pebbles. Then it was enough, and he halted. Rolled in weed there was a dead thing at his feet, a seal, and for no good reason he began to tug at the slippery stuff, to free it. He got the head clear and the flippers, then desisted. One eye had gone, the other was beaten in, the head, so shapely on a living beast in water, was monstrous. And all below was dead weight in a stinking winding sheet.

A wet light eastwards over home. Jack stood. In the narrow strip between the shingle and the surf a man and his dog were making their way. Jack moved from the cadaver as though he were guilty. The walker was Councillor Rabbit and his dog, a dachshund, trotted beside him on a lead. Meeting Jack, he cast down his eyes and halted to let him pass. But Jack addressed him. Wet, he said, I'm turning back. Councillor Rabbit was a big man in a trilby, which he had to clutch hold of or the wind would have taken it. He wore a very large herringbone overcoat and polished Oxford shoes. His face, when he allowed Jack to look into it, was as sorrowful as a bloodhound's. It had slipped, it had collapsed. Though Jack had hardly exchanged a word with him in all the years he grasped him now almost familiarly by the elbow and turned him towards home. He did not want the dog to go sniffing at the seal.

Councillor Rabbit was easily led. There was enough room for the two men and the dachshund to walk side by side between the pebbles and the waves. You never let him off? said Jack, nodding down at the adipose dog. Safer the way he is, said the Councillor. Besides, he's going blind. From under the brim of his trilby he was glancing fearfully at Jack. They made their way, exchanging remarks about this and that. What's he called? Jack asked. Billy, said the Councillor. The little dog's belly left a trail on the wet sand. He's not much of a runner, said the Councillor. As they neared the dunes and the wider beach below the Folly Field other dogs and their masters and mistresses appeared. I generally come out early, said the Councillor. You'll maybe want to go ahead. No, no, said Jack. I'm in no hurry. And again he touched the Councillor amicably on the elbow. First came the Minister's wife, Mrs. Blunt, and her alsatian. It was bounding free, in and out of the retreating tide, and others were advancing after her, more or less frolicsome and fierce. The Councillor was inclined to halt, it seemed he might have stared into the dunes until the trade and chapel people had all passed, but Jack with gentle touches to the elbow kept him going. So they shuffled forwards, Jack and Councillor Rabbit and between them, on a tight lead, Billy the little wheezing dog.

ASYLUM

Prison more like, said Madeleine.
Come now, said Mr. Kramer.
If I run away they bring me back, said Madeleine.
Yes but, said Mr. Kramer.

Mr. Kramer often said, Yes but to Madeleine. Something to concede, something to contradict. Now he said again how kind everyone in the Unit was, all his visits never once had he seen any unkindness and couldn't remember ever hearing a voice raised in anger against any girl or boy. So: not really like a prison.

Then why's she sitting there? said Madeleine, nodding toward a nurse in the doorway. The nurse did her best to seem oblivious. She was reading a women's magazine.
    You know very well, said Mr. Kramer.
    So I won't suddenly scratch your face and say you tried to rape me, said Madeleine. So I won't suddenly throw myself out of the window.
    That sort of thing, said Mr. Kramer.

The window was open, but only the regulation few inches, as far as the locks allowed. Mr. Kramer and Madeleine looked at it. She'd get through there, he thought, if she tried. Not that I'd ever get through there, said Madeleine, however hard I tried.

The walls of the room were decorated with images, in paintings and collages, of the themes and infinite variations of body and soul in their distress. A face shattering like a window. A range of mountains, stacked like the hoods of the Klan, blocking most of the sky, but from the foreground, in a red zigzag, into them went a path, climbing, and disappeared. Mr. Kramer liked the room. Waiting for Madeleine, or whoever it might be, he stood at the window looking down at a grassy bank that in its seasons, year after year, with very little nurture or encouragement, brought forth out of itself an abundance of ordinary beautiful flowers. At this point in his acquaintance with Madeleine it was the turn of primroses. The air coming in was mild. Behind the bank ran the wall of the ancient enclosure.

Asylum, said Mr. Kramer. What is an asylum?

A place they lock nutters up, said Madeleine.

Well yes, said Mr. Kramer, but why call it an asylum?

Because they're liars, said Madeleine.

All right, said Mr. Kramer. Forget the nutters, as you call them, and the place they get looked after or locked up in, and tell me what you think an asylum-seeker is.

Someone from somewhere bad.

And when they come to the United Kingdom, say, or to France, Germany or Italy, what are they looking for?

Somewhere better than where they've come from.

What are they seeking?

Asylum.

And what is asylum?

Sanctuary.

Sanctuary, said Mr. Kramer. That's a very good word. Those poor people come here seeking sanctuary in a land of prisons.

An asylum, he said, is a refuge, a shelter, a safe haven. Lunatic asylums, as they used to be called, are places where people disordered in their souls can be housed safely and looked after.

Locked up, said Madeleine. Ward 16, they took Sam there last week.

So he'd be safer, said Mr. Kramer. I'm sure of that.

Madeleine shrugged.

Okay, said Mr. Kramer. A bit like a prison, I grant you. Sometimes it has to be a bit like a prison, but always for the best. Not like detention, internment, real prison, nothing like that.

Madeleine shrugged.

Mr. Kramer's spirits lapsed. He forgot where he was and why. His spirits lapsed or the sadness in him rose. Either way he began to be occluded. An absence. When he returned he saw that Madeleine was looking at him. Being looked at by Madeleine was like being looked at by the moon. The light seemed to come off her face as though reflected from some faraway source. Her look was fearful, but rather as though she feared she had harmed Mr. Kramer. Rema says Hi, she said. Rema said say Hi from me to Mr. Kramer.

They both brightened.

Thank you, Madeleine, said Mr. Kramer. Please give her my best regards next time you speak to her. How is she?

Can't tell with her, said Madeleine. She's such a liar. She says she's down to four and a half stone. Her hair's falling out, she says, from the starvation. She says she eats a few bean sprouts a day and that is all. And drinks half a glass of water. But she's a liar. It's only so I'll look fat. She phones and phones. She wants to get back in here. But Dr. Khan says she won't get back in here by starving herself. That's blackmail, he says. She might, however, if she puts on weight. Show willing, he says, show you want to get better. Then we'll see. She says if they won't let her back she'll kill herself. Thing is, if she gets well enough to come back here, she thinks they'll send her home. Soon as she's sixteen they'll send her home, her aunty says. But Rema says she'll kill herself twenty times before she'll go back home.

Home's not a war zone, if I remember rightly, said Mr. Kramer.

Her family is, said Madeleine. They are why she is the way she is. So quite understandably she'll end it all before she'll go back there.

Rema told me a lovely story once, said Mr. Kramer.

Did she write it?

No, she never wrote it. She promised she would but she never did.

Typical, said Madeleine.

Yes, said Mr. Kramer. But really it wasn't so much a story as a place for one. She remembered a house near her village. The house was all shuttered up, it had a paved courtyard with a sort of shrine in the middle and white jasmine growing wild over the balconies and the wooden stairs.

Oh that, said Madeleine. It was an old woman's and she wanted to do the hajj and her neighbours lent her the money and the deal was they could keep her house if she didn't come back and she never came back. That story.

Yes, said Mr. Kramer, that story. I thought it very beautiful, the deserted house, I mean, the courtyard and the shrine.

Probably she made it up, said Madeleine. Probably there never was such a house. And anyway she never wrote it.

Mr. Kramer felt he was losing the encounter. He glanced at the clock. I thought Rema was your friend, he said.

She is, said Madeleine. I don't love anyone as much as I love her. But all the same she's a terrible liar. And mostly to get at me. Four and a half stone! What kind of a stupid lie is that? Did she tell you she wanted to do the hajj?

She did, said Mr. Kramer. Her owl eyes widening and taking in more light, passionately she had told him she longed to do the hajj.

So why is she starving herself? It doesn't make sense.

I told her, said Mr. Kramer. I said you have to be very strong for a thing like that. However you travel, a pilgrimage is a hard experience. You have to be fit.

Such a liar, said Madeleine.

Anyway, said Mr. Kramer. You'll write your story for next time. About an asylum-seeker, a boy, you said, a boy half your age.

I will, said Madeleine. Where's the worst place in the world? Apart from here of course.

Hard to say, said Mr. Kramer. There'd be quite a competition. But Somalia would take some beating.

I read there are pirates in Somalia.

Off the coast there are. They steal the food the rich people send and the people who need it starve.

Good, said Madeleine. I'll have pirates in my story.

Madeleine and Mr. Kramer faced each other in silence across the table. The nurse had closed her magazine and was watching them. Mr. Kramer was thinking that from many points of view the project was a bad one. Madeleine had wanted to write about being Madeleine. Fine, he said, but displace it. Find an image like one of those on the wall. I have, she said. My image is a war zone. My story is about a child in a war zone, a boy half my age, who wants to get out to somewhere safe. Asylum, said Mr. Kramer. He seeks asylum.

Tell me, Madeleine, said Mr. Kramer. Tell me in a word before I go what feeling you know most about and what feeling the little boy will inhabit in your story.

The sleeves of Madeleine's top had ridden up so that the cuts across her wrists were visible. Seeing them looked at sorrowfully by Mr. Kramer she pulled the sleeves down and gripped the end of each very tightly into either palm.

Fear, she said.

Mr. Kramer might have taken the bus home. There was a stop not far from Bartlemas where that extraordinary enclosure, its orchard, its gardens, the grassy humps of the ancient hospital, touched modernity on the east-west road. He could have ridden to his house from there, almost door-to-door, in twenty minutes. Instead, if the weather was at all decent and some days even if it wasn't he walked home through the parks and allotments, a good long march, an hour and a half or more. That way it was late afternoon before he got in, almost time to be thinking about the cooking of his supper. Then came the evening, for which he always had a plan: a serious television program, some serious reading, his notes, early to bed.

On his walk that mild spring afternoon Mr. Kramer thought about Madeleine and Rema. It distressed him that Madeleine was so scathing about Rema's story. How cruel they were to one another in their lethal competition! For him the abandoned house had a peculiar power. Rema said it was very quiet there, as soon as you pushed open the wooden gates, no shouting, no dogs, no noise of any traffic. The courtyard was paved with coloured tiles in a complicated pattern whose many intersecting arcs and loops she had puzzled over and tried to follow. The shrine was surely left over from before Partition, it must be a Hindu shrine, the Muslim woman had no use for it. But there it stood in the centre of the courtyard, a carved figure on a pedestal and a place for flowers, candles and offerings, and around it on all four sides the shuttered windows, the balcony, the superabundance of white jasmine. The old woman never came back, said Rema. It was not even known whether she ever reached Mecca, the place of her heart's desire. So the neighbours kept the house but none had any real use for it. Sometimes their cattle strayed into the courtyard. And there also, when she dared, climbing the wooden stairs and viewing the shrine from the cool and scented balconies, went the child Rema, for sanctuary from the war zone of her home.

Mr. Kramer was watching a program about the bombings, when the phone rang. Such a program, after the cooking and the eating and the allowance of three glasses of wine, was a station on his way to bed. But the phone rang. It was Maria, his daughter, from the Ukraine, already midnight, phoning to tell him she had found the very *shtetl*, the names, the place itself. He caught her tone of voice, the one of all still in the world he was least proof against. He hardly heard the words, only the voice, its peculiar quality. Forest, memorial, the names, he knew what she was saying, but sharper than the words, nearer, flesh of his flesh, he felt the voice that was having to say these things, in a hotel room, three hours ahead, on a savage pilgrimage. The forest, the past, the small voice from so far away, he felt her to be in mortal danger, he felt he must pull her back from where she stood, leaning over the abyss of history, the pit, the extinction of all personal relations. Sweetheart, said Mr. Kramer, my darling girl, go to sleep now if you can. And I've been thinking. Once you're back I'll come and stay with you. After all I cannot bear it on my own. But sleep now if you can.

Mr. Kramer had not intended to say any such thing. He had set himself the year at least. One year. Surely a man could watch alone in grief that long.

The Unit phoned. Madeleine had taken an overdose, she was in hospital, back in a day or so. Mr. Kramer, about to set off, did the walk anyway, it was a fine spring day, the beech trees leafing softly. He walked right to the gates of Bartlemas, turned and set off home again, making a detour to employ the time he would have spent with Madeleine.

In the evening, last thing, Mr. Kramer read his old notes, a weakness he always tried to make up for by at once writing something new. He read for ten minutes, till he hit the words: Rema, her desire to be an owl. Then he leafed forward quickly to the day's blank page and wrote: I haven't thought nearly enough about Rema's desire to be an owl. She said, Do you think I already look like one? I went to the office and asked did we have a mirror. We do, under lock and key. It is a lovely thing, face-shaped and just the size of a face, without a frame, the bare reflecting glass. I held it up for Rema. Describe your face, I said. Describe it exactly. I was a mite ashamed of the licence this exercise gave me to contemplate a girl's face whilst she, looking at herself, never glancing at me, studied it as a thing to be described. Yes, her nose, quite a thin bony line, might become a beak. Pity to lose the lips. But if you joined the arcs of the brows with the arcs of shadow below the eyes, so accentuating the sockets, yes you might make the widening stare of an owl. The longing for metamorphosis. To become something else, a quite different creature, winged, feathered, intent. Like Madeleine's, Rema's face shows the bones. The softness of feathers would perhaps be a comfort. I wonder did she tell Madeleine about the mirror. Shards, the harming.

The Unit phoned, Madeleine was well enough, just about. Mr. Kramer stood at the window. The primroses were already finishing. But there would be something else, on and on till the autumn cyclamens. It was a marvellous bank. Then Madeleine and the overweight nurse stood in the doorway, the nurse holding her women's magazine. Madeleine wore loose trousers and a collarless shirt whose sleeves were far too long. She stood; and towards Mr. Kramer, fearfully and defiantly, she presented her face and neck, which she had cut. Oh Maddy, said Mr. Kramer, can't you ever be merciful? Will you never show yourself any mercy?

The nurse sat in the open doorway and read her magazine. Madeleine and Mr. Kramer faced each other across the small table. All the same, said Madeleine through her lattice of black cuts, I've made a start. Shall I read it? Yes, said Mr. Kramer. Madeleine read:

Samuel lived with his mother. The soldiers had killed his father. Some of the soldiers were only little boys. Samuel and his mother hid in the forest. Every day she had to leave him for several hours to go and look for food and water. He waited in fear that she would not come back. There was nothing to do. He curled up in the little shelter, waiting. One day Samuel's mother did not come back. He waited all night and all the next day and all the next night. Then he decided he must go and look for her or for some food and water at least because the emergency supplies she had left him were all gone. He followed the trail his mother had made day after day. It came to a road. She had told him that the road was very dangerous. But beyond the road were fields and in them, if you were lucky, you might find some things to eat that the farmers had planted before the soldiers came and burned their village. Samuel halted at the road. It was long and straight in both directions and very dusty. A little way off he saw a truck burning and another truck upside down in the ditch. But there were no soldiers. Samuel hurried across. Quite soon, just as his mother had said, he saw women and girls in blue and white clothes moving slowly over the land looking for food. Perhaps his mother would be among them after all? At the very least, somebody would surely give him food and water.

Madeleine lifted her face. That's as far as I got, she said. It's crap, isn't it? No, said Mr. Kramer, it is very good. Crap, said Madeleine. Tell me, Madeleine, said Mr. Kramer, did you write this before or after you did that to your face? After, said Madeleine. I wrote it this morning. I did my face two nights ago, after they brought me back here from the hospital.

Good, said Mr. Kramer. That's a very good thing. It means you can sympathize with other people's lives even when your own distresses you so much you cut your face. I know the rest, said Madeleine with a sudden eagerness. I know how it goes on and how it ends. Shall I tell you?—Will you still be able to write it if you tell?—Yes, yes.—You promise?—Yes, I promise.—Tell then.

She laid her sleeves, in which her hands were hiding, flat on the table and began to speak, rapidly, staring into his eyes, transfixing him with the eagerness of her fiction.

In among the people looking for food he meets a girl. She's my age. Her name is Ruth. The soldiers have killed her father too. Ruth's mother hid with her and when the soldiers came looking she made Ruth stay in hiding and gave herself up to them. That was the end of her. But Ruth was taken by the other women and hid with them and went looking for food when it was safe. When Samuel came into the fields Ruth decided to look after him. She was like a sister to Samuel, a good big sister, or a mother, a good and loving mother. When it was safe to light a fire she cooked for him, the best meal she could. After a while the soldiers came back again, the fields were too dangerous, all the women hid in the forest but Ruth had heard that if you could only get to the coast you could maybe find someone with a boat who would carry you across the sea to Italy and the European Union, where it was really safe. So that's what she did, with Samuel, she set off for the coast, only travelling at night, on foot, by moonlight and starlight, steering clear of the villages in flames.

Sounds good, said Mr. Kramer. Sounds very exciting. All you have to do now is write it. You've looked at a map, I suppose? The nearest coast is no use at all. That's where the pirates are. You need the north coast really, through the desert. And crossing the desert is said to be a terrible thing.

You have to pay truckers to take you, I believe. Yes, said Madeleine, I thought she'd do better on the east coast, with the pirates. A pirate chief says he'll take her and Samuel all the way to Libya but it will cost her a lot of money. When she says she has no money he says she can marry him, for payment that is, until they get to Libya, then he'll sell her to a friend of his, who will take her and Samuel into the European Union, which is like the Promised Land, he says, and there she will be safe, but she'll have to marry his friend as well, for the voyage from Libya into Italy. I asked Rema would she do it and she said she wouldn't, she couldn't, because of the things at home, but she said I could, Ruth in my story should, it would save the two of them, they would have a new life in the European Union and God would mercifully forgive her the sin. She says Hi, by the way. She asked me to ask you are you all right. She said it seemed to her you were a bit lonely sometimes. Thank you, said Mr. Kramer, I'm fine. And guess what, said Madeleine, she doesn't want to do the hajj any more, not till she's an old woman, and she doesn't want to make Dr. Khan have her back here either. No, she's decided she'll be a primary school teacher. Plus she's down to four stone. So it's all lies as usual.

A primary school teacher is a very good idea, said Mr. Kramer. But of course you have to be strong for that. As strong as for a pilgrimage.

I told her that, said Madeleine. So she's still a liar. Anyway, another thing about Ruth is that when she's with the first pirate, as his prostitute, all the way up the Red Sea he sends her ashore to the markets—Samuel he keeps on board as a hostage—and she has to go and buy all the ingredients for his favourite meals, I've researched it, baby okra and lamb in tomato stew, for example, onion pancakes, fish and peppers, shoelace pastry, spicy creamy cheeses, all delicious, up the coast to Suez. So she makes her Lord and Master happy and Samuel gets strong.

Will they stay in Italy, Mr. Kramer asked, if the second pirate keeps his word and carries her across the Mediterranean? No, said Madeleine, breathless on her story, they're heading for Swansea. There's quite an old Somali community in Swansea. I've researched it. They've been there a hundred years. At first she'll live in a hostel, doing the cooking for everybody so that everybody likes her. Samuel goes to school and as soon as he's settled Ruth will go to the CFE and get some qualifications.

Madeleine, said Mr. Kramer, it's very hard to enter the United Kingdom. Ruth and Samuel will need passports. I've thought of that, said Madeleine. The first pirate chief has a locker full of passports from people who died on his boat and because Ruth is such a good cook he gives her a couple and swears they'll get her and Samuel through Immigration, no problem.

Rema should go to the CFE, said Mr. Kramer. I believe the Home Office would extend her visa if she was in full-time education. And if she trained as a primary school teacher, who knows what might happen?

She's a liar, said Madeleine, very white, almost translucent her face through the savage ornamentation of her cuts. She's supposed to be my friend. If she was really my friend she'd come back here. Then we'd both be all right like we were before she left me.

You want to stay here?

Yes, said Madeleine. It's safer here.

Why overdose? Why cut yourself?

The nurse was watching and listening.

Because I'm frightened.

My daughter was frightened, said Mr. Kramer, and she's twice your age. All the time her mother was ill, four and a half years, she got more and more frightened. And now she's gone to the Ukraine, would you believe it, all on her own and not speaking the language, to research our family history. She phoned me the other night from the place itself, a terrible place, I never want to go there, all on her own, at midnight, in a hotel. Write your story, won't you? You promised me. Somalia is very likely the worst place in the world and Swansea is a very good place, by all accounts. What an achievement it will be if you can get Ruth and Samuel safely there!

Madeleine's white hands with their bitten nails still hid in her sleeves. All the animation had gone out of her. I'll never get to Swansea from Somalia, she said. Never, never, never. I can't even want to get out of here.

First the story, Madeleine, said Mr. Kramer. First comes the fiction. Get Ruth and Samuel out of the killing fields, get them by the cruelty and kindness of pirates into a holding camp on the heel of Italy, get them north among strangers, not speaking a word of the language—devise it, work out the necessary means. You promised. Who knows what might happen if you get that lucky pair to Swansea?

WISHING WELL

Happiness. Some lines came back to him: 'What are we? Beings of a day / Shadows of a dream. But when / The light, god-given, the light / When that comes / Brightness is on us, brightness / And life is lovely.' And so it was: light coming, alighting, playing over all, but over the two of them in particular, like tongues. Well-being—in which he was aware of the passing away of trouble and tension, so that although light had indeed come over him, it was also like passing out of a sunlight that had been too brilliant into a grateful shade and suddenly feeling, under a dappling coverlet of leaves, a release and a relief, so that the features knew, with a shock, how tense and strained they had been and for too long. Lightness of spirit.

He looked about him. Rhos in summer is a busy place, busy and ordinary, and everything he looked at pleased him, especially the little harbour which had not made any effort to keep up with the world. He liked that. And that they were strangers here and he could sit with her at a table in the public view and take her hand when he pleased and they could stroll along.

She watched his enjoyment. He was quite transparent. She saw quite clearly what it felt like in him as his feelings climbed and held and he looked about him, pleased. He saw her watching. He knew that her own enjoyment at that moment consisted mostly in being amused by the sight of him. But he was not downcast and felt he could carry her away with him on his feelings, just as soon as he wished.

There's a lot you don't know about me, she said.

He was grateful for this topic into which he could direct his happiness. He answered that he was glad, they were at the beginning, it was an outset, he loved outsets, he would learn and learn and the more there still was to know about her, the better.

When I fell in love with you, she said, it grieved me that there were so many years of your life before my time, that I could never belong to and I could only learn about if I asked you and you told me.

Telling is good, he said. For both of us. When I tell you things you didn't know, I feel I hardly knew them myself before I told you. It's as though they are only becoming clear to me now, in the light of you.

And then—because of course this was at the heart of his happiness, this was lighting up the ordinary seaside town, lightening his spirits, relaxing the strain that for so long had tensed his features—then he couldn't hold back and he said: And after tonight, after we've slept together, it won't grieve you any more, once we know each other like that the rest won't trouble you, you'll see it the way I see it now, life for the asking, more and more, nowhere refused.

She looked at him wonderingly. Such innocence. He seemed to walk on faith without fear of disappointment. The very spectacle of him made her fearful. How was any mortal supposed to live up to a part in that? Then she thought him not innocent but, for all his intelligence, obtuse; and beginning to say, I hope you won't be disappointed, she felt almost a wish that he should be, that he should grow up, and she halted the sentence, shaking her head. And perhaps he was right. Certainly she had no more worries about the place. The place they had decided on was certainly right, she was on firm ground where she had feared she might sink in. That was one good stepping stone, she would believe him, the other stones would be there, step by step.

She stood up. I'll go and pay, she said. When she came out again she saw a hesitancy in his manner, as though in the brief absence her lingering anxiety had touched him. She took him by the hand. The well, she said. I have to show you the well. I have to begin showing you and telling you. Today's the day and tonight is the night.

Coming back is risky. He was glad to be a stranger there, with no memories. Soon she let go of his hand and walked apart, wholly given up to an anxious looking. This wasn't here then, she muttered. The sea came right in. To him the wall, the railing, the further defences were unexceptionable. But she said crossly, as though he were to blame, It was a shore, the sea came right up. There were floods, he said. You told me about them. They had to build a wall. Yes, yes, she said, they had to. Don't they always have to?

They had walked too far. She was wringing her hands, almost in tears. Don't say it's gone. Nobody would do a thing like that. Chapel and well. Nobody would raze a chapel and fill in a well. She turned and walked back, hurrying away from him. It's here, he said. He had to shout after her. She had hurried on. How lovely. He was leaning over the railing, looking down. The tiny humped chapel, squat and solid, crouched under the wall, out of sight of the road, like a shell, like something that would have housed a naked hermit crab. Between it and high tide ran a bulwark of quarry stones.

But it was on the beach, she said. Just above high water. Not protected at all. Why does everything have to be protected? Once or twice the sea came in. I know that. And my father told me he had read of other occasions. Seaweed on the flagstones, salt water on the fresh under the altar. But they cleaned it out. The sea went away again. The freshwater well renewed itself. Stink of salt and weed in that thick shell for months. Like being in a sea cave. But it freshened again, the sun came in, a breeze, people brought wildflowers. Why put a wall around it? He shrugged. Things are getting worse, he said. You know that. The floods further up the coast were terrible.

Slowly she was reconciled. She took his hand again. Come and see, she said, come down. I'm so happy that we are here together and I can show you the well.

Temenos, a little precinct—which he liked. She clung to her picture of a sacred house on the beach, just above high water, but conceded that the enclosure was decent. Inside, the memory took her by the throat, seized her around the heart with a hand of ice, the hairs on her neck stood up 'in holy dread.' One window by the altar, another in the north wall broadside on to the sea, a saint in each. An utter simplicity. It was a cave, a shell, the carapace of a spirit, furnished humanly with a table and a few chairs, not asking to be thought beautiful. The thick walls, rough as the hands that had fitted them, enclosed a presence of—of what, exactly? Human impress, people at their most serious, their most given up and most wishful. She went on her knees and pulled him down by her, not at the altar—which she disregarded—but at the well beneath the stone roof that the altar made. A square of clear water, as though a flagstone had been removed and there was the water, quietly arrived and waiting. She dipped in her hands, raised them up to his mouth. Drink, she said, drink and wish hard. He did as she asked, all the water, he lapped at her wet palms, drank and loved her and wished hard, looking into her eyes over the bowl of her hands. He had never seen her so sure and demanding. Now me, she said. Offer me. So he did, raised up some water in his cupped hands to her mouth. She drank, wished hard, looked him hard in the eyes.

Then she stood up, as abruptly as she had from their café table, and took him to the window that looked out towards the sea. The window was thin and the saint himself, in the coloured glass, rather blocked the view. But it was not so much a matter of looking and seeing, more of listening, of her murmuring and his listening.

We played down there, she said. You and your friend? What was she called, your friend? She was called Awen. A name like yours, he said. We were very like, she said. We came after school when the evenings were long and at weekends summer and winter when we chose. Nobody minded in those days. She was from here, I was an incomer, but I learned her language at school and together we never spoke anything else. Except we had our own speech too. Speech within a speech, foreign and secret. We used that sometimes, for the things which mattered most. When we found anything especially pretty we brought it in here, splashed it from the well, and laid it on the altar. A flower you mean? Or a shell? A shell, a flower, a starfish, a bit of whitened wood, anything pretty or especially strange. We wetted it and laid it on the altar under that saint's window. Nobody minded in those days. And if we found any creature that had died we brought that in too, splashed it and buried it outside, close under the western wall, and made a little mound of stones. An oiled-up seagull, a fish, even a crab or a rat, anything that had lived the way humans live and was dead. We looked out for such things as keenly as for pretty things fit to go on the table top. And always we drank, lifting our hands to one another, just as you and I have done now. And every time we drank we looked each other in the eyes and made a wish. There's a lot you don't know about me, and one thing is this: that I am afraid my friend Awen is dying. Do you have a pen? Do you have a scrap of paper? I didn't think I would do this but now I feel I must.

He carried a pencil. It fitted into the spine of a handy blue notebook. He tore out a page, handed her the pencil, she used the altar as a desk and wrote: Please wish for my dear friend

Awen who is very ill. She folded the note and slotted it in among others in a sort of lattice on the south wall.

Now come out, she said. I want to show you the sea properly, not through a narrow window. But as soon as they were out and had climbed over the rampart of new rocks and had broached the empty sands, she halted, turned to him and alarmed him by her helpless agitation. What is it? he asked. Oh, I should have written it in Welsh, she answered. But more people will understand it in English. But it's closer to her in Welsh. And it may work better. Do it then. And he handed her the notebook with the pencil fitted in. Can I even? Do I even know the words any more? Try. She closed her eyes, faced him, waited. Then said in a rush: *Gwnewch ddymuniad i Awen wella—mae hi'n sâl iawn.* Good, he said. Now go back and write it.

It seemed he waited quite some time. When she came out of the chapel she was barefoot, carrying her shoes. So he took his off also, stuffed the socks into them, laced them together, watched her cross the rocks. Your notebook is full of things, she said. So much I don't know. Then she took his hand and led him—so it felt—out where the sea must be.

I came out here with my father once, she said, with Awen, he walked between us, holding our hands. He didn't speak Welsh, though he knew many of the words because of his studies in local history. It was strange to be with Awen speaking English. My father asked her questions. I could tell that he liked the way she talked. She was very pretty. You would have liked her too. My father had read that before they built the chapel on the beach they built one out on the flats in what was then a forest. He asked Awen was it true. She said she believed it was. My father wanted to see evidence of the forest, if not of the chapel, and on that afternoon when, according to his chart, the tides were exceptionally big, he took us out, the two of us, to have a look. We walked and walked, like now, the sea was quite invisible. We were the only people out. I don't think he should have taken us there, do you? But he consulted his watch very often and kept an eye on the horizon, where the sea must be. And at last we did come to the forest, the stumps and traces of it, a sort of herd, emergent or disappearing, over a vast area of sand, as I remember now. We shan't go so far today. I'm not sure of the tide. But another day when the tides are very big we'll work it out exactly and I'll take you to where you can see the stumps of that great forest, if they are still to be seen. The sand moves, you know. It covers and uncovers. But the tide comes in very fast. Faster than a man can run, so my father said. He told us that out there in that vast graveyard of a forest. I don't think he should have told us that, do you? He told Awen particularly. I didn't like him doing that. So if there really was a forest, he said, perhaps there really was a chapel too, with its own well, of course, like the one on the beach. But we'd never find it, he said, not in a hundred years and we looked every day. Stones under the sand, a mouth of fresh water stopped up under the sand. My father! There was still no sign of the sea. You could almost believe it had withdrawn for good. But my father said we must go home. By his calculations we were still entirely safe, but we must go back in and not linger.

When we turned, then I was frightened. The shore looked to be infinitely far away. I couldn't make out the chapel at all. The distance looked to be quite beyond my strength. But Awen seemed unconcerned. She laughed and looked up at my father and he held her hand very tightly and said nothing to worry about we'd be safe home in no time. My hand he held tightly too, but I felt he hadn't even noticed how frightened I was because he and Awen were being so jolly together. We were the only people out there, the only upright things in all that flat space. You'd think with your own father if he said nothing to worry about, you'd believe him, wouldn't you? But I kept looking back, to see if the sea was coming after us, faster than a man could run.

My father said the chapel out here was the first building and the chapel on the beach just above high water was
the second. And the third, he said, was a proper church, at
Llandrillo, about a mile inland, on a rocky hill, quite safe
from the sea. I knew about that church already. Awen had
told me. And I knew something else as well, that she had told
me. And suddenly out here on the sands, in English, she told
my father the thing I thought was a secret between her and
me: that a tunnel went from the church on the hill to the
chapel on the beach, an escape way to Ireland, when the old
believers were in danger from the new. I heard her tell him
that in English when I had kept it secret even though he was
my own father and I knew how much it would have interested him. And indeed he was very interested. He stopped
dead in his tracks out here on the sands and said, Goodness
me, what a thing! We must find it, this tunnel, you must
take me and show me where you think it is. We have found
the forest together, and we believe there was once a chapel
in that forest, and now you tell me there's a secret tunnel
from the chapel on the beach to the church on the hill, so
certainly we must go and find that together. I was hurt by
Awen. Across him, I said to her in Welsh, You shouldn't have
told him that. It was our secret. Why did you tell him that?
But all she answered was, Will if I like. And we set off again,
him between us, and I couldn't get over it and hoped the sea
would come at a lick and drown us all.

Then there was worse. Much worse. My father was very
interested in wells and had visited a number of them along the
coast and inland. It's true this area is especially rich in wells.
Wishing wells, he said, I'm a great lover of wishing wells. And
then Awen said, Wishing wells are one thing. But I know a
cursing well. That was the worst. Never in my life, before or
since, have I hated anyone as much as I hated my friend Awen
when she said in English to my father that she knew a cursing
well. The tunnel was one secret. We hadn't been able to find

any likely flagstone in the floor of the chapel, nor any suggestion of an entrance behind its south wall above high water, but
we were planning to make a thorough search at Llandrillo,
both in the church itself and in the graveyard around. We had
hidden torches and a special notebook up there ready, in a
grave whose lid was loose, under an elder bush at the bottom
of the slope. When she told my father, all the fun went out of
that. But the well, the cursing well, was the secret of secrets.
We only ever spoke of it in our tongue within the tongue,
our speech that nobody on the planet understood but us. And
there she was, in broad daylight, in everyday English, ready
to tell my father what she knew. Don't tell him, I said, in
the secret tongue. Even in Welsh he would not have understood, but I said it in the secret tongue, to impress on her the
seriousness of the matter. But she smiled me a bad smile and
grinned up at him and answered me in English just the two
words: Why not? The well was on her farm, she told him,
at Llanelian-yn-Rhos, under hazels, holly and alders, where
the stream started, at the bottom of the steep field, and it was
the most famous cursing well in Wales, or had been until the
Bishop forbade it and smashed the lovely stone bowl of it a
hundred years ago. Now hardly anyone knew of that well
and nobody who came looking on his own would ever find
it, it was on private land, her land, and hidden away, but she
would show him, my father, whenever he liked, since he was
so interested in wells.

She stopped. We've come out too far, she said. We must
go back in. I don't know about the tides. I believe we are
nearly out where the forest was. The sea is so fast when it
turns and starts to come in. He was not so bothered, not
about the sea. Did he not believe that tide-flow came faster
than a man could run? Perhaps he did, but he was sunk in
her, how travailed she was, how girlish and much older than
a girl, how it was welling up in her through the deposits

of the years, through her eyes and through her mouth. He
was beginning to see what love would be like, with her. So
he stood, looking neither out to where the sea must arrive
from, nor in towards the chapel where they must return,
but only at her, at her face, at her standing disconsolate on
the flat infinity of wet sand, holding her sandals, wide-eyed
and as if in shadow in all the sunlight. I'm frightened, she
said. I'm frightened out here. I'm all alone, you know. Some
days it's like a black cloud around me, head and shoulders.
You are going to have to look after me. Come in now, let's
go and find the place where we will stay tonight. There's
more, you know, about the cursing well. Above it the air is
peculiarly healthful, they say, because the airs that come in
off the sea meet there with those that live over the land. And
there's more about what we did at the cursing well together,
Awen and I, raising the water to one another's lips, the way
you and I did at the wishing well. Much more. And what I
did there and said there and wished there on my own one
day, on her private land, unbeknown to her, in that deep
hollow out of sight. There's a lot you don't know about me.
Come back with me now quickly. There are things I can't
say in the daylight, but I will say them in the dark when we
have slept together.

UNDER THE DAM

1

Their first home was under the viaduct. Seth found it. His train slowed and halted, waiting for clearance into the station, and he looked down on the rows, the smoking chimneys, the back alleys, and imagined being down there looking up at a train strung out along the arches in the sky. Next day he went in among the little houses and soon found one to buy for less than it would be to rent a room in nicer places. He fetched Carrie at once, as though this opportunity were a glimpse into the heavens and might at any moment close. The back bedroom had a pretty tiled hearth but Seth was at the window craning up. The arches climbed higher than he could see, the track lay on an upper horizon out of sight. Okay, said Carrie, in a loving wonder at this renewal of his eagerness. A train crawled heavily over and away. The house trembled.

Now began a good time for both of them; different for each, but equal in its fullness. They would look back on it, separately, and marvel: that was us then! The house was solid; or if it wasn't, they never worried. The sashes rattled under the heavy trains, once a slate came loose and slithered down; but they only laughed, Seth with a kind of satisfaction. The house was never light, not with daylight, at least—how could it be? But they made it cheerful with lamps, candles, coal fires, bright paint, and with lovely things they had collected on their travels.

Carrie advertised, and got two or three pupils for the fiddle or the guitar. They came to her and played or listened in the front room, always lit and scented, under the viaduct. When a train passed overhead, they paused and smiled. Seth kept on his job at the art school, only a few hours but just about enough. In his free time he did his own work, still trying for a true style, he said, but with some hope that, if he trusted, he would feel his way. He worked, and looked about him with a lively interest, to see how the things were that he must try to answer.

Under the arches, where the little streets ended, were strange dens and businesses. Seth and Carrie had a scrap man for a neighbour. He lived behind a wall of old doors, corrugated iron and barbed wire. He was black as coal, except for a grizzly head of hair the colour of ash. He had lost the power of speech. His clients were humped old men pushing bicycles and handcarts. They brought him rolls of lead and lengths of copper piping snapped like the limbs of insects, stuff ripped out of a vacancy before the Council came to board it up. Seth sketched them from his window as they passed. They were like gleaners on the slag heaps. When Carrie bought a big brass bed and several knobs were missing, Jonah hunted out the exact replacements from a drawer. When she asked what she owed him he raised his arms and tucked down his head, to mime a fiddler. She fetched her fiddle and played him a jig. He capered like a bear, on and on, until she feared for him and paused. Then the energy left him, he slouched off into his shack. Carrie glimpsed his Primus stove and mattress. Seth marvelled. The man lay smack under the tracks!

They were mostly old people under the viaduct, or who
looked old. The young left if they could. The Council
accommodated difficult cases there; and one or two incomers, like Seth and Carrie, lodged or settled by choice. A pub
had survived very easily, a couple of corner shops by dint of
bitter struggle. Carrie soon got the feeling that they were
welcome. Their outlandishness was engaging. She felt people look at her and Seth with a sort of hope. Seth did a sketch
of the landlord's little girl, for her birthday. Then one or
two others asked him. He did it quickly, for free. They marvelled, and forcibly he had to quell in himself a rising pride.
Likeness, however exact, was not enough. He saw the hands
of the old miners, the broken nails, the blue–black fragments
of the job inhering under the skin like shrapnel; he saw the
flaky cast, like talcum powder, over their puffy faces. Then
he knew his uselessness and averted his eyes.

Seth did some research on the subject of the viaduct. He
learned the weight it was built to bear, and the weight that
nowadays it must. He gazed up, wondering at the difference.
All those blackened bricks, arches like a Norman cathedral, the
iron road, the thousands of oblivious people travelling north
and south. In the pub he edged the talk towards catastrophes.
There was one in 1912, coal trucks, the last two in a long line
somehow derailed and hanging over the parapet, emptying.
Street next to yours, somebody said. Coal through the roof,
coal on the bed. Then the iron. The Company rebuilt the
houses, paid for the funerals, let them keep the coal. Seth
wanted more. He had read of a suicide, a man dangling from
the parapet on a rope, discovered in daylight, a crowd of cit-
izens gazing up. All night there, trembling under the trains,
tolling in the breeze. Carrie watched his face becoming helpless under the pull of his wish to know. She tried to cover
for him, to veil an indecency. She feared for him. But that
night, thrusting a poker into the congealed coals and letting
the flames out, their warmth and dancing light, he said in the

story of the derailment it was the richness that overwhelmed him, the too-sudden, too-abundant giving of the fuel of life. She pulled a face, shook her head. Then he said: We'll get an allotment, they're dirt cheap, we'll grow what we like.

The streets, yards, rooms were not entirely dark. In summer the morning sun slanted in very beautifully; in fact, like a peculiar gift and grace. There were early mornings of nearly unbearable illumination: sunlight through the rising smoke, a blood-redness being revealed in the substance of the arches, through a century of soot. But the allotments, higher up the dip the houses were gathered in, enjoyed an ample and more ordinary helping of daylight. Seth was given a plot on the slope facing the railway embankment, just below a ruined chapel and a few wrecked graves, just before the viaduct began its stepping over the sunken town. There was an attempt at terracing, almost Mediterranean, he said. He went up there whenever he could and Carrie joined him. He watched for her climbing the path from the houses into the allotments among the sheds and little fences. She brought a flask and a snack. Then they worked side by side. Palpable happiness, real as the heavy earth, as the tools in their hands, as the produce. So it was. She said to herself: Nothing will obliterate this.

One of Carrie's pupils was a boy of seventeen or so. He was called Benjamin and had no home to speak of. He came to their house under the viaduct, said he wanted to learn the guitar, but had no money. Could he do odd jobs for them instead? Carrie said yes. He spoke a thick vernacular. He had black eyes that seemed to be seeing things he hadn't the words to utter. Seth saw how it would be and to all that he foresaw, like Carrie, he said yes. Soon Benjamin was in love with her, muffled and bewildered by it, but with the steady helpless gaze of a passionate certitude. The best he could ever say, including both of them, but turning back helplessly to Carrie, was: You're not like people round here. Seth watched Carrie shift so almost imperceptibly in her feelings that at no point was there reason enough to halt. From pity for the incoherent child—he wrings my heart—she passed through the troubling satisfaction of being loved by him into loving him, in her fashion, in return. Seth came home once and saw them in the music room together. Benjamin was making his best attempt at the accompaniment of a familiar song. He was bent down and away from the door, anxiously watching his own fingers. Carrie was singing, and watching him. Seth saw how far along she was in the changing of her feelings. She met his eyes and knew that he knew. Afterwards she said: It doesn't make any difference. I know that, he said; but felt a difference, of a kind he could not fathom. And she added: Whatever you ask, I will always tell and whatever I tell you it will be the truth.

Seth had been planning to restore the kitchen range. It should heat, like the back boiler, from the open fire, and once would have cooked and baked for a family. But all its intricate system of flues and draughts was blocked and useless, one door hung loose, a cast iron hob below it was cracked and tilted. For weeks Seth had been brooding on his project with a secret satisfaction, as though it were the promise of a break-through in his drawing and painting and he must bide his time, gather his energies, make a space, and finally set to. It was all his own, all his own dreaming, that he would act on when he chose. It amazed him therefore, one afternoon when Benjamin came in from the lesson, that without thinking he took him by the arm, stood him before the hearth and said: Know anything about ranges? Benjamin blushed. Here was a large opportunity. Aye, he said. Same make as my mother's. I always did hers till my stepfather moved in. And he went on his knees before it, opened the loose door, rattled gently at the damper. No worse than you'd expect, he said. He looked up at Seth, then quickly away. In the firelight on his looks Seth saw clearly how Carrie must love him. He said: I had a mind to get it working again. You could give me a hand. His project, disclosed, shared, made over to someone else. Suddenly he was deferring to the boy, who was local and knew about these things, knew better. He tested his feelings for regret and could find none. Benjamin was rolling up his sleeves. No time like the present. There should be a rake somewhere, and wire brushes. They're out the back, said Seth. In secret he had been making his preparations. He fetched the tools, a dust sheet, a tin bucket, overalls for them both. Soon he was taking out a pail of rust and soot. Thinking Benjamin had already left, it shocked Carrie to see him in Seth's overalls, crouched close to the fire, intently working at the blocked airways. Seth came in. We've made a start, he said. Feel. She put her hand into the open oven. The warmth was coming through. A long way off baking bread, but a start. Like cleaning a spring and the water beginning again. Ben's the man, said Seth. You both look the part, said Carrie, bringing tea, their filthy hands closing round the mugs, eyes whitened through a faint mask of soot, eyebrows, hairs on the wrists lightly touched up with dirt. She felt her own cleanness like an attraction, almost too blatant. She said: Why don't I go and ask Jonah for a new door? It's the hinge, Benjamin said. The door's okay. Well, a hinge, said Carrie. Why don't you? said Seth. And to Benjamin, as she left the room: She likes asking Jonah. Five minutes later Carrie was back, with Jonah himself. Couldn't remember the make. Thought he'd better see it. His appearance in their living room was astonishing, as though an order of things had been undone. He bulked much larger, blacker, more grizzled, more indifferent to any usual manners. He glanced and nodded, tapped the cracked hob with his boot, nodded again, departed. It's sunny out, said Carrie. Strange irrelevance. Under the viaduct they seemed to be making a life that would be all interior, by lamplight, intimate. Their feelings wanted sleet and hail, early dusk, the long nights. The fire would roar, the oven would heat up tremendously, Carrie would bake a batch of loaves, there would be a kettle whispering on the hob.

They were in a hurry to finish, but it took some days. Seth would only work at it with Benjamin, at which Carrie smiled. She went to Jonah for the hinge, he had found a likely hob as well, also a battered kettle that might polish up. He beckoned her into his shack and pointed to a can of WD-40 on the table. There was a notepad by it, to do his talking. He scrawled: FOR THE RUSTY NUTS AND BOLTS. And after that: YOU PLAY ME A TUNE? His oily hand had smudged the cheap lined paper. Carrie kissed him on both cheeks. A baker's dozen of tunes, she said. In town she bought the substance necessary for loosening rusty nuts and bolts, and a tin of the proper stove paint, glossy black.

Seth and Benjamin were at work, kneeling on the dust sheet side by side. Your mother must have been glad, said Seth. Why ever did he stop you? Benjamin shrugged. Whatever I liked, he put a stop to it. And after that he started thumping me. Your mother let him? Couldn't stop him. Didn't try? Little by little let the boy go, for the man, reneged on everything, betrayed him utterly, crossed over, stood against him with the incomer. Stepfather said he was a pansy, queer. Unbuckled, belted him, left him curled on the hearth rug swallowing his own snot. Then joined the mother in the room above, in the marriage bed. Benjamin said again: You're not like people round here.

It was Seth's birthday. They declared the kitchen range open for use. The burnished copper kettle boiled for tea. By evening the house smelled of bread. Red wine and brown ale shone in the firelight. Savorous things, all manner of plates and dishes, it was all their travelling gathered in. Jonah came, grinned, tapped with his dirty knuckle on the shiny iron. From somewhere in his throat came up a cheerful clucking. Two or three others were invited. Carrie played her promised thirteen tunes. After dark they went out into the yard. The arches stood supreme and along them, elongated, lay a halted train. The lights shone like scales. Nothing above until the infinitely distant constellations. When the others had gone Benjamin came to Seth and Carrie by the fire. I got you this, he said, handing Seth a thing in a plastic bag. It was the shape and weight of a bible, but cushioned to the touch and a lovely dark green and the thousand pages, closed, made a block of brilliant gold, and on the cover, ornately and goldenly inscribed, the name: Shelley. Benjamin was anxious. Okay or not? I wouldn't know. He shrugged, sorry on many counts. Seth looked from the gold to Carrie to Benjamin and bowed his head over the gold again. You've got no money, he said. It's only Oxfam, said Benjamin. And anyway I nicked it. Seth kissed him and left them by the fire. He wanted to be outside for a while, under the viaduct and the Plough, holding the book of poems. Carrie said to Benjamin: Don't go. We want you to stay.

2

In Rhayader they went first to the solicitor's, to sign. Seth had insisted that it be in Carrie's sole name, so she signed. He cradled the baby in his arms and watched. The man was polite, punctilious; if he found a client odd he would never show it. Seth felt as remote from him, fellow humans though they were, as one star is in fact from any other. All people in professions, decently dressed, decently doing their jobs, they were moving further and further away from him. He bowed his head over the sleeping child. He prayed his wife would never go from him into the icy distances while he lived. The estate agent's was a few doors along. They collected the keys. The man was jolly, heartily wished them both good luck, extended a little finger to touch the baby's cheek. Was there anything in his manner which said he was glad to be shot of the place and rather you than me?

Rhayader looked a nice town, simple on the axis of a clock tower. The waters felt very near, and the cold breath of the hills. Carrie remembered it well enough and they shopped quickly. It was late February, the daylight would soon give out, they wanted to arrive before dark.

Seth drove. Carrie held the baby on her knees, on the open map. The road climbed the river, which was rising, they heard it roar, the tires hissed over sheets of running wet. After a while they must take a junction left, out of woodland and across the narrow reservoir, a sinuous long water whose lapping edge they clung to. So far so good. The lake seemed to double the light of the clear sky, giving them more time, a reprieve. Then, sharp right, the thin road took up with another river, doubling it exactly. Carrie opened the window. Such a din entered, the river hurtling in excess of the course at its disposal. The hills, streaked white with headlong tributaries, opened and were revealed on either side, very beautiful, terribly exposed. Seth, as so often lately, viewed himself and his enterprise with fear and pity, like a spectator. As though from high above he viewed the cumbersome white van, in which was everything he owned and loved, crawling forward at the mercy of the universe. He admired the three of them, loved them intensely, wished for their safe arrival; but remotely, as though they were fictions, actors, a lively dramatization. Carrie was in doubt. She had begun to wish it should be dark before they arrived, that he saw the place for the first time in a fresh daylight. She felt answerable, the onus on her felt as vast as the opening hills. Not that he would not like it, but that he would like it too well. Was she not siding with him against himself? Was it not a conniving in his destruction? The daylight lasted, they were far west, the stars appeared on a sky still white.

Then the road ended, they were at the dam, up under it, up against it. A stream came tumbling off the hill, the hill came steeply down in rocks, and there in the angle, between rocks and sheer black wall, on a platform reached by a raddled track, stood the house. Carrie shook her head, wondering over

herself, appalled. But Seth had jumped out and stood marvelling in the cold air. He took the baby from her arms, helped
her down. Home from home, he said. Well done! He was radiant. He seemed shocked back into proximity. At once he had
energy, the spirits, the courage for anything. She unlocked the
door, it needed a heave to open it. Never to be forgotten, the
first breath of the place, the soot, the damp. The electric, he
said. Can you remember where? She could. They had lights.
Now for a fire, he said. I saw a woodpile. She followed him
out, stood by him. He turned with his arms full of logs, faced
the sheer black wall. Beloved wife, he said, I shall work here.
Under the stars they lugged their brass bed from the van.

Craig Ddu was a dead end. The road stopped there, it was
for Midlands Water and the few tourists. A car park, a public
toilet, a phone box, all like a failed outpost. And from under
the massive wall the original river set forth again, ignomin-
iously. True, in no time at all, fed fresh water by the free
streams off the hills, it had recovered and rattled along with
the dam behind it like a fading nightmare. The house itself,
older than the dam, a survivor of the colossal works and
shoved by them into a new relationship with the world—the
house itself wanted living in. There was an acre around it and
forty more vaguely up the hillside and a little way downstream. But the wall was so close and towering it seemed to
Carrie that at the least diminution of their resolve they must
lose the contest and be overwhelmed. Again she wondered at
her choosing it for Seth. Was it vengeful? But Seth went from
room to room and paced the territory blessing her name.
He said his love and gratitude were as vast as the backed-up
waters behind the wall. So she was reassured, but still with an
anxiety that his exaltation, her doing, was itself a precipitous
and dizzying thing. But they had days full of appetite and
savour and at nights their love was like a miracle at their disposal. The house warmed. They owned a copse of twenty or
thirty shattered firs, fuel forever, so it seemed.

Carrie drove into Rhayader, to stock up. They needed blades, paint, sand and cement, as well as food. Seth watched her out of sight, a long while. After that, with little Gwen slung on his chest, he continued to discover how rich he was. He found a damp place in the very angle of rock and wall, a lighter green and lit up with celandines. It was a spring, and only wanted cleaning. In a stone barn he found a collapsed tractor; and a scythe, a rake, pitchforks, all wormy wood and rusted steel, that he would surely mend and put to use again. He fed Gwen, laid her down for a sleep, sat on the boards and leaned against the cot, dozing. He felt fuller than the rivers. He must have slept for a little while soundly. His face was wet with tears when he woke. Only grasp it, even a small part of it, make even a little of it able to be seen! Joyful commission, courage to come up to it! Gwen was waking. Together they went and sat in a mild sun, to watch down the length of the river and the road for Carrie coming home. Scores of rabbits browsed and scurried below them over their ragged estate. Benign neglect.

It was a week before they climbed to see the lake. They might have gone down through the car park to the road which served the dam ordinarily; but they had seen, with a shock, a steep path, almost a stairway, starting behind their house, near the celandines and the newly discovered spring. That was the way they must go, arduous, secret, starting from their own ground. So cold, so damp—more than damp, the hillside oozed and trickled and spurted with more water than it could hold. The rocks were soft with moss, tufted with the ferns that, in their fashion, luxuriate in chill and wetness. Seth cupped the baby's head and steadied her against him, against his chest, in the warm sling. They were in an angle, almost a chimney, close into the join of dam and hillside, hard up against an unimaginable body of water behind its engineered restraint. At first, for about half the climb, they were in a shadow akin to darkness at noon, eclipsed.

Seth turned whenever the stairway allowed it, for Carrie to
come up. Over the bright scarf on her head he took in their
new home and beyond that the river, its recovered force, its
intrusion and insinuation through the resistance of the hills.
How slight and at the same time vigorous and cunning they
were, to climb an intricate and precipitous stairway under a
deep reservoir of water, the child pressed against him felt as
brave and tiny as a wren, he felt her pulse to be infused into
his own, married in, blood into beating blood. The day had
grandeur, like a heroic expedition, like a myth.Then they
were in the sun, the low sunshine of the dawning of the
spring, it warmed and illuminated the greens and the tones
of gold, they climbed with a faint warmth on their backs,
felt for it with their faces when they paused and turned, like
a whisper of earthly everlasting life, a breath, an intimation,
infinitely delicate and poignant against the immensity of the
immured waters up which they climbed.

Their arrival, a last steep haul, landed them in a grave
uncertainty of feeling, with no words. It was like surfacing:
there lay the level water. Come up through the depths they
were level now with miles of length and breadth, the far
reaches winding away invisibly in many bays and inlets and
the inexhaustible hills continuously contributing. The total
bulk exceeded comprehension, like a starry sky. From the far
head of the lake, or rather from off the hills and harrowing
softly over the face of the lake, came a cold breeze. The water
lapped steadily at the ramparts under them, the water came
on and on, without end, hit against the stone, each wave
that ceased in its particular self being at once renewed and
replicated. Somewhere in the distance, out of sight, was an
infinite spawning of waves against the dam. Quite suddenly
their little human enterprise seemed futile. They became
anxious for the baby, the necessary energy was lapsing out
of them. There was a watchtower halfway along, locked and
boarded up, but they hid in its lee, saw to little Gwen and

settled then without much regret on the ugly and ordinary
way to climb and descend, the Water Board's metalled road.
Clouds were driving up, such hurtling clouds, you might
stand and watch the world occluded in three minutes.

What are you thinking?
  About the dam.
  Don't.
  Not badly, I wasn't thinking about it in a bad way.
  What way then?
  Only about the water. How it naturally wants to be level.
  Not there it doesn't.
  No not there. There it wants to go headlong, and be level
later. Real lakes are different. They're serene in comparison.
When it's too much, they overflow. That's very gentle. But
the water up there, even when it's still, all the weight of it
doesn't want to lie like that. It wants to be headlong.
  Stop it.
  Can't stop thinking. I was thinking about the waves as
well.
  Kiss me instead. Love me. I want you.

Carrie was feeding the baby by the window. Such a view
from there, away from the dam, downstream through oaks
and rowans towards the little hidden town. On the draught
through the sash window she could smell a bonfire. Always
a bonfire, so much to clear and burn. Seth came in, went
upstairs, she heard him rummaging, floorboards and ceiling
were one and the same. Peaceful feeding; the quiet view, the
scent of smoke. Sometimes she dozed as the baby did. Seth
went out again, she glimpsed him, what was he carrying? She
dozed. Then it broke in on her. Oh no! Oh no, not that! She
ran out, her dress undone, Gwen's eyes flung open wide.

  He held a portfolio open on his left arm and sheet by sheet
he was feeding it to the flames. Carrie halted, clutching the

baby tight. He was like a man on a ledge. Should she snatch at him or quietly, quietly talk him to safety? Seth, don't, she said, soft as the small rain. He turned, his face was rapt. She hated to see it. Grief, despair, would have been easier to view in him, not rapture, feeding his work to a bonfire. No harm, my love, nothing wrong, he said in the voice of some peculiar wisdom. I see my way, I see I have to begin again. Seth, for my sake, stop it. She saw sketches and drawings, beloved likenesses, herself in the little churchyard above their allotment, a warm and vivid picture of their hearth, the burnished kettle, the rug, the glossy range. I have to, he said. One folder lay on the earth, wide open, wholly empty. Soon be over, won't take long. Then we'll begin again. They're ours, she said, they're not just yours. When they're done they belong to both of us. Herself in her sixth month, peaceable. The baby newborn. How can you? There was Jonah, seated at their kitchen table, manifestly content. And again and again, there were the heroic arches of the viaduct, striding across the town. Everything? All of it? He would not be talked into safety. Carrie made a grab for the portfolio, dislodged it from his arm, spilled out the remainder on the ground. Pictures lay under the sky, half a dozen of Benjamin. Seth's face jolted and altered, as though from a stroke. Bitch, he said in a voice like a ventriloquist's. Bitch, you are in my way, you and your bastard you are in my way. And he reached for the pitchfork, newly mended, wrenched it from the earth, raised it, stabbed and stabbed at the images and rammed home all he could of them hard into the fire. Gwen was screaming. Carrie went on her knees, scrabbling together what few sheets were left. Seth leaned on the new handle, worked the prongs free, and stood back. He saw her breasts, her weeping face, what he had done.

Listen to the rain.
　　So soft.

And the streams, can you hear the streams?

All of them, near and far.

It's gone again. I'm better. I feel you have forgiven me.

I love you. Nothing else matters. I will forgive you anything. Except the one thing which you know about. Do that
and I will haunt you day and night in hell.

Where is he, do you think?

Who?

Benjamin.

I don't know.

Does he know where we are?

How could he?

Gwen woke. Seth went naked to her room, reached down
into her white cot, lifted her warm and snuffling against him.
Carrie sat up, reached for her, all in the tranquil darkness. The
baby's whimpering became a focussed hurry; then she settled
into the blissful certainty of satisfaction. Seth stood by them
in the dark, Carrie leaned her head against him. The baby
had her hunger exactly answered. He went to the window,
parted the heavy curtains, looked down. He could make out
the water, like the ghost of the milky way, a soft luminance in
movement. He could almost believe that the dam was a natural lake that has no wish to topple but in a measured fashion
gives into the valley. Across the cold room Carrie said:

I suppose he visits his mother.

Did he say?

He said he always would.

He is very loyal. You could write to him there.

I suppose I could look for that address.

Seth came back to bed, obliterated his face against her,
dozed, woke when it was time to carry the sleeping child
back to her cot. Like a little boat, he always thought, a safe

241

little ark, into which he laid her, in which she drifted safely
on the waters of her sleep, returning, calling out in the dark
when next she needed a reassurance of the close connected-
ness and safety of her world.

The van tilted, rocked from side to side. The descent always
did look perilous. Carrie, watching, was glad when he reached
the girder bridge and the start of the road. There he paused, got
out, waved, blew her a kiss, departed. All the way out of sight
she watched him travel. Then she went indoors to prepare the
house. As for herself, she made an abeyance. She feared Seth's
changes. They were the abyss. Now he was marshalling events
the way she most desired. Or the way she dreaded most. Or
both. And between her and him, one flesh, it was never certain whose proposal they were following, either might serve
the other for the self's obscure desires. She knew that much,
but it appeared impenetrable and induced in her a passivity
and a fatalism, under which, like a spring making for daylight,
ran the irrepressible force of self-asserting life.

In the late afternoon Carrie and Gwen went down to the
bridge and the junction of the little stream with the river
creeping out from under the black doors of the dam. They
were less in the wall's shadow there, the sunlight lingered a
while longer. The rabbits fled; watched; soon resumed their
trespassing. At the waterside Gwen was absorbed by all the
babble and movement. A yellow wagtail flitted over and
stayed close. Carrie lost her consciousness almost wholly in
the child and the bobbing, darting soft-coloured bird. Her
particular complexities were postponed.

At the waterside she heard the motor but could not see it.
The rhythm was unfamiliar, the arrival might be somebody
else, though scarcely anyone ever came so far. Having no wish
to see a stranger, she took Gwen in her arms and climbed
the track home. The engine still approaching made her nervous, like a pursuit. Not till she was on the level, at their

usual viewing place, did she turn. The vehicle, an old estate car, long as a hearse, was riding grandly over the bridge and embarking, with great caution, on the rocky track. Seth and Benjamin. Where's the van? she asked. Seth was pleased with himself. Sold it. More seats in this. Carrie said: What about our bed, if we move? We're not moving, Seth replied. Here we are now. First job tomorrow: improve our approaches. Benjamin stood to one side, smiling, very uncertain. An army surplus haversack seemed to be all his luggage. Again that gaucheness, again his black eyes seeing more than his tongue could utter. It lurched under Carrie's heart. So here we are, to stay. Again; anew; as before; wholly new. So be it.

Then began a good time for the three of them; for the four of them, since Gwen among the childish grown-ups continued in gaiety and satisfaction with only little bouts of fret. That very evening, in a lingering daylight, in fire-light and candlelight, Seth begged their forgiveness and explained as clearly as he could what he must try to do in his drawing and painting henceforth. He said: I look at you. I look from you to my hands. I can make a like-ness of you but it will not be enough. It won't be what it is truly like. So my premise is failure. My axiom is that whatever I *can* do, whatever my hands *can* make, will not suffice. Carrie was anxious, wanted to halt him, she saw him raising the precipice. No, no, he said. Through what I *can* do, its manifest failure, I will feel my way towards what I should do, always by failure, I'll know what isn't right, what manifestly will not do. Carrie stood up and stopped him softly with her fingers on his mouth. We haven't had enough music lately. She fetched the guitar for Benjamin, the fiddle for herself. Benjamin shook his head. You men, she said. So fearful. Start, it will come back. Listen to this.

Seth said he would go and stock up. Food, and we need a sledgehammer and a pickaxe, he said. Gwenny's coming with me. Back for lunch. Carrie strapped her carefully in; leaned over her, kissed him on the mouth, feeling for his tongue with her tongue. Benjamin stood in the doorway.

A bit uncertainly, Carrie first, Benjamin hanging back, they came out of the house, to greet him. They were like children, he laughed at them, how he loved them, he laughed aloud over them and him, he exulted, the life there lifting up before his very eyes filled him with a wild glee. Guess what, he said, handing Carrie the sleeping child, guess what, or perhaps you knew, and he kissed her lips, perhaps you knew already when you brought me here? What? She asked. Such a shop I did, food and alcohol for a fortnight and tools for eternity. He was handing the plastic bags out to Benjamin, overburdening him. What did I know already perhaps? Carrie asked. Shelley's down there, him and Harriet, under the second reservoir. They were alive down there and planning a thorough revolution of our ways of being in the world, in the summer of 1812. They came up here for picnics. It's all in a book, I bought a book, it's in that bag Ben's holding with the cheeses, five different cheeses. Truly, there's no end to this place. He faced the towering black wall. That wasn't here then, of course. It was a high valley with the little river hurrying down. He cupped his mouth, tilted his head and shouted at the dam. Back came the clearest sound of craziness imaginable—the sole name: Shelley, fracturing and chiming. Gods, said Seth. Did you know that as well? No, said Carrie. Benjamin stood like a beast of burden with the shopping, watching Seth and Carrie as he had under the viaduct when they appeared like an enchantment on his life. Shout, Ben, said Seth. Shout out who you are. Echo it to Rhayader that you're here. Benjamin looked called up for an ordeal. Shout, said Carrie. Stand where Seth is and shout your name. First time no sound came, none from his mouth at all. He licked his lips, raised his head, called out his

name. The echoing fell away in a cadence that was utterly
forlorn. Carrie ended the game. Food, she said. Then work,
said Seth. Work and pray. Work and play. But work first, the
chain gang. Anchor me with a ball and chain, don't let me
float away.

That afternoon, with pickaxe, sledgehammer, shovel,
wheelbarrow, in boots and heavy gloves, they worked at
smoothing a way from the girder bridge to their platform
under the dam. Parts had become like a riverbed, from frost
and sun and torrents, and it was with some reluctance that
Seth made them carriageable. He worked next to Benjamin,
or parting and returning as the tasks required, almost without a word, in the intimacy of a shared hard labour. At first
Benjamin was shy, watchful, but Seth won him over, slowly
and surely into something akin to his own present state. By
four the job was half done. Enough, he said. The sun was
behind the dam. They went indoors, made tea, sat at the table
in a too-early dusk. Carrie was at the window with Gwen.
Not far down the valley lay the sunlight still, the shadow
advancing very slowly over it. She felt the haste more characteristic of Seth. We must show Benjamin the water, she said.

All they had seen so far cried out to be seen again, to be
seen and shown, and he was the only fellow human they
wanted for the revelation. The climb was eerie, chilling; the
wet trickled on them as though night and blackness were
exuding an icy dew. They felt the cold of the body of water
through its concrete shield. But all the while, as in a seaside
town when a street heads at an incline for the sea, Carrie
and Seth were expecting the enormous light over the brink
and treasuring it like an imminent gift for Benjamin. At
the last they sent him ahead and waited, looking down over
their own chimneys to the pool of sunlight on the woodland
very far below. Then they joined him on the rampart of the
dam. The breeze; but gentler, warmer, a zephyr if there ever
was such a thing. And sunlight dancing, a shattering white

radiance further than they could see, more than they could bear to contemplate. They drifted apart, drifted together, gauche and ineffectual, brimful of love and joy and their mouths silenced with shyness.

So their days rose, whatever the weather, they had work to do, they played like children, were passionately companionable. Benjamin went back to the echo, he became the master of it. He positioned Gwen on the ground to listen to the names returning strangely. He invented birds and animals, he brought them forth for her, as though from an ark.

In the evenings they read or Seth painted, Benjamin withdrew as far as the room allowed, turned his back on them, strummed softly at the guitar and in an undertone, barely audible, hummed and mumbled some words of his own invention. Seth said aloud: Nantgwyllt went under the water in 1898. The Shelley Society lodged a formal protest. The Welsh were evicted from their homes, where they had lived for many generations. Carrie went for her bath. The clock ticked more audibly. She came in naked and kneeled on the hearth rug between her husband and her lover, bowing her head, towelling her long hair, the curve of her spine in the lamplight. She sat back on her heels, the firelight on her knees, her belly, her breasts. She slung her damp hair forward in one hank over her left shoulder. What else is under the water? she asked. The house of his cousin Thomas Grove, where he stayed in 1811, wondering what to do, when they had sent him down from Oxford for professing free love and atheism. Nothing under our dam here? Some sheepfolds, one or two cottages already given up and the ruins of a chapel at the very far end with a holy well, a hermit lived there in 1300, he had moved further and further into solitude and come this side of the hills from the Cistercian community at Strata Florida.

They trekked over hill and bog and down through woodland to a vantage point over the second reservoir from where, closely comparing Seth's old maps and the reality, they believed they must be looking on the surface under which Nantgwyllt and the house belonging to Shelley's cousin lay submerged. On a long day, first climbing the stairway that started from their liberated spring, they circumambulated the reservoir, the highest, under which, night after night, they slept, and located, to their satisfaction, the place a diver would have to sink himself who wished to visit the anchorite's roofless cell. Question, said Seth. Does the well still bubble up oppressed by tons of water? They took out the deeds of their home, Craig Ddu, and climbed the little stream, to see where they began and ended, their forty or fifty acres. But this was harder than imagining a village or a dwelling fixed forever under sheets of water. The walls had collapsed, the bracken and sedge were over all. At the head of the stream, where it split, where its three strands were plaited together into one, there was a ruined fold, one hawthorn clinging on, its roots in rock, its shape, set by the wind, offering a threadbare roof over a waterfall. Emblem: the survivor. I don't know what we own and what we don't, said Seth. Whatever, wherever, the land was given up, for humans it was long since finished and the crows, the kites, the buzzards and the kestrels were left at liberty to scour it lot by lot.

Seth's work was changing. Carrie looked over his shoulder now and then, his concentration was intense, he did not mind. She loved to watch his hand, so quick, so deft. But what came of it troubled her. At first she thought she must make a new effort of understanding, to do him justice. He had said his way must be that of groping through failure towards the truth. But in truth she had to confess to herself that she understood him perfectly well. The lines of his art were forfeiting all insistence, one figure elided into another. One that by the shock of black curls and the steady eyes most resembled Benjamin had the bodily shape of an adolescent girl; she saw herself with Seth's short hair and features haunted by all his previous alienations. Everywhere there was doubling, tripling, echoing, fragmentation and dispersal, fleeting as Welsh weather, faithless as water. Even that she might have said yes to, and praised his courage. They were change, flux, movement, or they were dead. That was their principle, was it not? What distressed her were his trials with colour, the way he exceeded and overrode his slight outlines with a willed carelessness, like a child's smudging and genial mess, the watery colours running and giving up their selves whilst the draught of some elusive shape ineffectually showed through. But this was a man with the keenest sharpest gaze she had ever known. She had watched him when he bore on a thing and truly saw it. She knew how exact and knowing he was: when he dashed off a likeness for a favour; and in the devising and execution of a particular pleasure. So why this allowing a world in which nothing belonged, nothing had shape or fixed identity or an outline marking it off from anything else? She remembered his axiom, and it chilled her: Whatever I *can* do will not do. He was reneging on his peculiar abilities. For what?

Seth took off his boots and entered on stockinged feet, quite silently, though he had no intention of stealth. Carrie and Benjamin were sitting in the window. She was buttonng her dress, he was cradling Gwen and murmuring over her. Carrie was contemplating him and her baby with a contented love. The light from outside was on the three of them. Seth stood, he saw the beautiful ordinariness of their intimacy, the daylight fact of it. He turned, quitted the room, his movement alerted them, Benjamin came out to him as he was putting his boots back on. Seth kept his face averted. Nothing, he said. I was going to show you something. Benjamin touched him on the shoulder. What then? Seth shrugged, still averted, but walked across to the stone barn, allowing Benjamin's arm along his shoulders. And step by step he felt the virtue going out of him.

In the barn, standing still, he couldn't for the life of him remember what he had wanted to show Benjamin. He was attending dumbly to the transmutation taking place in him, a sort of petrifaction, the replacement of every atom of faith with an atom of hopelessness. He stared in stupidity at the tractor. It had slumped forward on burst front tires. He motioned vaguely at it. The weights? said Benjamin. No, no, said Seth. Nothing. The weights, a couple of cast-iron pyramids, were still slung from their rings under the tractor's front bar. Stop you going over backwards, said Benjamin. He was staring at Seth, who at last looked him in the eyes. Tell Carrie, will you, Ben. I'm very sorry. Then he covered his face. The tears forced through his fingers, the wells of his hopeless sadness burst their strong restraint.

He curled up on the bed of love, tight as an embryo, and sobbed; he choked on his own snot; he was a grub, a grown man with his knees up to his brow, smelling his own terror and despair; in overalls, with dirty working boots, a competent man, weeping over his exile from all fellowship with love; shoved into space, into the cold and the dark of the interstellar spaces, turning forever like a finished capsule. For an eternity, for an hour or so. After that, uncurled and lying quietly in his wife's embrace, behind the curtain of her hair, he said in a level voice he was not fit to live, he had a coward soul, he cringed in shame that he had ever associated himself—in a far-off laughable mimicry—with any of his saints and heroes, the artists and the poets. He begged in the flat, the leaden voice that she would burn every scribble of his or daub she ever found. He begged her to promise there would be nothing left, not a scrap or jot to show the world his folly and ridiculousness. And he said again that he wasn't fit to live, that on her house and home and child and love he was unfit to have the smallest claim. Then shame over these his speeches. Dumbness then, the mute inability. And a vague terror, hard to pinpoint, hard to lay a finger on its whereabouts. Inside or out? The air he breathed, the wreath of atmosphere around his neck and shoulders. Or in the blood, coursing around him for as long as he was he. The nights had terrible gaps in, rents and pits, and every morning waking he felt sheeted under lead.

Ten days of this, a bad passage. He came out lachrymose and vastly sentimental. He sat with Gwen in the bedroom window like a grandfather, her hand clasped tight on his little finger as though she anchored him and nurtured him. With a large benevolence he watched Benjamin, like his own younger self, labouring at the finish of their steep track to the bridge and the beginnings of the outside world. The thistly grass was gay and innocent with rabbits, like a tapestry. Carrie, her hair coming loose from under a red headscarf, pushed manfully at the wheelbarrow. She waved, said something to Benjamin, he looked up and waved. They swam in tears as far as Seth could see.

Then his return began, unhoped for, miraculous, never biddable but somewhere in the depths of him insistent as a germination or water forcing up. He wandered about in the house and out of doors with Gwen on his hip, she was easiest to be with, he could babble at her or murmur like a breeze and what delighted her in the early summer delighted him, thistledown, dandelion clocks, forget-me-nots around their neatly stone-flagged spring whose water was a clear continuous beginning again. He viewed himself with more indulgence now, with a wry friendliness. Held up the child against the soft blue sky and intoned while she kicked and chortled: My own heart let me more have pity on; let/ Me live to my sad self hereafter kind ... Brought her close, kissed her nose, went down on his heels and toddled her towards him. Her cool hands warmed in his; he marvelled with her over the unpractised action of her legs. Scooped her up to admire the woodpile, Benjamin's special pride, and the new plots set as well as possible for the growing season's sun. The stone barn, the very sight of it, tilted his spirits towards a steep collapse, so he walked away, down the slope past Benjamin and Carrie smoothing the last few yards, to the water where the wagtail liked to visit and sat there till they called him, willing his fears into submission in the happy consciousness of the child. Returning, admiring, he suddenly saw where a new plot might be dug, on the slope itself, with some terracing, almost Mediterranean; he would begin it next day.

That evening he read in the Shelley Benjamin had given him. He read Mary Shelley's notes on the poems year by year, until the last. They were brave, these people, he said. It's brave just being in a place like that, so far from anywhere, facing the open sea. And Mary collecting everything afterwards and writing her notes, that's brave. What happened to Harriet? Benjamin asked. Seth made no answer so Carrie said: She went in the Serpentine. He had left her for Mary. They married and went to Italy. Seth was thinking of her heavy clothes, sodden, the mud, the weed. And her heavy belly, she was very pregnant. They didn't look after one another, Carrie said. One to another they were a catastrophe. I suppose everybody is responsible, Seth said. I mean for what he does. They left one another their own responsibility. He was feeling bolder. He was thinking about his terracing—whether to tell them or not, or make a start first thing, for a surprise.

Next morning Seth appeared at the foot of the bed. He whispered a strange sentence: the boat has come. It was early, he had parted the curtains slightly and the sun shone on the black paint and the golden brass. Carrie woke. Benjamin was asleep on her left arm. He looked, to Seth at least, much as he had lately in his drawings and paintings, only more beautiful, the black curls, the lashes. Carrie smiled, gently disengaged herself, sat up. Seth said again: the boat has come; but with his eyes on Benjamin shook his head in wonder and added the words: sweet thief. Carrie joined him outside in the sunlight. You've been working already? Yes, he said. Come and see. He took her to the edge and pointed down to where he had begun hacking out a terrace. We shall grow what we like, he said. Carrie put her arms around him. Was I dreaming, she asked, or did you say something about a boat? I did, said Seth. That's the strange thing. But not strange at all really. Not for this place. I was working and I looked up at the dam and thought how lovely the water must be with the sun on it already. I thought I might go and swim and when I got up there I saw the boat, a little rowing boat with the oars in. It was bumping against the land where I might have gone in swimming. It's nobody's, we can use it.

Everything from the far end drifts before the wind and arrives sooner or later up against the dam or lodges in a near angle. They claimed the boat and the shipped oars until they should hear of someone who had a better claim. They made a mooring in a tiny inlet, out of sight of the rampart should anybody walk there, which was almost never, and whenever they liked, which was often, the four of them were out on the water. There was nearly always a breeze but rarely too strong to make headway against. And besides, by keeping close and following on water the path they had followed or made to the far end of the lake, they could creep along, like a yacht skilfully tacking. They packed a picnic, landed where they pleased: by two or three hawthorns, by the broken line of a drystone wall where it descended and entered the water. Poignant, these traces, these indications of a connection and a use gone out of sight. Keeping an eye on the weather—they were never foolhardy—they crossed with steady strokes the width near the far end, to experience, said Seth, the imaginable tremor of the hermit's holy well still bubbling out of the ground invisibly below. And best were their returns, scarcely rowing at all, idling down the centre, confident of safety within reach on either bank, wafted by the breeze and what felt like the bent or inclination of the water always to be coming from the west and heading, however quietly, towards the ruled line and the little tower that made the limit and the brink. It was sweet to drift like

that, as though to a sheer falls but knowing they could halt
when they chose, safe in a secret harbour, and disembark
and descend their secret stairway into their house and home.
Often they had a soft music on these returns. Carrie sat in
the stern, holding Gwen and singing; Seth rowed, his eyes
on them, and behind him in the bows Benjamin, become
accomplished, played and murmured an accompaniment.
Seth was between them, between their music. Their last
such return was at full moon. They had not thought of it.
They were idling down the length of the water, the music
dying behind them like a wake, there was the merest breeze,
and the blue of the sky was becoming pale so very gradually they were beginning to drift into nightfall before they
would notice. Then Seth saw in Gwenny's face what she had
seen. Her eyes were all amazement, she thrust out her pointing finger, as though she were the inventor of that gesture of
an astonishment demanding to be shared, then Carrie saw
too and suffered likewise a childish shock and pause or gap
in her adult comprehension. Moon! The moon! White as a
bone, frail as a seed, big as a whole new earth, the moon was
rising over the rim of the dam, dead centre, clearing it, first
with the ugly stump of tower intruding, then free, sover-
eign, beyond measure beautiful and indifferent. Seth turned
sideways on, so all could see, and like that they drifted nearer
and nearer, in silence but for the water lapping.

Carrie woke. The curtains were slightly parted, which
made her think he must have stood there and looked at her.
She went to find him on his terraces. There was fresh earth
dug but the mattock had been flung down. She turned and
called for him, the echo came back, a single note, distended.
Benjamin came down. He'll be swimming, he said. Or in
the boat. Look for him, will you, Carrie said. Benjamin
began the climb, Carrie went indoors, dressed, saw that
Gwen was still asleep. Then downstairs again, uneasy, and
met with a shock, an absence: the table was cleared of his

sketches, drawings, paintings; the portfolio, that had stood by it, also absent. She ran out, Benjamin was coming down from the dam, too fast. She waited by the spring, he hurried by her, not a word, averting his face. His breath was coming in sobs. He ran to the stone barn, she followed, the door was open, he took a step in, bent forward, turned to face her, ashen, smitten white. The weights, he said. He's filed them off. They're gone. He began to whimper, a queer unstoppable distress, bolted like an animal for the cliff again. Carrie fetched the child and laboured with her oblivious up the stairway to the ugly level rampart of the dam. She saw Benjamin already distant, small, making haste along the bank, visiting every inlet, in all his bearing, his sudden leaps and halts, hurting her even as he diminished with his manifest dread. How large the water, vast the hills and without bounds the sky.

Now she must wait on the dam in a steady breeze. Everything drifts that can sooner or later down the length of the water and bumps against the terminus, the ugly wall. The little boat will come, with its oars shipped, empty. Everything that can float will drift this way, the work, the distorted likenesses, they will be for a while like spawn, like a flotilla of vaguely coloured rafts, till the colours run and all weighs heavier and they sink. The boat will come. But what cannot kick free, anchored at the feet, what cannot rise on the body's insistent buoyancy, pulling towards the daylight on the will to live, that must stay where it is and in her lifetime will never rise, only toll like a bell, like a sunken, silent and useless bell. On the dam, the baby on her hip, Carrie reflects that she has said she will never forgive him.

CHARIS

Charis, Zoë and Felix, said Zoë, daughters and only son of Prosper and Felicity, christened as they were so that their names should be a blandishment, like calling the Furies the Eumenides, the Kindly Minded, and just as futile. For in truth, she said, mumble all the apotropaic spells you like, bribe all the greater and the lesser gods you've ever heard of, still they fuck you up, your mum and dad, and in our house, no less than in the House of Tantalus, they do so with a vengeance. Dear sister Charis, third of the first-born daughters who have killed themselves, I was not at your cremation nor at the Service of Thanksgiving for your Beautiful Life nor at the scattering of your ashes in the Sacred River Alph, farewell, dead sister, I weep for you. Our brother in Jesus, Felix who is full of shit (though he tells all and sundry he had the shit kicked out of him at a tender age by Mama in one of her rages), our beloved brother Felix, who escaped soon as he could to sweet New England to do good works for a Community of Fathers, this sharp-suited executive announces to the world that he has seen you in the arms of Mary Mother of God and that she loves you better than her one and only boy and that you are in the light there and at peace and radiantly happy. No soul among the millions in his Facebook does not rejoice with him at this glad news, said Zoë. Dear Charis, forgive me if I don't forgive you for leaving me in the world with him.

You should see your website! I tell you, one glance at it, all the anti-emetics available on the NHS would not keep you from throwing up. He calls it his choir of angels extolling you, my sister. And he has posted there the rhapsody he delivered at the Service of Thanksgiving, for the world to see: Charis is in the Light. Charis was brave. Charis prays for us. Charis asks our help to create a Church of Light. Charis is the Butterfly. For after the scattering of your ashes on the effulgent surface of the Sacred River Alph, a butterfly landed on the basket which had contained them and stayed there for a while, quietly. In truth, my dearest, being dead, you have brought out the very best of the worst in him, said Zoë. But this will make you laugh. If you really are safe and sound in the arms of the Virgin Mary this will make the pair of you wet yourselves laughing. Remember that photo of you and me and his daughter Allegra (!) dancing? Was it in Powys, when you returned from the waterfalls? Or at Beaurepaire, before I gave up the unequal struggle, and we were dancing the crane dance, the labyrinth dance, that turn by turn was to bring us deeper into Gaia's mysteries? Oh that dance! There were three of us, Charis, Zoë and the radiant child Allegra, all dancing the crane dance in pretty dresses. And he emails me to say he has airbrushed me out on the grounds that I was looking miserable and spoiled the picture. So now there are two, Allegra and Aunt Charis (deceased), with a hole between them where poor Zoë was till our brother in Christ Jesus disappeared her because she had a face like a wet Whit Week. And that, sweet sis, is how the website opens, on a nice big lie, and goes on that excellent beginning from strength to strength through the ninety-nine delusions with links along the way to multitudes more, said Zoë.

Is there Internet in Heaven? Do you spend much time online? I tell you, Charis, Zoë said, it would take eternity and then some to mark and inwardly digest the half of what's already there under your beloved name. The Other Photograph pops up everywhere. I mean the one of you striding purposefully up the long slope towards Seaford Head, all alone, my dearest, and nothing before you but the empty slope, the summit and the sky. Taken a couple of years ago, I believe, in May or June, by that fat holistic potter—Angie? Fran? Isolde?—who told you she could heal you. And there you are climbing out of the busy little town where hundreds of lucky people are having a nice time in ordinary ways. No sooner were you named in the local newspapers, the fat lady emails it, the photo, to our Felix and from him in seconds it goes forth and multiplies and humans in all five continents have it on their screens. Did he weep much for you when you were living, Charis? I don't remember that he did. But now he shows you to strangers on his BlackBerry and takes off his glasses and dabs at his eyes with a snowy white handkerchief and says what a comfort that photograph of you climbing Seaford Head in the days of your almost hopefulness has been to him and Father. Tell me, Charis, did you ever understand our brother Felix? Does Mary? Does the Trinity, all three of them combined and thinking hard? In truth though it is an excellent photograph, said Zoë. You are turning away, you are heading off up the long slope alone. I have never been there and I never shall but I imagine the air to be a pure delight and surely there are skylarks and the flowers that love the chalk and all around you space and the feeling of the nearness of the sea. But the white face, the sheerly final face, the flatly vertical height and fall, how could a human being employ a thing so utterly inhuman? Don't worry, big sister, I shan't go anywhere near the place.

That book I lent you about Eleanor because I thought it might fortify you in the locked ward but which you couldn't bear to read, they posted it back to me. I was rather worried that they knew who I was and where I lived, said Zoë. But I'm glad to have her book.

Father skipped the ceremony at the Sacred River, Zoë said. But he attended your cremation and the Service of Thanksgiving, leaving early, of course, to drive back to Ealing and put Mother to bed. To annoy Felix, I asked that she, Mother, be remembered with everyone else among the prayers because if anyone is in hell, in this world or the next, she is. Felix wouldn't allow it, needless to say. He said it would not be appropriate. He said he had consulted the Carmel Fathers and had been told by them that it made no sense theologically to pray for a soul in hell. So I thanked our Felix, Zoë said, for saving the congregation from doing something nonsensical.

Email, mobile phones and the Internet are a marvellous facility, Zoë said. Here I am in Swindon miles away all on my own and nonetheless *au courant*. Alas and God help me, it was the last thing I wanted and surely not your intention but doing what you did has brought us closer, me and the blessed Felix. Now the Word comes from him to me in superabundance. As do the images. He sent me one of those slide shows so I can view you through the years approaching nearer and nearer to that sweet summer morning in the Year of our Lord we are still suffering in. I see you on a trike in Ealing, setting off, and the look on your face is more fearful than hopeful. Your schoolgirl years distress me. By then it was obvious. And you on courses and retreats, you dancing, singing, painting, drumming, weaving, making masks and pots and doing tai-chi and meditating among bare ruined choirs or in a glade. So many stations, photograph by photograph, sent to me by Felix, of your road to Seaford Head.

And would you believe this? (Of course you would.) When he flew in from Boston to visit you on the trauma ward he called at Martha's first and phoned me from the

place itself, as he called it, her attic room, with the neighbour who found you, the Good Samaritan, standing by
him at the open window. The sill is quite high, he said.
You had to put a chair there to climb on to it. He said that
beyond the damaged roof he had a view of the garden, the
blossom, the little white clouds on a blue sky and to him
they were proof perfect of the love of God. He did not
mention the psychiatric hospital, whose beech trees, lawns
and wards are also visible from that window, just over the
wall at the bottom of the garden, as you and I, my dearest,
know. But there was, he said, a blackbird—he thought it
was a blackbird—singing from the rooftop above his head.
He held the phone so I could hear it, sister.

Flying back next day, said Zoë, Brother Felix emailed me
from the airport to say you had told him you were damned
but that he had promised you Mary loved you and would
lift you down from the Cross into her lap. And he added
that the Fathers could not do without him for more than a
day or two, however urgent his own family responsibilities
might be. He begs the world to google Carmel Fathers. Every
hit, he says, feels like a shot of the love of God. And when
people see the photographs of the work-in-progress on that
donated land in a glade among the ancient redwoods of New
England, when they see the ruined chapel and the cloisters
of Beaurepaire, where you were happy, Charis, being resur-
rected in effigy by the holy work of the Fathers' hands, they
put their money where their amazed eyes have been. Charis,
by moving from Martha's house to the bosom of Mary you
have greatly increased the blessed Felix's fundraising pow-
ers, he says. On the ten million dollars he had drummed up
already, two million more have come in since you left. He
tells me the Fathers tell him he is what they had been praying
for: the man abundant in both money and the Spirit. In their
Norman and Early-English ruins, by a virgin spring, there
will be a place for thinking prayerfully of you, sweet Charis,

so he told me, Zoë said. He also tells me he is considering lit-
igation against Beaurepaire for not allowing you to stay there
indefinitely and against the psychiatric hospital for allowing
you out of their sight. And he has asked the Carmel Fathers'
legal advisers to advise him on the soundness of his case.

Felix says you have stepped off a white cliff into universal
love, said Zoë. He says you have quitted the Earth of Agony
for the Sea of Peace. Stella Maris illuminates you, Mary Star
of the Sea illuminates you for all to gaze upon. And Mary
has spoken through our brother Felix and said, Go, sisters
and brothers of the sister in my lap, go tell the story that
must be told and let it touch the hearts of all in all the world.
And there is more, said Zoë. Every day he updates the site
and emails me and phones me more and more.

How I despise myself, said Zoë. I should shut the system
down, drive the whole fat box to the tip and throw my phone
in after it and lie still in the dark and see you clearly, Charis.

Charis, when you came back from the waterfalls you
were radiant, Zoë said. It was in Powys, early evening in
May or June, and although you asked me would I like to
come with you I could tell you wanted to walk up the stream
alone. Now, if I close my eyes and concentrate, I can see you
as you were when you came back and found me reading
and watching for you in the grounds. And it is easy for me
to remember and imagine what the walk was like out of
the grounds, following the stream to the waterfalls that you
did not know were there. Though you walked alone you
carried with you up the stream the loving fellowship of the
house whose trees and lawns and flowers you were leaving.
You carried in you the quietness, the expressive dancing, the
hours of song and of silent meditation under the stars around
a fire, all that and more, as you climbed by the thread of a
stream that came down out of the mountains and all the
things that made the body and the spirit of the stream, its
hurry and abundance, its endlessly varying polyphony, the

brightness, the leapings, the passages almost of stillness and the hazels, alders, willows, harebells, ferns, rocks and mosses through which the water felt and expressed itself, all that and more, said Zoë, you carried with you in a joy rising to ecstasy as you stepped out from under the cover of greenery and found yourself at the opening of a large horseshoe, an almost sheer embrace of hillside around a pool into which three waterfalls fell with a steady force and noise and overflowed and ran as living water down and down into the grounds of the house in which you felt at home. And at that place under the waterfalls, so you told me, Charis, Zoë said, you prayed, as you had never prayed in your life before, that having looked and listened hard and breathed the smell in of the thunderous falls and taken a palmful to your lips, you would be enabled to follow the waters down and be forever in your slight person a vessel and a bringer of love and joy not just into the fellowship of that blessed house but into any house and any company you ever thereafter entered. That was your heartfelt prayer, said Zoë, as you turned your back on the waterfalls and the high horseshoe wall and began your careful descent through the watery greenery to me.

You don't know, said Zoë, unless with the love of Mary comes omniscience, that the only time I visited you during your second incarceration in the locked ward I knew at once, even before you mentioned Seaford and your barmy potter friend, what you were planning, sister. And I didn't try to dissuade you and I didn't alert your keepers. And really I cannot tell whether my conscience troubles me on that account or not. When Felix emailed me his report—from Father—of the hours you spent dithering on Didcot Station and then of your foolish leap from Martha's window my chief thought was, If this must be let it be clean. Naturally he attached his pictures of the hole in the tiles and of the soil pipe, aerial and a section of the gutter hanging off. What a mess you made! What on earth were you aiming at? Quits with Mater? Another dagger in the heart of Saintly Pater? Believe me, Charis, I should not have liked to see you alongside her in a wheelchair and him ministering to you both till he dropped dead. I know about vengeance, I have thought about it and I know there are better forms of it than that. So when in the locked ward I saw how spruce you looked, how mobile you were again, no walking frame, scarcely needing even a stick, and I learned they trusted you to go into town and get your hair done, I had a pretty good idea what you were up to. And when you spoke of Seaford in that lingering way, how happy you had been there with that dippy potter woman, I thought that would be clean at least. Does it weigh on me or not? Worse to bear, said Zoë, would have been your sisterly hatred had I warned your keepers and they took me seriously and stopped your little privileges and put you under obs twenty-four hours a day. You wouldn't have liked that, would you, Charis? Zoë said.

Seeing Felix's photograph on the Carmel website, seeing him among the jolly American Fathers who clap him on the back and call him Jesus or Midas as they please, it struck me again, said Zoë, how strong the family likeness is between him and you, my Charis. You have the same black greying hair, the same thin face, the same spectacles behind which the black eyes look out like insects backed into a corner and expecting to be trodden on. When I left you in the locked ward, a doctor, passing, said to me, Much better, wouldn't you say? Indeed she is, I answered. Sweet, these physicians who think their suicidal patients want a cure. I saw you playing passably the role of a woman on the mend. But behind your spectacles I saw your cowering eyes. You have the eyes, Charis, the family eyes, frightened.

Having announced on the website that you are a butterfly, said Zoë, Felix phoned me to say that in a vision he had seen you ascending through the stratosphere doing bravely on your frail and beautiful wings. And that you had come to the very house of Mary and entered at an open window and settled on the sleeve of her sky-blue gown. Then after a silence, said Zoë, he asked me in a different voice did I know about the ichneumon wasp. Yes, I answered, but he told me anyway. The female lays her eggs in the pupa of the butterfly, the larvae thrive by eating it, the butterfly harbours what is eating her. That's it, he said, said Zoë. That's it, the whole story, plain and simple. But resuming his Mary voice he told me he believed the butterfly could choose to die and by dying stop giving sustenance to the killer parasite and so by self-immolation end the curse. Charis was the butterfly, he said. Charis was brave.

Felix tells me Father arrived in his invalid wagon just in time to see you departing in an ambulance. And I wonder is that why you changed your mind at Didcot. Did you think you would be wasted under a train? So you decided you'd give him a nice surprise when he arrived from Ealing with a duvet and bags of shopping for you in your new home in Martha's attic bedroom? Oh, Charis!

I miss you, Charis, Zoë said. I am quite alone. I fear the family will look more my way now. It weakens me that you are dead. We were arm in arm, whatever the distances. Remember our pact to get through childless so the curse would end with us? You kept your word and I will too. Not that there's much temptation. It seems to me I walk with a clapper in my hand and shout, Unclean! Unclean! I feel I have it cut into my forehead, I am of the House of Labdacus, keep away from me! And any I might have loved and wanted children with do keep away from me. What is it about Felix? Did he take a test? Does he have a certificate saying his seed is good? Pity Allegra. Her best hope is that her fool of a mother—whom Felix has deserted, by the way, he emailed me last week to say the Fathers and their phoney ruins need him wholly—will carry her off to a secret place in a forest or on a boundless prairie or in some colossal foreign city and bring her up with never a mention or any clue of our family name. But you know the myths as well as I do, Charis, Zoë said. One day when she's stopped worrying a messenger will come from Delphi or a man on a train will stare at her and say, I know your face, and they'll be back again, back in the mechanism, and the helpless girl will breed.

In therapy once, said Zoë—did I ever tell you this?—they asked what the worst thing was I'd ever seen at home. And I had to answer quick, not giving it any thought. Up popped the image of Mother in her wheelchair in the open lift ascending out of the living room into the bedroom and halfway up she stuck. Her pasty face empurpled fast with rage, she swiped at nothing in particular with her stick. Father fiddled with the controls fixed to the wall. I heard him whimpering. Mother by then could not make proper words but clearly the blurtings of her mouth were meant as curses. In the midst of it she shat herself. She was halted halfway up, just above my head, I raised my eyes to her, and Father, turning helplessly towards her, did the same. So we stood either side of her thwarted ascension, looking up at her who fumed and stank. Father said he would have to telephone the Services and she would have to be patient a little while until they came or could give him good advice. That was the image that came to mind when they asked me to say, without any searching through my thesaurus of horrors, what was the worst. Mother flung her stick down, trying to hit Father, but of course she missed and when he went to the telephone and left me standing there she slewed her bloated purple face my way and from her mouth, already slavering, she tried to land a gob of spit on me. I'm fairly sure I never told you that, Zoë said. Needless to say, in the leisure of sleepless nights I've thought of much since then to equal or excel what sprang to mind when they said, Say quickly what's the worst.

According to the therapist, Zoë said, some go to terrible lengths to command if it can't be love at least attention. Aiming at paraplegia from an upstairs window is not unheard of, so he said. But it takes two, of course, there has to be somebody you can do it to and you have to be sure on some deep level that he or she is fit material for your scheme. It's quite a risk. In the case of Mother and Father, that particular therapist said, and I agree, said Zoë, she must have known that she had in him a man supremely capable of cruel and abject servitude. Who would not fail or flee however vilely she used him. He was her reciprocity in person, superhuman in his lust to be enslaved, and strong, so strong. I have always pitied Father for his fortitude. Would so much bad have happened had it been obvious he could not bear it? Perhaps he excited the Fates to try him worse and worse by the very fact that he stood so tall and had lived so long. There can't be much pleasure in tormenting a man who will give up the ghost at once.

Possessing Father, that therapist said, Mother possessed the children too. He fed her them whenever she said, Do it. Does that make sense to you? the therapist asked. I shrugged, said Zoë. What do you think, Charis? He fed us to her piecemeal on demand, the three of us? And now there's only two.

Charis, Felix and Zoë, spawned at the confluence of two poisoned streams… I wonder, Zoë said, did the ancestors, dragging their heritage, advertise in the Soul Mates columns of the Daily Telegraph? Clytemnestra seeks an Oedipus with a view to further damage. Thyestes, hungry for children, seeks a Medea.

Charis, said Zoë, I plan to disappear. I know it is said to be very difficult nowadays but I intend to do my best. The day they found you I noticed that my passport would soon expire. I hurried to Boots and photographed myself; got the forms from the post office and applied for another ten years, using the Express Service they offer. I can't see why I should be refused, can you?

But what I don't want, Zoë said, is the police out looking for me. Father and Felix, bless them, when they phone and email me and I don't respond, are bound to think, Oh dear here we go again. I don't want anyone looking under cliffs for another missing woman face down on the tide. So I have told Martha, who will surely tell the world, that once I've put my affairs in order I shall walk alone to Compostela in hopes of easing my mind after the terrible events of spring and summer. Of course, she is delighted by this fiction—the first of several I will compose—and agrees I must walk alone. The love feast in the evening and the fellowship of the dormitory will balance me, she says. She drove to see me with a bundle of maps and leaflets and hours of practical advice. Now I could blog my way to Compostela quite convincingly without ever leaving Swindon and this detestable bedsit. But I shan't do that. I'm not sure what I'll do or where I'll go when my passport comes and even when I've decided I might not tell you, Charis. I expect you'll be haunting Ealing and Carmel for at least a year and I don't want you blabbing to Father and Felix in big-sisterly concern. But whatever I do, it won't be clean, Charis. It won't be the cleanness you got to in the end. Wherever I go, I'll still be among the anniversaries, I'll be in the world of Mother's stick and spittle, of Father's liver spots, his rheumy eyes, his terrible staying power, I'll know that Felix still operates in his dark blue suit, his light blue shirt, his moccasins, his glasses just like yours, his snow-white handkerchief, I'll drag the Ealing torture chambers after me, the soil pipe, the wheelchair and the insect walking frame, my Charis. I'll be in the foul rag-and-bone shop of the heart. For a while at least that's where I'll be, perhaps for the duration of my brand new passport, perhaps forever, said Zoë, I don't know. It's not what I want, of course, but it's where I have to start.

I shall be all right, Zoë said. And if I'm not I can do without help from Father and Felix, thank you very much. Bear in mind, Charis, that when Mother gets hungry there's really only me to supply her now. Felix is pretty safe, I'd say, in New England among his Holy Fathers and their reproduction Beaurepaire, so it's me our unholy dad will come for down the fast M4 in his paraplegic carriage when Mother says, Get me a pound of flesh and a pint of blood and a dram or two of soul by nightfall, will you, dear. So I must be off somewhere neither they nor you, sweet Charis, nor any other remnant of our blighted tribe can find me.

In my passport photograph I don't look a bit like you or Felix, which must be an advantage to me on my travels, Zoë said. I haven't decided yet what I'll call myself in circumstances where I don't have to prove it with a signature or a document. But it will be something ordinary, something, like Joan or Margaret, that doesn't tempt Fate or raise impossible expectations—Joan Thompson, Margaret Evans, how about that? At nights when I can't sleep I try to calm myself by making up little biographies that in a café, say, or at a bus stop I could come out with to a stranger, as my own. The most I thought I'd say in the general direction of the truth is that I've recently suffered a bereavement, a beloved sister, and think a change of scenery might do me good. Then last night I expanded on this little scrap in a way that gave me a thrill of pleasure. I'll say that I intend to travel abroad but that before I do, to fortify me, I'm going to spend a few weeks with a dear friend on a small holding in the north of England, a woman of my age, recently widowed but determined to stay where she is, high up in the snow, the wind, the rain and the sunshine. Yes, she'll stay up there and manage the couple of fields and the animals just as she and her husband together did. And I say how well she is doing, though profoundly deaf. Charis, said Zoë, I love this bit of a story. I get off a bus high up in a village I've never been to before and there to meet me is my dear friend Eleanor and she is wearing the bright woollen scarf and hat and gloves that she knitted herself in the deep mid-winter with wool from her own sheep, wool she spins and dyes herself in many cheerful colours. And how glad she is to see me! And I believe her when she says in the strange flat voice of the profoundly deaf that I will be good company for her and the sheep, the dog, the cat, the chickens and the ducks. She promises to show me things up there on the fells that I will never forget but will cherish forever, wherever I go, my Charis, Zoë said.

MR. CARLTON

After the cremation Mr. Carlton's two daughters invited people back to the house for tea. Not many came and there was none of the hilarity—relief—you sometimes get on these occasions. After an hour or so only the daughters and their families remained. They washed up, cleared everything away, put the table and chairs back where they belonged. Then Mr. Carlton said, You go now. I'll be all right. His daughters weren't so sure. Yes, yes, he said. I've got to be on my own. Best start at once.

As soon as they were gone Mr. Carlton went upstairs and stood for a moment in the bedroom. Then he took the bag he had packed two days before, locked up the house and drove away north. It was midsummer, the long evenings. At the first services, sitting in the car, he sent a text to his daughters: I'll be out of touch for a few days. But don't worry. All will be well. Love, Dad. Not knowing, not wishing to learn, how to send a message to two people at once, he composed his text twice and dispatched it west and south. That done, he got out of his car, fitted the phone under the nearside front wheel, drove slowly over it, reversed, drove over it again. Should be enough, he said to himself. But, to be sure, he retrieved the thing, which was indeed flattened, and walked across to the nearest bin with it. Getting back into his car he noticed that he was being stared at by a woman parked twenty yards away. That's one witness, he said. No matter. And having filled up with fuel he drove off, north.

Mr. Carlton feared and hated motorways. He kept to the nearside lane and only moved out if absolutely necessary. In the middle lane, enclosed in ranks of metal travelling very fast, he felt as vulnerable as a snail among marching men in boots. Rarely did he cross further right; but that evening, just north and west of Manchester, he was obliged to and from there, the fast lane, he noticed that no traffic whatsoever was coming south. As soon as he could, Mr. Carlton crossed back left. Ahead of him warning lights blinked, the whole vast speeding entity slowed, clogged and stopped. In no time at all many miles of track were plated over with many thousands of vehicles come to a standstill. Rapidly the solidifying continued south, every minute another mile of it. The engines idled for a while, then hushed; and this hushing extended down the lengthening lines. A helicopter hurried over, north. Fire, police and ambulances went by on the hard shoulder as fast as they dared. But the stronger feeling was of a gathering silence. Whatever could be done further north was being done. In the long repercussion behind that violent point there was no movement. The evening was mild, stretching itself towards dusk and a distant nightfall. People got out of their cars, lorries, coaches and walked where pedestrians are not allowed to be. They climbed into the central reservation and gazed in something like wonder at the vast and empty southbound carriageway. Others strolled along the hard shoulder, leaned against the crash barrier, smoked, chatted, phoned.

Mr. Carlton stood apart at the barrier. That stretch of the motorway is raised up on columns. They carry it over a flat moss whose chief beauty once was birchwoods, of which there are still remnants. You can also tell which parcels of land had once been drained and farmed. But first Mr. Carlton looked half a mile or so west and saw the feeder road, also raised up and its traffic halted solid and shining in the sun. Had you stood at the junction of that road and the motorway and looked back, your sense of the moss might have been of its opening, widening and escaping; but from Mr. Carlton's viewpoint you saw it narrowing and stopped. But the strange silence and stillness and the mild westering light lay over this segment of surviving land like a blessing or a reminder or a haunting. Mr. Carlton orientated himself in relation to the silenced roads and the moss, felt the queerness of the time and place, and only then looked nearer and down.

Below, barely thirty yards from the nearest concrete column, was a house and home. It was a brick house, it stood in its own close, hedged all around, a comfortable rough square, with a gate on the far side into a kitchen garden, more raggedly fenced and a scarecrow hoisted and tilting over the produce. In the far corner of the close there was an apple tree and a swing by it with a green iron frame and a red seat. Washing hung on a line down the dandelion lawn. And there was more, oh much more. Mr. Carlton felt himself presented with something he would not have the time to take in. It was an interlude, he would have to leave, he would never come back, his knowledge of the place would be small and so poorly ingested how should it do any lasting good? What do they grow there? He could distinguish runner beans and broad beans and at least four rows of potatoes. Those might be beetroot, those were surely carrots. Raspberries and currants in a coop. That was the toolshed, with a pipe from the guttering into a water-butt by which stood the can. A wheelbarrow, a compost heap, a patch of nettles and docks. What fuel do they burn? Behind the house Mr. Carlton saw a coal bunker. Who would deliver to such a place? Mr. Carlton

271

found a track, it departed from behind the house and proceeded, with many right angles, towards and then alongside
the feeder road, south. Would a lorry manage that track? In
the wet, in snow and ice? Perhaps the man of the house had
to fetch the sacks himself. From where?

Mr. Carlton had just noticed a means of transport, a squat
black car, parked outside the south hedge of the kitchen
garden, when a man joined him at the barrier and pissed
through the bars of it steadily in a bright gooseberry-yellow
arc, towards the house but falling far short, of course. That's
better, he said, zipping up. Then: Fucking silly place to live.
I suppose they were there before the motorway, said Mr.
Carlton mildly. I suppose they were, said the man, pulling
up his white T-shirt to wipe his neck. But who in their
right mind, he wanted to know, would stay? He had a hairy
belly, over-folded. That there, he said, pointing at the black
car, that there is a Ford Popular 103E. I know a man who
collects them. Mebbe I'll come back here and buy it and
sell it him.

An old woman came out of the house with a basket and a
bag. She wore a floral dress and heavy shoes. She moved the
foot of the pole back just far enough to bring the line down
within her reach, then worked her way along it, clothes
into the basket, pegs into the bag. When that was done she
turned, holding the full basket with the bag of pegs on the
top, and looked up to where the traffic and the spectators
stood. But she gave no sign of any thoughts or feelings, only
turned and went back into her house. As though we're not
here, said Mr. Carlton to himself.

An old man came out. He wore boots, faded and quite
baggy blue trousers, a smock of a darker blue and a brick-red
cap. He took away the clothes pole and laid it flat and close
under the gable end; came back, untied the line from its two
posts, coiled it and took it to his wife who was waiting at
the door. She took the coiled line from him and went in. He

crossed the close into the kitchen garden, fetched a hoe out of the shed and with his back to the motorway set to work.

You married? asked the fat man who had pissed. Yes, said Mr. Carlton. Yes I am. He said this aloud in answer to the question, said it without any hesitation, feeling it to be true. And having said it, he felt he must abide by it, in a sort of reservation within himself, and certainly mustn't try to be more exact, in the world's terms, with a stranger. I was, said the fat man. Still am, sort of. They were side by side leaning on the barrier, watching the man below at work in his kitchen garden. Swallows flashed out from under the concrete of the motorway, dipped up under the eaves, adhered there briefly with an audible twittering, and flitted off hunting again. Heavens, said Mr. Carlton. Swallows live here too. The man in the garden leaned his hoe against one of the six wigwams of canes that his runner beans were climbing and went to fill the watering can. She fucked off and left me, said the fat man at the barrier. Mr. Carlton turned to face him: his eyes were bulging and watery. Took the kids as well.—I'm sorry, said Mr. Carlton, face to face. Thank you, said the deserted man. You meant that, didn't you?—Yes I did.—Dozens of people I've told it to and never one till now, till you, ever said they were sorry. Mostly they look at me and it's as clear as daylight they're thinking, Can you blame her? Why wouldn't she fuck off and leave you and take the kids? And they're dead right, of course. Why wouldn't she? But at least you said you were sorry and I believe you when you say you meant it.

The man in the kitchen garden was watering his beans. The water showed pure silver in the lowering sun. Plainly the job contented him, he took his time over it, so much time he had. Mr. Carlton felt he had never before witnessed such leisurely and contenting work. Three times the man went to fill the can again. The sound of it filling, the changing tone of water filling a can, lifted like a memory of itself as far as Mr. Carlton at the barrier. And the man in the garden stood with his hands on his hips watching the water leave the green tub through the black tap and enter the green can. He watched; it entranced him. The deserted fat man offered Mr. Carlton a cigarette. No thank you, said Mr. Carlton. The fat man lit one for himself. I'll toddle over and see what's doing, he said. And he added, leaving, Before she left me I wasn't this bad. I didn't always look as bad as this.

The woman came out of the house and walked through the close into the kitchen garden. Now she wore a dark shawl over her shoulders. She stood with her husband. If they spoke it was too softly for anyone on the motorway to hear. The swallows came and went, at speed, intently, with a clean skill and grace. A blackbird sang from the apex of the roof. Was it so or similar, changing with the seasons but in essence just so, all fitting, all in place, all pleasing, was it always so even under the usual traffic?

A helicopter flew away south. Did that mean anything? Mr. Carlton wondered whether the swing meant grandchildren visited now and then. The colours were bright, the seat and the ropes looked strong. Would children mind about the noisy motorway? Was there anything to interest them outside the house and its bit of land? Mr. Carlton began to look for paths. Towards the south, where the moss widened, he thought he could make out a way which, like the carriageable track, advanced in right angles, perhaps to find bridges over ditches. He saw a couple of trees that did not have the appearance of birches. They might be ash or sycamore and a house had stood there once. If the children had been his grandchildren he would have taken them looking for frogspawn in the ditches. Surely the man and his wife knew where to find whortleberries and mushrooms. A moss was a rich place if you were born there or if you came in as a stranger and got to know it.

The old man had finished watering. He put the can back by the water-butt and the hoe back in the shed. The light coming over out of the west was golden now and almost level. All visible things partook of it and became truly themselves. Most astonishing, from under the motorway itself, the route the swallows were familiar with, half a dozen fallow deer appeared. They paused and were illumined; then moved sedately in single file around the north edge of the close and at greater speed bore away south. The old man and woman, her arm in his, watched them out of view and continued standing there in no hurry to leave the light.

A young woman came up to Mr. Carlton at the barrier and said, You wouldn't lend me your phone, would you? I'm very sorry, said Mr. Carlton. I don't have a phone. Oh, said the young woman, so you haven't told anybody you're stuck, you'll be late, they needn't worry? I had already told them, Mr. Carlton replied, that I'd be out of touch for a few days. I was speaking to my husband, the young woman said. Then my phone gave out. It frightens me being stopped up here. My husband was telling me not to worry. But what if we're here all night? I've never left him for a night before. Perhaps that helicopter was a good sign, Mr. Carlton said.

The old man and woman had left the kitchen garden. They were crossing the dandelion lawn towards the house. They halted, looked up, the old man pointed. Bats, said Mr. Carlton. It's not us he's looking at. He has seen the bats. The swallows have roosted, the deer have gone to where the moss is wider and perhaps there is still woodland for them to hide in. Did you see the deer? I've been watching the swallows. And now the bats. All those creatures have come out from under the motorway. I'm pregnant, the young woman said. I only found out yesterday. I went to tell my mum and dad. I wanted to tell them face to face. And now I'm stuck here. I don't want to be away from home in the night.

The old man and woman went into their house. In rooms to the left and right of the door the lights came on. Oh they've gone in, said the young woman next to Mr. Carlton at the barrier. They've shut the door. In the room on the left, on view, the old woman busied herself for a while. Then that light went out. She appeared at the window of the room on the right, stood there for a moment, now without her shawl, then drew the curtains.

The young woman at the barrier took Mr. Carlton's arm. I'm frightened, she said. You don't mind, do you? What do you think has happened? It must be very serious to close both carriageways. I heard a man say it was a fire. And somebody else said ten minutes earlier we'd have been in it. My husband said not to worry, they'll clear it eventually, if we're here much longer they'll bring food and water round. He's right, said Mr. Carlton, patting her hand that was gripping his arm. We're quite safe here. How still it is. I was wondering do they have grandchildren who visit occasionally. I hate it when you're on a train, the young woman said, and you stop in the middle of nowhere and after a long time they tell you there's a fatality on the line. Yes, said Mr. Carlton, that is a horrible expression. And everybody's only wanting to get home, the young woman continued, and they don't care about the fatality in person. But it's horrible sitting there knowing that someone is chopped to pieces further up. And this is worse than that. It has blocked both carriageways.

The after-lingerings of a midsummer sunset last forever. Infinitely slowly pallor passes towards blackness. The vanishing light edges north, smoulders on earth long after the source of it has gone below. But with an utter abruptness the light went out in the old couple's downstairs room. They're going to bed, the young woman at the barrier said. Mr. Carlton shuddered. The bedroom light came on. The old woman in her floral dress stood at the window illumined and looking out. Perhaps she stood there every night, every soft summer night at least, and looked down on the close and the kitchen garden for a minute or two, taking it in. She drew the curtains. You're crying, said the young woman holding Mr. Carlton's arm. What is it? You're crying? What's the matter? No, no, Mr. Carlton replied. I have two grown-up daughters, older than you, with children, a great joy, as yours will be. No, no, all is well. The light in the bedroom went out. They're going to sleep, the young woman said. Is it that? Is that why you're crying? Yes, said Mr. Carlton. It's that.

The southbound carriageway opened. Down it in a flickering torrent of blue lights the police cars and the ambulances screamed. After them, bulkier but quietly, came the fire engines. Carnage, said Mr. Carlton. A few minutes later the normal traffic followed, three lanes of it, headlong, heedless. Now we'll be moving soon, said Mr. Carlton. Do you want to go back to your car? I'll stay here, if you don't mind, until it starts, said the young woman still gripping Mr. Carlton's arm.

David Constantine is an award-winning short story writer, poet, and translator. He has published four collections of short stories in the UK: *Back at the Spike, Under the Dam, The Shieling*, and the winner of the 2013 Frank O'Connor Award, *Tea at the Midland and Other Stories*. Constantine is also the author of the novel *Davies*, and a work of biography, *Fields of Fire: A Life of Sir William Hamilton*. His collections of poetry include *Caspar Hauser, The Pelt of Wasps, Collected Poems, Nine Fathom Deep, Elder,* and *Something for the Ghosts*, which was shortlisted for the Whitbread Poetry Prize. He has translated Hölderlin, Goethe, and Kleist, as well as Bertolt Brecht's *Love Poems* (with Tom Kuhn; Liveright, 2014). In 2003, his translation of Hans Magnus Enzensberger's *Lighter Than Air* won the Corneliu M Popescu Prize for European Poetry Translation. He lives in Oxford and on Bryher, Isles of Scilly. Until 2012 he edited *Modern Poetry in Translation* with his wife Helen.